I Got Here as Fast as I Could

Rebecca L. Del Giudice

In memory of the 1,800 lost and the 250,000 whose homes were destroyed.

I remember sitting on my front stoop [a few days after Katrina] when a disheveled and seemingly disoriented guy pulled up in front of me in his pickup truck. He had Michigan plates and was pulling a boat behind him.

"Which way?" he shouted to me. "Who's in charge here?" he said.

I had to laugh at that part. No one's in charge, I told him. But if he wanted to put that boat to good use, I said, "Keep going straight and you'll hit the water."

He nodded. And then he started crying. "I'm sorry I took so long, man," he told me. "I got here as fast as I could." And he drove off.

I saw him two days later on Canal Street, looking fresh and invigorated. He had been rescuing people and pets ever since I'd seen him.

—Chris Rose, *1 Dead in Attic*

Prologue

August 1980

East Tamarack, Maine

Up here, Leo's lights burn bright; he readies the sky for summer. He shines down on the water that drew the Penobscots and the Passamaquoddys. He burns the fog that concealed English fishermen on its back. But Leo descended, and the water took everything in the end.

The last time Ava saw her father, it was the summer of her tenth year, right before Labor Day, before school started in the village of East Tamarack. Two hours before the last minute of her father's life, she was sitting in the kitchen of their old saltbox cape, legs curled under her, reading a book. The day had been perfect. There was a blue, nearly cloudless sky, and the seagulls were gliding in lazy circles. It was warm but not hot, like so many Maine summer days. At first Ava ignored how her mother was banging cupboard doors closed and scraping chairs on the floor. It was one of the ways she often registered her displeasure with her daughter. Ava used to ask what was wrong but eventually realized that she was supposed to know; Abigail Cabot was not a patient woman, and asking got her into more trouble. When the banging got louder, Ava put down her book and announced, "I'm heading to the beach."

She walked into the mudroom and grabbed her sweatshirt off its hook. She stepped out into the bright afternoon and went down her street and across the main street of town to the tiny, rocky beach, where her dad and Grandpa Noah were each carrying a kayak to the water's edge. Ava's dad's head turned, his tortoiseshell glasses glinting in the sun, his tall frame still bent toward the sea. He waved at her. She smiled at the sight of him, because he looked so happy. He loved summer up here. It was so much cooler and more forgiving than the summers he had experienced as a boy in New Orleans.

The Cabot family had been forced out of Canada like so many other Acadians in the eighteenth century. They steered their vessels all the way down the spine of the Eastern Seaboard, around Florida, and through the long tail of islands spreading out of Louisiana like a shower of embers from a Fourth of July sparkler. They had been there ever since.

But John Cabot surprised his parents, his uncles, and every relation on both sides with his move to Maine. They could not process why he would want to move North, nearly back to Canada, to the land of lobstermen and hunters of the sacred cod, the home of Yankee fishermen who rode out to the North Atlantic and the Grand Banks, a submerged continent ruled by storms, once the fishing domain of their ancestors. He loved New Orleans, though he loved it with a broken heart, unlike his parents. He was an active participant in the civil rights movement, a movement most of the elders in his family found threatening. But he hoped the city and his family could change.

Moving to Maine was a betrayal. Everyone expected he would return some day.

John had accepted a scholarship at the University of Maine. He got his PhD and taught the history of American architecture there. Ava often saw her dad bent over at the desk in his study, wearing his red cardigan that reminded her of Mr. Rogers pecking at his typewriter. Behind him, on the wall, was a framed print of a ghostly black-and-white photo of the old New Orleans. He had explained to Ava many times over the years—forgetting in his enthusiasm that he had already told her—that the Opera House was the finest example of Greek Revival architecture in the city and that it had been designed by an African American architect, a Creole named Benjamin Hamilton, whose name was lost to all but a handful of architectural historians. It sat on the edge of Treme, a once-grand denizen of that musically rich neighborhood. She had seen it in person on one of her many trips to New Orleans. It was careworn, to put it kindly. It was shabby and in need of restoration. In the print her father had it was bright white, a solid structure with a soaring columned entrance worthy of the Greeks. Her father would take her on a tour of architectural landmarks, sometimes dragging her cousin Ellis along because, Ava suspected, he was the son of the controversial Creole daughter-in-law, and her father worried about how he was treated when he was alone with his grandparents.

"Look at the bones!" he would say when he saw Ava looking at the print, and she would always look closer, expecting the old landmark to reveal skeletons sitting in the audience, waiting for a performance that would never begin.

Her father was writing a book on Hamilton, a book he had been meaning to finish for many years. This kayaking excursion was a rare break for him, as he had spent much of his summer holed up in his study.

"Coming with us, pumpkin?" he said, and even though he said it in that New Orleans drawl that the Mainers in their family always made fun of, Ava could never hear his accent; to her, it was just her father's voice.

She knew her dad was glad to see her there for a couple of reasons. There was the fact that he hadn't been able to spend much time with her this summer and had been disappointed when she, deep into her book, had declined his invitation earlier. But also her dad and grandpa had a strained relationship, although they tried to hide it when she was around. Grandpa didn't like southerners. He was still angry about the Civil War even though his side won, and he never missed an opportunity to mention it in front of Ava's father, whom her grandfather seemed not to notice was a modern and progressive man, southerner or not, and was certainly no southern apologist, despite what the Cabots had to say about it. Even at ten years old, Ava found it incredibly ironic that while her father, the southerner, was not racist, Grandpa, the proud great-grandson of Union general Joseph T. Pierce, was the worst bigot around; he just didn't realize it.

Grandpa hated that Ava and her parents spent every other summer (and every other Christmas) in New Orleans with the other grandparents. He was a man who liked to get his way every time. This son-in-law/father-in-law bonding time was probably for the sake of Ava's mother, or maybe it was Grandma's suggestion. Either way, Ava was a welcome buffer. It irritated her that they didn't think kids noticed stuff like that. It irritated her that her grandfather would always say she looked just like her mother, when everyone, including her mother, knew that she was the spitting image of her father—same black wavy hair; same pale, freckled faces; and same green eyes.

"Hey! Ava, my favorite granddaughter," Grandpa said. His thick Irish English face beamed at her.

"I'm your only granddaughter," she responded, tired of the joke. Her dad's kayak was a tandem, so she went over to him, rolled up her pant legs for the wading part, and hopped in while he held it steady. He took off his lifejacket and gave it to her to wear. Grandpa was "too much of a man" to wear a lifejacket and had made fun of her father for wearing one. Her dad had bought this kayak last summer, thinking he and Mom would use it, but they seemed to have trouble coordinating their paddling when they tried it, and Mom wanted nothing to do with it anymore.

Ava's dad loved the water and always said he felt safer in the water up here because it was too cold for sharks or gators, unlike the waterways back in the Gulf or Louisiana, where he grew up. He was traumatized by a close encounter with a gator in Lake Pontchartrain when he was a child. He told the story many times, as he told so many stories of his youth in that city that seemed so foreign and exciting to Ava. One time when they were in New Orleans for Christmas, he even got out of the car to show her the spot near the shore where he had punched the gator in the snout in a desperate attempt to save himself from getting pulled into the gator's death roll. Ava never wanted to go near that lake. She never understood how Louisiana families could live so comfortably with those creatures lurking in every watering hole. The worst you'd find in Maine was a snapping turtle.

As they pulled away from the beach, Ava rolled down her pant legs. The water was cold, but it was always cold up here, and Mainers were used to it. The few tourists who showed up in this little town were the only ones who were surprised.

Ava's father had a sweater and a vest on; her grandpa had only a long-sleeved shirt. "How far are we going?" she asked, not wanting to commit the entire afternoon to kayaking, when she still had all this reading to do.

"Egg Island," Grandpa said.

"Not too far," her father said at the same time. He looked at his father-in-law.

"We'll see. Probably not as far as Egg Island."

"Come on, John! What's the point in even going out?" But Grandpa was already paddling fast.

Ava's dad ignored Grandpa. He paddled faster.

Ava tried to keep up, but next to her father she felt awkward and useless wielding the paddle. She wanted to impress him; she was a daddy's girl and did not want to let him down from want of effort, so she plowed ahead although she wasn't even sure she was paddling correctly.

Soon Grandpa Noah was flying out ahead. He moved farther and farther from the shoreline, which made Ava nervous. She liked it when they hugged the coast; she liked watching the summer people in their handed-down houses. She was watching an end-of-season party on the grand lawn of the Green Estate, one of the finest homes in town. After they had been out on the water for a few minutes, she noticed that people were heading inside. Fast-moving clouds were appearing from the south. The wind was picking up. It would likely pass quickly. These summer storms always did.

"Wanna go home, John? Arms gettin' tired?" Noah taunted him from across the water.

Ava's dad increased his pace. The paddle lightly sliced the water: left, right; left, right. He was an athletic man, and although they moved quickly, he seemed unaffected by the effort. His breathing was steady.

A few minutes later, high above them, Ava watched as sea gulls were buffeted by gusts and gannets made crooked, wind-blown kamikaze dives for fish. The wind was steady now. As it blew around her, she was cold, even with the sweatshirt and the big, puffy lifejacket. Her father glanced at the sky, too. He let up his paddling for a brief moment as he wiped the spray off his glasses.

To the east, the contours of Egg Island started to materialize behind the waves. The water was churning faster and higher. Egg Island's shore was marked with slick black rocks, debris from glaciers that had gouged and scraped their way across the continent during the last ice age. Grandpa Noah was laughing, saying, "John, this is why your people lost the war! You give up too soon!"

The shape of a seal melted into the waves. Ava's stomach clamped down; she tried to breathe deeply. She remembered her father told her once when she had to give a presentation at school that taking deep breaths could keep her from being scared. But her breathing was quickly forgotten as she scanned the sky. They shouldn't be out here.

"Dad, we should go back," Ava said, and he put his glasses back on and looked around. His face set into a frown, and he realized she was frightened, so he called out, "Noah, let's head home! I don't like the look of that sky." But Noah wasn't going to turn back until he had proved to himself that he could get to the island and turn around before John could reach it. That's where he said he wanted to go today, and that was where he was going to go.

So they kept paddling.

And then, in the space of a breath, a towering wave rose up and over the sharp edges of Egg Island and headed straight for them, and Ava watched, frozen, as her grandpa's silver hair disappeared under a wall of water. Her father shouted at her to hold on. They rolled and flipped, tasting the shocking bite of saltwater in their mouths, noses, and throats. Ava was struggling to get out but could not get out; her dad was pushing, jerking around in an effort to right the kayak; and Ava was underwater and could not hold her breath any longer. Just as she thought her heart was about to burst, her father finally had yanked himself out and upright and rolled the kayak with his frantic hands; she saw his face, and his eyes met hers, and he was so afraid it made her more afraid, and he pushed her up with a force that shocked her, propelling her back into the air and back into life, and then she found herself sitting in the kayak, soaking wet and gasping for air.

She sat for a moment, confused, coughing, waiting for her dad to swim over. But he wasn't there. And Grandpa wasn't there. She had water in her eyes and nose and cold stabbing pains in her lungs; she coughed, and every time she drew in a breath, she felt a vise squeeze her chest, and she screamed with panic, "Daddy! Daddy! Grandpa!" AndBut nobody answered her. She scanned the water over and over, looking for them. But she never saw them again. Not even at the funeral, where both of the coffins were closed.

Chapter I

On Saturday morning, Ava stood in front of her family's old green-black cape, surveying the work ahead. Summer was nearly over, and up here that meant it could snow in a month. The gutters needed to be cleaned out so the snowmelt could flow freely. The front garden needed work; this summer the deer had ripped up some of the perennials, bulbs and all. She was behind on her weeding. She needed to stock up on firewood. Inside, the water heater was on its last legs, and the upstairs windows really needed replacing; the draft was brutal in winter. It was a lot for one person to take on, but Ava could not bring herself to sell the house. Lord knows she would make a good amount of money on it. For years now, people from New York and Boston had been snatching up old houses all along the coast, from Kittery to Bar Harbor, including many houses here in East Tamarack. If you had a view of the ocean, you were going to get a call from a realtor. If the local laws allowed them, the summer-home crowd would wreck the old capes, colonials, and Victorians and replace them with architecturally uninteresting behemoths, stretching their necks in front of their neighbors to hog the bay, its timeless expanse framed in windows that stood in front of granite countertops and easy-to-maintain gas fireplaces.

Three hours later, weeding done and perennials replanted, Ava sat at the kitchen table staring at her paternal grandmother's recipe book. She was terrible at doing nothing. Even though it was a day of rest (she long ago stopped going to church), for her Sunday was a day that stretched out for too long. She had to do things, keep the mind busy. She was driven to accomplish things. It staved off loneliness. So now she would cook.

Besides, the news had been making her nervous, and she needed a distraction. She had called her cousin Ellis twice already, and he didn't answer, so in her anxiety she perused the old recipe book, smeared with decades-old grease and butter and Crisco and flour and salt, its pages shedding from the binding. As Ava flipped through it, a familiar photo fell out. It was her and her cousin Ellis, in the yard of her grandparents' home; behind them was a wisteria-covered wrought-iron fence. They were both ten years old, all limbs and grins, wearing those athletic-style shorts that were popular in the '80s. Ava smiled at the memory. Grandma had given it to her the last summer she spent in New Orleans, more than twenty years ago. When she was restless, Ava would pick a recipe, go to the village grocery store, buy whatever ingredients she could find (she often had to improvise, since things like Andouille sausage and alligator were hard to come by in coastal Maine), and then cook and bake New Orleans style: oyster po'boys, shrimp etouffee, dirty rice, collard greens with bacon, cornbread, and pecan pie. It didn't always come out well, but she felt better for trying to create something. And she would sit at the old kitchen table, her napkin in her lap, her dog Tiras's eager face at her knee, and cut away a small portion from every bowl and plate. She would save a couple of meals' worth of food for herself and then wrap up the rest to bring to work on Monday; her vulturelike coworkers would make sure nothing went to waste.

Before her father died, Ava's mother would cook any number of Maine staples on the weekends: seafood chowder or fisherman's stew, roasted cod, apple pie, blueberry cake. Mrs. Cabot didn't cook New Orleans food unless she had been in a fight with her husband and wanted to make nice. She would cook in one fell swoop, leaving a massive tower of dishes and copper-bottomed pots to be cleaned in her wake. Ava hated that; she cleaned as she went. A messy pot was best dispatched immediately. The Cabots would eat leftovers most of the week, except for Fridays, when, following a tradition established by Ava's grandparents, they went to Harry's Lobster Pot.

After her father died, Ava's mother checked out a library book on southern recipes. There was a section on New Orleans, and one night, sitting up late with a stack of student papers in front of her, Ava's mom opened the book and meticulously copied each New Orleans recipe onto an index card. She cooked New

Orleans food frequently after her husband died. At some point Ava asked her, "Why now?"

And her mother said, "Because it reminds me of your father." It was a couple of years later that Ava got her grandmother's recipe book.

Now Ava stared at her plate of fried turkey, cornbread, and beans. It was a winter meal. It might seem odd in August. But it was very nearly September; in Maine, there was already a bit of a chill in the night air, and winter was not so far away.

Ava got up to check the news, something she had been doing every time she tried and failed to reach Ellis today. The TV screen showed the swirling blue weather map with a curling white hurricane. The blue and white of the map matched Ava's old kitchen-fireplace tile paintings of whalers pursuing their prey. *This one is going to be really bad.* She wished Ellis would call her and tell her he's already left the city.

The summer after her dad died, Ava and her mother went to New Orleans, as they would have if her father were still alive. They stayed for two months as usual. To Ava, New Orleans had always been a magical place, with lush, palmetto-flanked yards and shotgun houses in bright yellows and mint greens and mysterious, shaded Victorians ringed by palms and oak trees. She spent hours exploring her grandparents' yard and the neighborhood with her cousins. The oppressive heat alone was exotic and otherworldly to a girl from Maine. But without her father, the city was ghostly and painful. She would plant herself in the far corner of her grandparents' ancient kitchen or in a rusty lawn chair under the crumbling trellis in their garden and read. She imagined her father curled up in the same spot. They both lived in the world of books.

The only good thing about being in New Orleans after Ava's dad died was her cousin Ellis, the lanky boy with black eyes and skin the color of a walnut shell. They were born just a few months apart, and as she got older, Ava would often marvel at how different their lives were. But when she was in New Orleans, even after her father died, Ellis would always find her and pull her away from her books. They would explore their grandparents' neighborhood like they used to when they were really little, and ride their bikes around all of Uptown and the Garden District. Sometimes they would head over to the Mississippi River levees and explore the shoreline. Ellis was a sensitive boy, and he knew what had happened to his uncle, but he never asked her about it. He just gave her new things to do and think about. She would come in the house at dusk, after a day of spying on neighbors or exploring the neighborhood's supposedly haunted house, having said good-bye to Ellis at his parents' gate just blocks away, and feel her happiness fade as she sat in the old kitchen—the kitchen where her father used to sit with his parents while they drank chicory coffee, and watch her mother, whose family had been in Maine since the end of the French and Indian War—quiet, miserable, and out of place, wandering like a tourist into rooms she did not feel comfortable in. When her father was alive, he would practically drag Ava and her mother out to Magazine Street and to the French Quarter and those dusty shops, where they would look at figurines of straw people with shocked, open-mouthed expressions and bright folk art that spoke of grueling work, the respite of church, and the challenges of family life in poverty. They would visit the French Market, where they would smell tiny vials of strong-scented oils and touch the teeth of alligator jaws piled up in bins. Ava would read the plaques and shiver to learn that this market was where men, women, and children were once sold like cattle. She would look around at the faces of black New Orleans and wonder whose ancestors had endured that horror.

None of it interested Ava's mom after he died. Her mother used to have fun exploring New Orleans with her husband and seemed impressed that he could point out the genius in the shape of a crumbling pavilion seemingly transported from the ruins of ancient Greece, set down for display in Audubon Park. They would always visit her father's beloved Opera House. And her father would point out a grand house in the Garden District or a wrought-iron beauty in the Vieux Carre and say, "That's Hamilton."

Ava's mother would ask him questions about the history—his history and his city's history—and they seemed sometimes like a young couple on a date, with Ava as their underage chaperone. Ava liked to see her father on his turf; it seemed to balance the power in her parents' relationship.

The last time Ava and her mother went to New Orleans together, five years after Ava's father died, Ava's grandmother talked about how her son was born in the middle of a three-day storm that brought twenty inches of rain to New

Orleans and how he should never have moved north. He was the only family member to move north for generations, and clearly it had been a mistake. Ava's mother sat, her face like stone, at the kitchen table. Ava knew then her mother would never come back to this house again. Ava, who no longer believed in fantasies, had watched as her grandmother waxed nostalgic about her son's perfect childhood, and her mother countered with whitewashed memories of their perfect marriage. John had gone to Maine for a professorship, and he met the beautiful redheaded schoolteacher Abigail at a lecture about Alexander the Great. Six months later, they were married. It seemed like a faraway, unimaginable time: this time when they existed, whole, happy, untouched by tragedy. It never really was anywhere near perfect, but Ava would have given everything to go back to her mother's version of things.

The Maine house became Ava's after her mother died. It was built in 1790, set at the top of a long, hilly street that looked out over the docks, wharves, and lobstermen's shacks. The old pine floors, mostly original, were marked with more than two hundred years of scrapes and dents. Sometimes at night all the ghosts of that house would sit in Ava's room, at the foot of her bed. She would not open her eyes, but she could feel their presence.

Ava listened for a moment to the TV's breathless droning about the threatening storm churning out in the Gulf. She remembered how her dad and grandfather used to argue about weather. Her father would shore up his firewood in September in preparation for a tough winter; her grandfather would make fun of him for being a southern boy who couldn't handle the cold. A storm warning would push her father into a flurry of preparation: batteries, bottled water, canned goods, loaves of bread, and portable radio at the ready. Ava's mother would come back from an administrative meeting or a tutoring session and confront an absurd mound of groceries on the kitchen counter. Her husband had vivid memories of violent summer weather, of roads washed away, neighborhoods deluged in New Orleans. He had endured Hurricane Betsy, and everyone in New Orleans remembered her and Camille. They hit Mississippi even harder, but the levees failed, and there were bodies floating in New Orleans.

Ava remembered Grandpa listening to Dad's stories and countering with stories of his own, about '38 and the unnamed ice storms and nor'easters that did more damage than most hurricanes in Maine. Whenever Dad talked about New Orleans hurricanes, Grandpa always remembered bigger storms, stronger winds, and higher body counts.

After Ava ate, she wrapped up plates to bring to work. She tossed a few pieces of turkey to Tiras, who shadowed her from sink to fridge and back again. After she had put all the food away, she went to her dad's old office upstairs. She hadn't changed it much over the years. She hadn't changed much in this whole house since she inherited it. She had renovated the kitchen with her uncle's help and paid for a new roof. But she had barely touched the bedrooms or the office with its '70s shag carpet and dusty rows of books stacked on the built-in bookshelves. The Opera House was still on the wall. Her dad's old desk still stood there, midcentury modern plopped down on a carpet the color of split pea soup. His old typewriter sat on top of it, untouched for decades. Rather than disturb it, Ava had set up her computer on a side table.

She tried to call Ellis again. There was no answer. They only talked rarely; mostly they exchanged Christmas cards and would occasionally instant message each other when Ellis was off duty. But this was one of those times when you hear from everyone because people see the news and somehow assume that you don't also watch the news, so they call to make sure you know what's going on. He was probably getting tons of calls from extended family. She told herself that hurricanes were exactly the type of news story that were overblown by the rabid cable news networks and that she should stop pestering him. The storm would likely veer off into the Gulf the next day, and the slobbering media would drop it without mention, too busy moving on to the next heightened drama. Ellis and all of her dad's family who still lived down there would be fine. New Orleans would be fine. Still, because she dealt in worst-case scenarios, Ava scanned the office shelves for a particular book she remembered reading as a child. Her eyes fell on title after title—the built-ins covered two entire walls—until she spotted what she was looking for, a book about New Orleans hurricanes, one of probably more than one hundred books in her father's office that had New Orleans in them. She flipped through the grainy old photographs of destroyed telegraph lines, flattened barns and buildings, an amusement park carousel plunged into Lake Pontchartrain, and boats washed ashore, sitting in ravaged streets two miles inland. The book went back to the apocryphal storms of the seventeen hundreds, with stories of local French and Spanish forts wiped out, and huts and pirogues—the canoes the Acadians used—full of furs lost to the floods. Back then, they didn't even know it was coming unless they watched the birds like the Indians did. Famous storms: 1909, Grand Isle; 1915, the rather plainly named New Orleans Hurricane. One page had a journalist's sketch of the aftermath of the storm of 1856, which washed the "pleasure resort" on Last Island into the ocean, along with two hundred souls. One hundred and fifty years later, the island was still half-submerged, home only to seabirds.

Ava closed the book and held it in her hands. From the television downstairs, she could hear the mayor of New Orleans repeating himself on a fevered loop: "We're facing the storm most of us have feared."

Her cell phone rang.

"Hey, Ava. You at work?"

"No, I'm home, Uncle K." He knew she often worked weekends.

"Ah. Are you cooking up something good?"

"Just finished up some fried turkey. I'll bring you some."

"Nah. It sounds great, but your aunt will kill me if I eat anything fried. We still on for tomorrow night?"

"Yep. How are you feeling, though?" Her uncle had had knee surgery just a few weeks ago and could barely walk.

"Eh, I'm all right. So I'll see you there at six, honey?"

"Yep, definitely."

Ava thought about going into work. It would be a distraction from watching the weather and waiting to hear from Ellis. She imagined her quiet little office at Eastland Publishing, in the corner of a dusty room in that gloomy old half-renovated Gilded Age mansion, a wedge of stone with turrets and arches and five floors of pine and walnut, the spoils of a lumber tycoon.

Before she could decide if she should go in, her phone rang again.

"Fuhuuuuck."

"Hey, Rem. Yeah." It was Remy, a good friend of Ava from college. Not coincidentally, he was Ellis's best friend from high school. When Ellis found out

Remy was going to the same school as his cousin, he told Remy to look Ava up when he got up there. They hit it off and had been friends ever since.

"My mom is heading out. Hopefully Dad too."

"They're not staying?" Remy's parents famously threw hurricane parties; they didn't evacuate. They lived in Uptown, near where Ellis's parents, Tess and Alex, still live, and it hit Ava again that maybe Ellis was not evacuating, either. She remembered one year when a big one was aiming for New Orleans, and Remy, weirdly nostalgic for the threat of dangerous weather (or perhaps just distracting himself from getting too worried about home), held a hurricane party at Bowdoin. It was a novelty in Maine…attending a hurricane party. The storm veered back toward the Gulf at the last minute, which Remy said was what usually happened. He was too young to remember Hurricane Betsy the way Ava's father did.

"What do you mean, 'hopefully'? Is your dad staying?"

"Dad's down in his hurricane hole in Port Sulphur, thinking he's going to ride it out."

"That seems like a terrible idea."

"It's a fucking stupid idea. Mom is freaking out. She had a bad feeling about this one, so she's going to go visit my uncle Bobby in Shreveport. Hopefully Dad will get his ass up there."

"Well, your dad's a smart guy, right?"

Remy Devereaux, with his almost ridiculously Cajun name, was the descendant, on his father's side, of Cajuns from Baton Rouge and Shreveport. His mother came from mostly English stock, an upper-middle-class family that had lived in the French Quarter since the mid-nineteenth century.

Ava heard a faint tap, like a cigarette hitting its package. "Are you smoking?" she asked.

"Nope," he said. They both knew he was lying. He kept telling her he had quit.

"Have you heard from Ellis?" she asked.

"Called but haven't heard back," Remy said.

"Yeah, me too."

He exhaled, breathing out smoke. "Oh. Well, let's keep trying."

"Maybe he's on duty and just can't answer his phone," Ava said. Ellis was a state trooper now.

"Maybe. Listen, I've got to make some more calls. Talk to you later."

Ava flipped her phone closed, turned off the TV, and took Tiras outside. She thought about the drive up to work, the hulking building abandoned, the hum of the office refrigerator and the buzzing lights above her desk deafening in her loneliness. No, she was not going to bury herself in work today. She walked down the hill to the main road, and an elderly man driving a truck waved her across. She went down to the beach and let Tiras off his leash. She watched him chase seagulls into flight. She looked out at the distant dot that is Egg Island, and then she looked above and beyond it to a sky that was nothing but blue.

Chapter 2

Saturday, August 27, 2005
New Orleans—The Shores of Lake Pontchartrain

Down here, Leo's lights hang in the soft heat of spring. He sits over the treacherous tides of the mouth of the Mississippi. For thousands of years he has looked down on the water as it has flooded out every incarnation of man's settlement. Man rules for a time. But the water always comes back, and Leo is there to usher it in.

I'm on call this weekend. Normally that means getting up at 5:30 a.m., which actually isn't too bad as far as doctors' schedules go. But because there's a hurricane headed our way, and I'm the lucky bastard who was elected to be head of the activation team this year, I don't have the luxury of sleeping in until five thirty. I have a staff to direct and preparations to make. And meetings. Always meetings.

If I'm being honest, even on a regular day, driving to work doesn't fill me with the same sense of excitement and anticipation that it used to. Ever since the merger two years ago, when our crotchety but principled old president—who knew this city and made a life of helping the people of this city, and whose grandfather had founded this hospital—was forced out, things have gone downhill. Now it's all meetings and memos and signatures and corporate attorneys. They are changing our name now, too. St. Liberatus, according to the sign on its front, has officially become NewCare, the meaningless name of the corporate conglomerate, and it will sound like any other hospital in any other city.

I had gone to bed at 8:00 p.m. but had just drifted off to sleep, before I woke up dripping with sweat. It was still Saturday night; my 2:00 a.m. alarm was hours away. Usually I wake up because I hear some dumb kids getting wasted on their parents' boat or guys listening to sports on the radio or music coming out from somewhere along the marina. But this time it was the heavy, stifling quiet of heat that woke me. I got up and looked out the porthole and realized the electricity was out; the harbor, normally dotted with boat lanterns and outlined on one side by brightly lit docks, was shrouded in darkness. My air-conditioning unit had gone off. No wonder I was so damn sweaty. I stumbled around until I got out the door. Dim emergency lights sputtered in a sporadic and unhelpfully vague outline of the dock. I walked carefully, not wanting to end up in the water, until I made my way to the harbormaster's office. I almost bumped into him on his way out.

"Hey, Pete, what's—" I started.

He interrupted. "Doc, you stayin' here?"

"Well, I'm on call—"

He shook his head. "You can't stay here, Doc! You gotta get out. We're all leaving." I looked behind me, and it was then that I noticed there was only one other boat there besides mine. And it's a boat I've never seen anyone use, let alone sleep in.

I had been so dead tired when I got home that it hadn't registered.

"I'll secure her," I said.

He said, "No, Doc, you gotta get her outta here, too. She will definitely be bashed up against this dock and by whatever else is flying around, no matter how well you secure her. This one's gonna be bad. There's going to be a hell of a storm surge comin' up that waterway and crashin' right into us. Haven't you been watching the news?"

The quiet told me most people did watch the news.

There are people who evacuate for every hurricane. There are people who evacuate occasionally, if a storm is a four or a five, when it's headed in our general direction. And then there is Pete. He has never, to my knowledge, left town when a storm was on the way. He strikes me as the kind of guy who would laugh at people who did. So catching him locking up and leaving town gives me pause.

"Well, shit, Pete. I don't have a place to stash her at the moment; it's been on my to-do list—well...it's been on my to-do list for about seven years."

"I warned you a couple of days ago, man," he said, shaking his head as if he felt bad for me but wasn't going to let me blame him for losing my boat.

I didn't remember this, but that was not surprising, as I am perpetually sleep deprived and exhausted and often forget mundane conversations that I deem unimportant. I guess that tells you how seriously I take hurricane warnings.

But most New Orleanians—at least most I know—have taken their chances that whatever storm is coming isn't the Big One. And even the ones that threatened to be monsters just never scared me enough. I got lucky with each one so far: glancing blows, debris on the deck, things that I could easily fix. If the storm really looked serious, I just stayed at the house of whichever friend was having the best hurricane party. My ex would say that's typical. Irresponsible. Dangerous, even. She was born here, and I was born in Baton Rouge, but there is a state of mind that true New Orleanians, born and bred or transplants, always have. That state of mind is how we live down here. We deny a lot of things and have a good time; we overlook the rot, because there is so much richness to look at. We burn everything we have, until one day we are surprised to find we've burned ourselves up too.

Since I have been unable to sleep, and it is miserably hot in the boat with no working AC, and apparently Pete is going to give me shit if I hang around any longer, I go back to the boat and get ready for work. I dig up my flashlight and some batteries, a rain jacket, a change of clothes, and my Dopp kit. I root around the cupboards for what turns out to be a pretty sad little collection of snack-sized bags of chips and granola bars that have been there a little too long. You know you need to go grocery shopping when even your granola bars have expired. I shove everything into my backpack and a gym bag and grab my cell phone and charger and head out. I am halfway out the door when I decide to turn back and grab Dad's watch and the flag from his funeral, sealed in its triangle case. I laugh at myself; Pete has me nervous now.

I do my best in the dim light to secure *The Good Life* the way Dad once taught me. Longer lines, so she has room to move with the wind but not so long that she'll be bashed to pieces up against the dock despite what Pete says. I take one look back at her, and then I walk down to the parking lot, throw my bags in the back seat, and head to work.

Chapter 3

Saturday, August 27, 2005
New Orleans—Gentilly

"Rob," my wife calls from the bedroom. "Did you get through?"

"Nobody's picking up," I say. I am sitting in the dining room, where I wouldn't worry her with my repeated unsuccessful attempts to get us out of here. I'm sitting in one of our formal chairs that we use maybe twice a year (not even now that the girls aren't home for most holidays)—chairs that have been unchanged since we bought them with wedding money back in 1961, their cream upholstery long ago turned yellow. On the wall hang our Sears family portraits, our little family growing up and growing older in tight golden frames.

It's the fourth time I have called. I rub my eyes—the damn eyes are killing me; I need a new prescription. But it's another errand to run, and our days are already full of errands and doctor's appointments, and since we can't drive now, I pick and choose how many times I will ask the visiting nurses' association or the home health aides and our friends' daughters for favors.

I start to stand up and then sit down again. My knees are giving me trouble too. My father was right: growing old ain't for sissies. He had always said that; he was a sharecropper's son with his big neck and hands, a strong back bent by labor, and a strong and seemingly unbreakable mind that withstood the withering reality of being black and poor in rural Louisiana and then being black and poor in prewar New Orleans. At least I had some hope as a young man, watching Martin Luther King and Medgar Evers and all the other people who gave me reason to believe things could get better. I never had to wreck my body like my father did. I did not have the same nightmarish stories that he did. I had a good office job when I got out of the army; I was an accountant and bookkeeper for thirty-five years.

Dad always seemed stronger than me. If my mother got Penny's diagnosis, I think he would have charged right through. He would have just pretended that she was fine. No complaints, no moments of panic.

Besides, Dad saw brutal injuries that left people maimed; he saw relatives die from scarlet fever and botulism. He would recount these events with a detached air, dropping these conversational bombs in a matter-of-fact way that my brother Charles and I used to joke about but also found devastating. We'd be standing out in the yard with him, gathered around my barbecue, and Charles or I would mention something on the news, like the gas crisis back when the girls were very little. And he'd say, "We're lucky to have any gas at all and to have cars to put it in. Speaking of gas, my uncle Simon got gasoline poured on him as a child. They tried to light him up, you know. They didn't have any hospitals where we lived, so he died. I never met him." And then he'd say, "Is the food ready yet?"

It is hard to see Penny like this, but at least I don't stop and think about it too much like I did in the beginning. We don't really accept, at least not on purpose; we just endure. Some shadow part of our minds stubbornly believes the promise that things will get better and that they will somehow get back to where they were. I remember when Dad found out my mother had cancer. I remember his assumption that she would beat it, as though it was just a bad cold or a broken leg. The stoicism, the refusal to talk about it. Dad's denial, I always thought, helped him survive as a black man in America. Sometimes you have to have these blinders on so you can go through the day without exploding in rage at everything you experience. I don't have his toughness. But I also don't have his denial. When the doctor told us Penny had Parkinson's, I cried. I'm not ashamed of that, but my father would be. Penny cried too. What I regret is not being stronger for her in that moment.

When I was a little kid, I remember how every morning when Mom was still sleeping, when it was still dark, Dad would put on these Coke-bottle glasses he had and read the paper, a ritual I had seen him struggle to hold onto even in the years when he was working two jobs and barely had time to eat. Sometimes when I couldn't sleep or got up too early, I would wander into the kitchen and find him there at our little beat-up kitchen table, the paper spread before him like a puzzle he was trying to solve. If he only had two minutes before he had to leave for work, he would scan every headline and read every photo caption. Even though we had so little money, he always paid for a newspaper subscription because he said he wanted his sons to grow up knowing what was going on in this world. It wasn't until I was much older that I realized my mother had taught him to read after they got married.

"I want you to be aware," he would say. And he would quiz Charles and me when he got home, often late at night, well after dinnertime. I still subscribe to the paper today, even though I need one of those ridiculous magnifying reader gadgets to read it or risk getting a headache.

Dad stopped reading the paper for a while when Mom was really sick, in the weeks before the funeral. The papers had piled up while we were all busy sitting with her and then grieving and arranging plans and greeting relatives. One day not long after Mom died, Charles started to gather up the papers to throw them out and my father stopped him, saying, "I'm going to read those."

I wonder what my dad would do if he were me right now. He'd probably be boarding up the windows and sitting back with his coffee already, prepared for the storm. He wouldn't even think to evacuate. The man never had the privilege of owning a home. He was proud when both his sons achieved that goal. If he had a home, he would never leave it. I know he would be sitting here with a shotgun, waiting to see what would happen if the storm got really bad and anyone got any ideas about looting in the aftermath.

But I am different. I'm worried about my wife, and I don't feel strong enough to take care of her if we go without power or drinkable water for too long. Sometimes these storms come, and they're not so bad, but there is street flooding, and they tell you to boil your water for a few days or the power is out for the better part of a week. I don't have the strength to deal with that right now. The heat will be unbearable.

We were supposed to be picked up by the visiting nurse association. The association had hired two big vans for their clients in Gentilly. The nurse who called on Thursday told me that was the plan. She told me the driver would have my address, and if the evacuation ended up being mandatory, we would be picked up. The mayor made it mandatory yesterday. I didn't like waiting on these folks; I wanted to just get my wife out of here. But without a car, there wasn't a hell of a lot I could do.

Now it was probably getting to be too late to evacuate anyway. And I've been watching that traffic—the contraflow, all six lanes headed the hell out of Dodge—and I'm glad I'm not in it, too. These storms often turn. Except for Betsy. She had actually been worth evacuating for, and we had lived through that. The memories gave me nightmares every year when hurricane season rolled around. When the girls were young, we always evacuated; we had to protect our babies, house be damned. And we evacuated last year for Ivan too. We took up Russell's offer that time and felt guilty for doing so when the storm turned out not to be a threat. It's a hassle; you're out of house and home for days. And it's expensive; we spent a lot on hotels and gas, getting up to northern Mississippi, where we thought we would be safe from the storm.

I pick up the phone again, this damn phone I hate because it has these huge buttons, like a child's toy, because of my eyes and my slowed-down, clumsy hands, and I called again. I have lost track of how many times I have called. I am starting to worry, because I know Penny wants to leave.

I get a busy signal again.

As I dial once more, I run a finger along the top of the dining room table. I look at the gray dust that sticks to my fingertip, and think about how when Penny was better, she never let a room get dusty or the pantry get bare or the flowers go untended. I took her for granted when I was working; my mind on other things, I would come home and ask her what she did all day. One week when Penny had the flu and the girls were little, I had to take care of them. I realized what a stupid question I had been asking.

It was different after the girls left home. But Penny still kept our house immaculate, helped count donations at church, watched the neighbors' children when their mothers had to work and the regular babysitters cancelled. She took care of everyone.

I stand up, knees protesting, and walk over to the kitchen, take one of the dust cloths out of the cleaning closet, and come back and wipe down the dining-room table. I don't really care about the dust, but I know *she* does.

I turn on the radio in the family room as I think again about Stacy's offer to move to San Diego and live with her. The radio is tuned to our local news station, and they are bleating out warnings about the storm. Stacy, our oldest, had been the first to go far away, to California. San Diego. She had been in love with it ever since we took a trip out for a far-flung family reunion in the early '80s. Stacy got a scholarship to San Diego State, and before she graduated, she met a marine.

Then there was Michelle. She went to Georgia Tech and met a navy man down there. Penny teased me that they went for military men because their dad was a military man. Now Michelle and our son-in-law Robert were near San Diego, near Stacy and Darryl, their third move since they had been married after they graduated in Georgia. Sometimes Penny and I would mourn the fact that the girls hadn't stayed in New Orleans, or at least stayed in the region, close enough so that they could visit more often than once or twice a year. I have always been sure that they would come back. Now it was getting harder for Penny to travel. She had really been looking forward to more visits out to San Diego, especially now that we have four grandchildren—grandchildren who are already growing so fast.

Penny calls from the other room again. I know she is getting anxious that I'm not coming in there and giving her a report. I wish I had better news to give her; I know she wants to evacuate not just because of the storm but because she's afraid taking care of the house during a power outage and cleaning up branches and such will be too much for me and this old ticker. She wouldn't believe me when I said I could handle it, but that's the thing with old love and marriages like ours, which have mostly been good: we each want to save the other and would give anything to help our spouse live forever.

When Penny's motor skills really started to deteriorate, she would get so angry trying to open a pill bottle or a door or just trying to work her way around the garden in the backyard or her little patch of flowers out front. The things she used to do with ease. The things she and I used to take for granted, nearly every Sunday for forty-five years.

I fell in love with her in the summer of 1957. We were just kids, barely out of high school. I had been in boot camp at Fort Leonard Wood up in Missouri. I was on my way home for a visit before I got transferred out to Germany, and I took a side trip to Memphis on my way back to New Orleans with a few of the other guys. She was a waitress at a local barbecue joint, a cute caramel-skinned girl with beautiful brown eyes who intimidated me with her bright smile and witty responses to my flirtatious buddies. I would never have had the guts to talk to her if I hadn't felt I had to show off a little in front of those guys.

Before I left that night, I got her number, and two days later, I called her from my parents' house in New Orleans. We talked for a while, and I asked for her address. I was stationed in Germany for a year, and we wrote letters. I'm not a great writer, but I could not forget about this girl, and I wanted to stay connected to her. So I would write about the base, about what the Germans I met were like…anything I could think of. She, on the other hand, wrote beautifully. She described her customers and her family, little things that happened to her. She wrote about her dog and her church meetings and the classes she was taking at a local college. English. French. History. She wanted to be a teacher. Each time I got a new letter from her, I would keep it in my pocket all day, and my hands would shake from anticipation and nervousness. I would wait until right before lights out to read it, which was stupid, really, because then I couldn't get to sleep. I was too busy thinking about her.

I visited her a week after I got back from Germany; we had been planning it for months. We got married before I was assigned to Texas the following year. She was so beautiful, with her hair all done up, and a pretty white dress that she had made with the help of her sister.

Now Penny spends a lot of time lying down, her limbs shaking, her head nodding. She was always so active, full of energy, quick with a funny joke when I came home each night, in the early years of our marriage. She would tease me because she always beat me at cards. She worked as a kindergarten teacher by then, when the girls started going to school, and she got up early to get ready for her day. She would be home before I got back from my job at Louisiana Oil, taking care of the girls after school and making dinner. At night after the girls had gone to bed, we would watch a little TV and play gin rummy or cribbage. Those times are precious to me now.

"Can we call the girl?" Penny had said from the other room. She meant the nurse who had promised there would be a ride.

"I only have the number she gave me for the van," I said. "And the number for the agency, and I've tried both."

"I guess we won't be leaving," she said. Her voice dropped, her brow heavy with thought.

She's thinking of Betsy. It happened in 1965, the year we moved back to New Orleans. When I had fulfilled my military duty, I was honorably discharged. I thought about staying on, out of guilt; besides, with the draft and my experience, I knew I would get called back. Penny was terrified of me going to Vietnam, though, so I left. And I never did get that call.

Betsy came two years before Stacy was born. When we first moved back, we were living on the edge of 8th Ward, renting a house not far from my parents' apartment. We rode out the storm in my friend Russell's attic, because their house was farther away from the levees than ours was.

I still remember the walk back to our home after the floodwaters receded. We had a wall of mud in our front yard, covering everything, caked over, and ruined furniture, bicycles, and trash lay strewn all over the neighborhood. Down at the cemetery, cars crashed into tombstones, splitting them into pieces, and in the street were suitcases and trunks broken open, spilling muddy beads and fabric from ruined Mardi Gras Indians costumes. We saw the bodies of an elderly couple who had brought us a Doberge cake to welcome Penny to New Orleans. Now whenever I see one of those cakes, with its layers of chocolate and lemon pudding, I think of that elderly couple lying in the street a block away from what used to be their home. Shoes off, half-clothed.

Betsy blew right over those levees. Not just our neighborhood in the 8th Ward but Gentilly and most of the 9th Ward, and Chalmette and Araby. The floodwaters didn't go down for more than a week, and for months afterward, they would still find people who had died in their homes, in their attics. President Johnson came to survey the damage.

This is why we evacuated nearly every time. And why we were trying to now.

I go into the kitchen for our coffee. Baron, our little beagle, has finally roused himself from bed and pads into the kitchen. "Hey, buddy," I say, patting him. It was on Michelle's first birthday that we got our first dog. Penny grew up with dogs; my parents weren't dog people and didn't want to pay for one—not that I blame them. After they moved to New Orleans, Dad worked in a factory in Algiers off and on; sometimes he got laid off, and he would take jobs at the docks or in one of the restaurants—whatever he could get. He and Mom saved every spare penny they had. One year they dressed us all up in our nicest clothes and took us out to the best restaurant in 8th Ward to celebrate my mother's fortieth birthday. It was a big deal to my father to be able to take her there. I have a bitter memory of watching a white trolley driver talk to my father as if he was a moron. My father, who could have beaten that man to Mississippi and back, sat there and said nothing, but it cast a pall over that special night for all of us.

My mother worked as a nanny for a white woman in Uptown for many years. She rode a bus and a trolley to get to the woman's house. My parents had never made it past fourth grade; they were at work with their sharecropper parents when they turned eleven. They both had the hands of workers. I remember looking at their hands when I was little, playing with the skin, rubbing the calluses on their palms. I've worked hard in my life but not like the way they did. My father had moved to the city for a job after his parents died. He met my mother in Treme, where he had gone to see a jazz band play on Friday night, a rare night out for him. But soon after they were married, the Depression hit. They lived in a room in a boarding house and struggled to find work like everyone else. Then the government stepped in, and my father was able to get a job through the WPA, helping to build wharves on the city's waterfront. When the war came, they both found good factory jobs, and that's when they rented the apartment we had grown up in.

When Penny and I got this house, we tried to have them move in with us, but they always said they weren't ready yet. They lived in that apartment, paying rent to the grandson of the man they first paid rent to, until the men from Charbonnet Labat Funeral Home came to take each of their bodies away.

I feed Baron and then go to make the coffee. I have been on this mission to get us evacuated since yesterday and have been sitting at that phone when I first woke up; we barely slept last night, worrying about all this nonsense since the forecast kept getting worse. Now for just a moment, the storm fades to the back of my mind as I move into my familiar routine, the rhythm of my mornings:

make the coffee, take a cup outside and walk the yard with Baron, bring a cup to Penny, and sit and drink another one with her.

I listen to the machine heat up. The water starts to gurgle. I spilled some grinds pouring them into the filter, so I stop to clean them up. I take out the mugs that I had let dry in the dish rack the night before. These mugs have been with us forever; they have the familiar brown-and-orange color palette that was so popular back in the '70s when we bought them. We never did get around to installing a dishwasher. Penny always wanted one but had never asked for one. I knew she wanted it because I saw her eyeing them in the stores and at our friends' houses. We could have afforded it when I was still working. But she was too frugal. She didn't like to make big purchases. She had been washing and scrubbing pots and pans and dishes and silverware and Tupperware by hand for all these years, and since it was just the two of us after the girls left home, Penny insisted it was silly to spend money on a dishwasher. I have a small pension, and we have Social Security, but all our pills are expensive, and Medicare does not cover everything.

Last year the girls came for Christmas. It's tough to fit everyone in the house, but it was great to have the girls and the grandkids here. We put Michelle and Robert and their boys out in the den with the pullout and Stacy and her girls (Darryl was deployed again—Iraq; these boys have seen far worse things than I ever did, which sometimes makes me feel ashamed) in the girls' old bedroom. I puttered in the garage with Robert, and he helped me—not that I asked him to—with some projects I had been meaning to finish for some time, like putting a new door on the shed and cleaning out the gutters. We brought the grandkids to Audubon Park and the movies; we took them on a trolley ride. They're West Coast kids, so they didn't marvel at it being in the '60s at Christmastime, but they marveled at how old everything is. Secretly, I wanted them to love it. I wanted the girls to fall back in love with it and talk their husbands into coming back to New Orleans. Of course, they couldn't control where they were assigned, but they could leave the military or retire early.

I get carried away. It's just an old father's wishful thinking. The girls aren't coming back.

We were up late one night when the girls were here, and they brought us up moving out there. The girls had talked about it, and they thought we should move in with Stacy. She had the larger home, and I think as the big sister, she felt it was her responsibility. My heart sank, because I knew my foolish dream of them moving back to Louisiana was never going to be realized.

We put them off, saying we would revisit the idea later, and since then we had pretty much avoided the subject. Neither of us want to move, as much as we would love to be closer to the girls and the grandkids, because we're concerned that if we move out there and the sons-in-law get transferred somewhere else, we'll have to move again to some other place we don't know.

New Orleans is home.

Penny takes her coffee black. I head back through the living room, passing the shrill tones of the radio. I double back to turn it off. Peace and quiet, for just a few minutes.

"Did you leave a message?" Penny calls from the next room.

"No," I say as I walk in. "The first few times, I got a busy signal. Then a few times, nothing but ringing," I continue. "They've probably evacuated and forgot we were on the list."

Soon it will be too late to get out whether we have a ride or not. She's coming either very late tonight or early in the morning.

"Your knees?" Penny asks me, her still-sharp eyes catching my attempts to walk normally despite the pain. I nod.

"Must be the storm," she says. "Barometer's wreaking havoc with us old folks."

I hand her the mug, slowly, making sure she has a good grasp on it. I am always careful not to fill it too high or give it to her too hot. The table next to her has a well-worn coaster. I sit down on the chair beside the bed. This chair is older than our marriage. It's an antique but then, again, so are we now. Penny picked it up somewhere in Texas at an estate sale. I never liked the chair because its dark fabric reminded me of Penny's parents' house. That house and their disapproving looks. A dark house, still decorated in the 1930s working-class style, with lace on the backs of chairs like this and rooms darkened by heavy drape curtains. The chair had a floral pattern in black and blood red originally, although it had faded to a gray and maroon. Penny had sat rocking our babies in this chair. I can still picture her here, her hair pulled up in a scarf; the baby, Michelle, resting against her; and Stacy playing on the floor nearby. Music on in the background; always music. She had loved Ella Fitzgerald and Billie Holiday when we first met. But down here was where she truly fell in love with jazz, with Louis Armstrong and Wayne Shorter. She later liked some of the music the girls liked in the '80s; she tried to be one of those moms who was open to change and wouldn't grumble about her girls' taste and all the scary trends in popular culture. She wanted to be engaged in their lives and to understand who they were. Her own mom never came down to visit us once. In her mind, Penny had abandoned them when she married me. Penny was the one her parents thought would always stay in Memphis and take care of them. They turned their backs on her, and it broke her heart. Her mother cursed her by saying she hoped she would have a daughter who would turn her back on her one day and abandon her too. And now both girls had moved away. It was different, though, I tried to console her; they love their mother, and she loves them so fiercely. It hurts me to hear how much her voice perks up when one of the girls calls. She misses them so.

"What's Russell doing? Did he leave?" Penny asks.

Our friend Russell had called a couple of days ago. I had told him we were all set, that we had a ride if we decided to evacuate. I thought we did. I didn't want to impose such a task on him again; it felt like we had asked Russell for too many favors already.

"Yeah, he and Ronny went up to Baton Rouge to stay with her sister. They left earlier this week." Russell and I grew up together down in 8th Ward. He went off to join the navy when I went into the army. I had seen him occasionally when he was home on leave, and briefly when the girls were little and he was stationed in New Orleans for a couple of years. Twenty years later he retired and came home, after serving all over the world—Vietnam, California, Alaska—with his wife and their two sons. Ever since then we'd been seeing him and his wife, Veronica, at least a couple of times a month. Sometimes we'd just go to a bar in Marigny, where we used to go when we were in high school, and shoot the shit, and sometimes we'd get together with some of the guys I used to work with at the oil company, and because Russell always had a bit of a rebel bent, we'd go to a place we never would or could have gone when we were young men, because it was unquestionably a white place—like the Carousel Bar at the Hotel de Monteleone. We'd ask him why he wanted to go to a hangout like that, but every time we went there, he would go on about the people who couldn't go there before, and in the case of the Carousel Bar, he'd yammer on with all his literary knowledge about the authors who used to sit there and get drunk, mostly Tennessee Williams or Faulkner. Russell should have been an English professor. If things were different where and when we were growing up, he probably would have been; instead, he delivers these drunken sermons and gets quite poetic in his mockery of my miraculous escape from serving during the Vietnam War.

But it has been a mostly good life. It was better when Penny was healthy and I was still working. The army and then the oil-company job. I was a bookkeeper and practically an accountant without a degree in accounting; every assignment I had on active duty was related to numbers once they realized I was good at it. In the late '60s, they would still hire you without a degree, if you could find a company that wasn't run by a bunch of racist good ol' boys. I had always done well in math as a kid, so accounting made sense. Russell used to make fun of me because I would always finish my math problems well before him and do better on the math tests than he did. He called me a teacher's pet and a nerd. But then I made fun of him for his reading habit. I never saw someone check so many books out of the school library.

I was lucky in more ways than one when I came home after my service. New Orleans wasn't exactly the headquarters of equality, but there was already a black man working in my company by the time I got there, and he had done the Jackie Robinson—I know he had endured a lot, and he was never particularly nice to me, but I would have done anything for him anyway, because I knew he put up with a lot of shit before I arrived. Not that it was all sunshine and rainbows for me, either; don't get me wrong. All the guys there thought I was a janitor; they talked to me as though I am not intelligent. They thought I was hired just to fit a quota. And the pay. I knew what everyone in that company was paid, and I made less than every single person there except the college intern. But I clawed my way, slowly, determined, from one year to the next, doggedly checking my work (you can't make mistakes when you are someone like me). I watched a lot of men who came in after me get promoted before me.

There was the oil bust in the '80s; they fired us all and eventually hired us back. Until they did, I worked three part-time jobs to try to keep our finances in check. Those were tough times. But they were tough times everywhere down South, including in New Orleans.

I love New Orleans, even though I get tired of it sometimes. The poverty in this city is the fate of too many black folks. I get tired of getting watched like a hawk in every white store I go into, especially if I am not with Penny or my girls.

But in the end I did all right. In the '70s, things got a little better; maybe it was the mayors, Morial and Landrieu, pressuring the bigwigs to stop being so damn backward. Or maybe it was just that some of the higher-ups at my company found a conscience. Or maybe they just feared a lawsuit. I got a few promotions, and by the time I retired, I was a senior manager. We paid off our mortgage the year before I retired. We were very ceremonial about it; we burned it over the grill in the backyard. I had a small savings and a pension; it wasn't a huge pension, but it was enough to pay our utilities and groceries every month, which helped stretch the Social Security check, so we could occasionally buy gifts for the grandkids or new toys for Baron or pay for dinner if Russell and Ronny took us out.

And that pension still helps us pay for all these damn pills.

As Penny sips her coffee, I stare at the big labels on the pill bottles next to her on the nightstand. It's hard to accept rides from people as if I'm a charity case, when I've been driving this many years and never once had a real accident. But before we got rid of the car, I had come so close many times. With my eyes and my old-man reflexes, every trip to the store was like a drive through an obstacle course. I was driving too slow and getting honked at and hitting the occasional curb. It was damn humiliating. My depth perception just wasn't there anymore, and sometimes it felt as though my eyes were wrapped in cotton, all fuzzy. It was tough when we sold the car.

I notice that Penny's left arm is shaking, jerking more than usual. I wonder if her medication is wearing off. But it is too soon for another dose.

"They forgot about us," Penny says, head nodding, her hazel eyes, still beautiful, dimmed with worry. "The nurses."

"I'm sure it will be okay, honey," I say. "These things always turn away at the last minute. I love you," I say, taking her hand.

"I love you too," she says.

Chapter 4

Sunday Night
Maine

At 5:45 p.m., Ava drove through the heart of East Tamarack to go meet her uncle. Like most New England villages, East Tamarack had a proper green town. At the edge of the green was a white clapboard Congregational church with a bright steeple and a black-and-gold painted clock. In the middle of the green stood a statue of a contemplative Union infantryman staring out into the town, a list of his dead brethren spread over stone below him. Past the green, windy streets led down to the docks and Penobscot Bay, and all along the main street stood still-proud houses slouching with age. The old houses were well tended, with freshly painted shutters, unsullied American flags, and shining doorknockers in the shapes of ships and whales and lobsters. Their front yards burst with lavender, chokecherry, and witch hazel.

Ava drove past the heart of downtown and looked out at the twin lighthouses, born from past disasters, marking the edges of opposite shores. The pines crept up nearly to the water in many places, with only a sliver of rocky beaches between them. Soon the loveliness of the houses started to fade, and the landscape gave way to the outskirts of town, dotted with dive bars and strip malls.

At the cemetery gate, Ava's truck bumped along a frost-cracked path. The tall ancient trees that gave the Cemetery of the Pines its name stood guard at the edges of the green, rolling hills dotted with monuments.

Her uncle was leaning against his old truck, his back to the graves, looking out at Penobscot Bay. "Hey, Ava!" His face broke into a smile. He started to limp toward her.

"Hey, Uncle K." She hugged him, breathing in the old familiar scent of Old Spice and coffee. He drank coffee all day.

He brought something, as she did, for all four of them. He brought cigars for Grandpa Noah and Dad and flowers for his mother and sister. They walked up the small path and down past a row of familiar headstones.

The air was heavy with the scent of balsam pine. They stopped in front of four sleek slate-gray stones:

John Stephen Cabot
Abigail Beal Cabot
Noah Oliver Beal
Janet Sewall Beal

Keenan walked up to his father's stone and balanced the cigar on top. Ava laid the flowers she had brought at the base of all their stones. Then she pulled out the little postcard she had ordered online for her father's grave: a reprint of the inside of the old New Orleans Opera House. You could see enough detail to make out the numbers on the old box seats.

Ava felt that dull ache flare up, sharp, into her chest, throat, and mouth; the heavy, crushing memory of wrenching loss; and the dim, sad awareness of everything she had missed since.

They stood there for a while, while the sun got lower in the sky and the breeze blew through the trees.

Eventually Keenan asked, "What do you think, Ava? Time to go?" She nodded, so they did what they did every year—they went to Harry's Lobster Pot.

When they got there, they settled into the 1970s-era dark wooden armchairs in the bare-floored dining room and toasted their family.

After they finished, the waitress came over to check on them one more time.

"Can I get you anything else?" she asked, looking down at the decimated haddock on their plates. They shook their heads.

While she tore off the check, the waitress asked, "Did you see the evacuation down in New Orleans?" She turned toward the bar, where two TVs were affixed to the wall. She pronounced it New Orleeeens, like most Northerners.

Ava's father had explained to her long ago that as far as New Orleanians were concerned, it was only okay to say it that way if you were Louis Armstrong looking for a word that rhymes with "means" when singing "Do You Know What it Means to Miss New Orleans." It was one of his few pet peeves with the Mainers, and all other Yankees, for that matter.

"Looks like it's going to be a big one." The waitress continued as she gathered up their plates. Ava and Keenan nodded and followed the waitress's gaze to the bar, where the bartender's customers were mostly quiet. They stared at some weatherman talking with a map of the Gulf behind him. There she was, the storm that had already hit Florida, now a clear, bright, swirling mass with a black hole in the center, a Chinese star aimed at the throat of the Mississippi.

"Have you heard anything from your dad's family?" Uncle Keenan asked.

She shook her head. "I tried to call Ellis a few times. He's the only one I'm still in touch with at this point." Her uncle's face betrayed his disappointment for her, but he didn't know what to say, so he decided to change the subject.

"Are you going to take a vacation this year before you end up losing your time?"

"I don't think so," she said, eyes still on the screen. "Nothing planned right now."

"Ava," Keenan said, "use it. You've earned it. Go visit one of your friends. You don't go anywhere."

"I don't like to leave Tiras," she said, feeling her defenses lock into place.

"We'll take care of him! We'll spoil him like you do. He'll be fine." Keenan leaned forward, his elbows on the table. "Your aunt Rosa and I worry about you. You spend too much time alone. Go visit some of your college friends." He paused. Ava noticed how gray his beard was getting; she remembered back when her dad and grandpa died and her uncle seemed so young. He himself was just a kid then, newly married at twenty-three.

He had her mother's eyes, dark chocolate brown.

"You are just like your aunt, always taking care of everybody else. Do something nice for *you*." This was a theme with her uncle. Aunt Rosa was a social worker and constantly going above and beyond for her clients. She would spend her own money on little things like phone cards and lunch at a local diner, warm food for someone's kids to help them get to the next paycheck on Friday.

Ava was like her, and she was proud to be, for the most part. But there was a darkness to her attempts to help; sometimes she wore herself to the bone helping people who did not want to be helped. After college, Ava had moved home to live with her mother, who was not doing well mentally and had never really recovered from what happened. Ava got a job, helped around the house, and obsessively tried to please her mother. But her mother could not be pleased. After two years, Ava was at work when she got the call that her mother was dead. She had suffered a major heart attack. Luckily it was after the kids had left for the day; one of her colleagues found her at her desk. She wept, and she was so sad for her mother and what her mother's life was like in those final years. Darker than it had to be. But she was also relieved, and that made her grieve too.

At first Ava had wild thoughts of escaping; she wanted to leave this town and never come back. One year she had a plan that she would move to New Orleans for a while to see if she could reconnect with her dad's family. She told everyone, but then she didn't move. The following year she had a new plan: Boston or New York. She told everyone and even did research and started looking for jobs. But she just stayed where she was. She took care of the neighbors and her mom's bills and remembered every birthday of her high school and college friends and her mother's friends. She took care of her dogs. First Jessie, and then a year after he passed away, she got Tiras.

Ava, tired of having variations of this conversation because she had no good defense, avoided her uncle's eyes and looked around the restaurant. She watched red-faced tourists wrestle with their dinners, their tables littered with lobster body parts, a multitude of tiny crime scenes.

Uncle Keenan changed the subject as he looked down at his placemat. "They changed this," he said.

Ava looked down at it. "Wow, they did," she said. "They've had the same placemat since I was born." She remembered drawing on it when her parents and grandparents would take her here. It had one of those '60s-era cartoony drawings of Tamarack and East Tamarack with cartoon caricatures of local business people and tourist attractions. Now the illustration was modernized with a crisp aerial photo of the town and the bay flanked on either side by advertisements for local merchants.

"It has Pop's story," Keenan said, pointing to the back of his placemat. There were three short stories on it. The first told the story of Harry and how he founded the Lobster Pot when he came home from World War I. The second talked about Tamarack and how the whites abandoned it during the French and Indian War and then resettled. And the third was about Egg Island:

The very unfortunate Captain James Egg was an Englishman looking to found a fishermen's settlement in 1765, two years after the end of the French and Indian War. His ship ran aground on Egg Island, three miles from the shores of East Tamarack. Not even fir trees could take root on Egg Island, as they do on thousands of other islands along the Maine coast. The crew had no shelter and no water to drink, for it hadn't rained. The one hapless gull the sailors had caught on the rock wasn't enough to feed the seven survivors, and so they resorted to cannibalism. Only two of the sailors survived. One was Captain Egg, and the other was a boatswain, Robert Black. Back home in England, the captain claimed he was haunted by the outraged ghosts of his murdered crew, and he committed suicide. Black, whose popular and gruesome account of the incident made him rich, retired high above his station, and he never went to sea again. He wouldn't even cross the Thames.

"Pops used to love to tell this story," Uncle K said. "It's funny, but even though he has been gone so long, I still sometimes remember things about him that I hadn't thought about since he died." Ava nodded. She remembered being scared by this story as a child, but it was nothing compared to what Egg Island invoked in her now.

An hour later, Ava was walking up her crooked front path, stretching her legs so her feet would land only on flagstones. She passed her neighbor's front window and glimpsed people sitting in folding chairs, drinks in hand, talking and laughing. A light breeze brought the smell of the ocean up into the neighborhood. The gulf coast's wind warnings and dire predictions were a world away. Here the hot green summer was moving out over the water, where Leviathan would wrestle it down and bring the cool night air to cover Maine and all her people.

Chapter 5

Sunday, 10:30 p.m.

St. Liberatus

The wind has picked up. It had been still and quiet until now; in fact, it had been still and quiet for days, and for a moment I imagine this is how it was one hundred years ago, in places like Galveston, when they had no warning: it was just another night, and then the wind picked up, and everything changed forever.

The streets are always deserted when I drive into work, but they are even more so today. It is eerie and made more so by the ghostly light from my headlights. A transformation occurs when I drive from my neighborhood to the one that I work in. The streets get shabbier; the homes get slouchier. The neutral grounds here are overgrown with weeds, and the palm trees wave shaggy fronds in the rising winds. I park my car in its usual spot on the floor of the parking garage adjoining the ICU. I walk through the hallway connecting the two buildings, the concrete walls sweating around me. Then I curse, realizing I need to go back down to Administration on the first floor to get my Code Yellow bracelet. Things can get hectic during a storm. We all have to wear our bracelets so people know at a glance who works here.

On my way out of the elevator, I glance in at the goings-on in the emergency room; it is noticeably quieter than usual, though not empty. It is never empty; we are a city of six hundred thousand souls. There is always somebody in New Orleans who has a heart attack or got beat up or overdosed or caught the stomach flu or has finally come here out of desperation because something has been hurting them for a long time but they were terrified to come because they couldn't afford to pay the bill.

One of the administrative staff who serves on some committees with me calls out. "Doctor Ray! You stickin' around for this madness?" I nod. I'm the chair of the Emergency Preparedness Committee this year. Basically, I lost a coin toss with Dr. Peck. And for this particular emergency, I am the Emergency Incident Commander and Head of the Activation Team. So much bureaucratic bullshit—basically it's my turn to be in charge when the shit goes down.

I go to the security desk and see Judah Robbins, the head of security, already checking names and handing out bracelets. He is training one of the guys on his team; the young man, whose name I don't know, looks nervous and tired and seems to be struggling to pay attention to what Judah is doing. The fluorescent lights are buzzing above our heads.

"Hey, Doc," Judah says, "ready for the big one?"

"I don't know, man," I say. "We'll do our best, right?"

He nods. "Yup. See you at the nine a.m." Our team meeting. One of many we are scheduled to have throughout the next twenty-four hours.

"See you."

I go back upstairs.

It is quiet on my floor. The night nurses and physicians on call are working on paperwork, eyeing monitors, and talking softly. I'm covering for a few of my fellow physicians today. Doctors Jain and Osgood are going to be in, but the three of us are covering for all nine partners in our practice. We have lung-cancer patients, an accident victim, a teenager with renal failure who is waiting on a transplant, and some older folks who are recovering from surgery and too sick to go home. I check in with the night nurses, getting updates on my cases. It's early for rounds, but I do mine anyway, waking up patients, because I want to transfer anyone I can transfer out of here. I can't discharge anyone straight from an ICU, of course, but if I can send someone to a less-critical floor, now is the time to get the ball rolling on paperwork.

During rounds I find that two patients are improved enough that they can leave the ICU and go to a less-critical floor. Afterward I go down the patient list, updating my notes for everyone.

I save my youngest patient for last, wanting him to get as much rest as possible because he is also one of the most vulnerable patients we have. Andy's just a kid—only 12 years old—but he was born with only one kidney, and it's in failure. If we had a pediatric ICU, he'd be there, but right now we don't, since we are renovating half of the peds floor. All we have is a NICU and an adult ICU, so here he is. His other organs have been compromised to the point where he needs help breathing, and now he's fighting an infection. He's been on dialysis for a long time, and while one of his family friends has stepped up to help, and thank God he was a match, we need to get Andy stable enough for the operation. Andy's nephrologist, Dr. Shery, is in charge, but she has also evacuated with her family, and we don't have a nephrologist on site. She will consult with us by phone as needed. It's my job to keep her informed.

"How's our young man?" I say to Andy's mother. She is half-awake, looking exhausted as she sits by her son's bedside. She has hardly left since he was brought up to our floor four days ago. She is dressed in jeans and sneakers, her hair in disarray, her face drawn, her eyes red and bloodshot.

Andy is sedated right now. We would often avoid sedation for cases like these, but it is stressful to be conscious and on a ventilator, and Andy was terrified when he was awake on that machine. Now he is lying there, a bean pole of a boy entangled in all the entrapments of modern medicine: leads, lines, and plastic tubing. I check his chart and find that he is little changed from last night. I want to see the fever go down more, and I need him to beat this infection. I've been doing this for almost two decades now, and I never get used to the sight of a kid in an ICU bed.

"I know it's tough," I say, looking at his mother. "But he's fighting the infection, and we just need to give him more time."

She nods. But she has something else on her mind now too. "What are we going to do about the storm?" Her forehead is a crease of worry.

"Well, we have supplies here, and we'll be safe, so we're all going to ride it out. Are your husband and your daughter still in the city, or have they evacuated?"

"They've evacuated," she says. "My husband brought the baby up to my parents' house in Bossier City so I can stay with Andy."

I nod. "Okay. We're all just going to hunker down. Call the nurse if you need anything."

I check on one last patient before I allow myself a coffee break. Then I check on Michaela Good. She's young too, car-accident victim, just a few years older than Andy. I believe she is a sophomore at LSU. She is brown haired and freckle faced. She will have some scars from this, but that is the least of her worries. She is recovering from a pretty major surgery that repaired numerous internal injuries she had from the accident. She was not driving. The passengers always seem to get it the worst. I nod to her mother and father after reading her vitals.

The looks the parents, wives, husbands, girlfriends, and boyfriends give me are one of the few parts of this job that I hate. The reliance they have on my skill is humbling. I always want to give good news, but, of course, so often I cannot tell them what they are longing to hear. In this case, I am hopeful; her youth is on her side, and her chances of a full recovery are quite good. I remind them of this, and their faces brighten. I say her vitals are holding steady, which they are; I am reaching for every detail I can honestly tell them without inflating their hopes too much. I do not want to downplay the extent of what she has gone through.

I go back to the break room and grab a cup of coffee. It is terrible as usual. I find this oddly comforting, as if this is just another day at the office.

I leave to walk the two blocks over to my practice. Our hulking hospital is flanked by a handful of mismatched medical-office buildings, a couple of parking garages, and a physical plant. My office is right next to the physical plant. The buildings are all slick and gray-green with morning dew and the heavy summer air that suspends us all in anticipation of this monster storm. When I step outside, I'm surprised at how much more the wind has picked up already compared to when I drove in. A couple of trashcans are bumping around the parking lot. Plastic bags are blowing around, getting stuck in trees. Somewhere I hear metal clanking on metal. I think of *The Good Life* smashing her hull to bits against the pier.

I walk into my building and nod to the security guy, who is relatively new, and I'm embarrassed that I don't know his name because he knows mine.

"You getting out of here, Dr. Ray?" he asks. He is a young kid, barely twenty, I would guess. I only know his name because it is on a tag he is wearing: Chris.

"Nope, I'm on call," I say. "What about you? I hope you're taking off?"

He shakes his head. "Nope! I want to get paid, and nobody else wants to work this weekend, so extra cash for me!"

I smile, but then I think about this kid being alone over here. "If anything happens, come over to the hospital, okay?" I say. He nods, looking slightly irritated, as if I've suggested he can't handle it.

I walk up the stairs and unlock the door to our practice. I walk through our empty waiting room. Our waiting room is just about what you would expect, with terribly outdated magazines and gauzy, out-of-focus paintings on the walls. I actually hate this place. I don't like coming here. It's gotten too big, and it's not what I envisioned when I started this business eighteen years ago with one of my friends from my fellowship days. I feel like I spend half my time filling out forms and talking about billing issues with our staff. I hate insurance companies. They serve no purpose other than to stress out my patients and me and to deny care that I thought was necessary and administered for a reason. People around here do not get enough health care as it is, and the ones who have insurance barely have it any better sometimes. And so often we end up seeing the ones without insurance in the emergency room when it's too late to do much good.

I go back to my little office, which is tucked in a corner next to one of the exam rooms. I start to make a half-hearted attempt to organize my paperwork and return emails. I check to make sure I don't have any appointments that need to be rescheduled tomorrow. It's hardly necessary; we talked about this last week, and it looks like most people have already cancelled. Our office manager, Viola, has taken care of the others. She's in Tennessee right now. Two of her childhood friends drowned when Hurricane Betsy hit. Since then she has evacuated for every hurricane, including Ivan in 2004. She sat in traffic and said she would do it again.

I look out the window. The streets beyond our complex are empty. I look at the photos on my desk of my parents, both gone now, and my brother and his wife and kids. Greg's in Wisconsin now, teaching math at a state university up there. I'm a terrible uncle. I send the kids birthday cards (I finally figured out how to set my calendar reminders so I would remember the dates), and I send them Christmas gifts. I haven't been to a Christmas up there in four years. They don't come down here anymore now that Mom and Dad are gone, and my schedule is not very accommodating. When I was with Jane, she would be more proactive about these things. She would have the cards picked out and would sign them, leaving a space for me to sign my name next to hers. Jane took care of all those little things—little things that I never thought about, because I didn't have to. She also took care of the house, when we had a house. And the dogs, which she took with her when we split up. I still miss the dogs. And I miss Jane too—I have to admit that. But I'm never home, and she had a normal nine-five job. Something in marketing, that's what she does. I never truly understood what she did. I never took the time to understand it. I can be a bit of an asshole sometimes.

The cars…she even took care of those. She took care of my parents' presents, and I let her do it all; it's like I put my home life on autopilot and merely checked in when I was asked to. She took care of everything, and, eventually, she got sick of the fact that I never took care of her. She couldn't compete with the true love of my life. No woman can.

As if on cue, Jane calls. We haven't talked in over two years. But she is calling now, I know, because she wants to make sure I'm going to take care of myself and evacuate. I don't answer. I don't want to tell her the truth.

But in the end, I don't know if my love is good for me. I didn't think it would be like this. I was the kid who won first prize at the eighth-grade science fair with my report on the different types of blood cells. I labored over those poster boards. I loved biology class; I actually read ahead to find out what I would learn in the next chapter of that hefty, well-worn high-school textbook. I still remember the look and feel of it; the smell of the paper shopping bag I had used as a book cover, the sharp colors of the illustrations, the corners that had started to wear, and the scrawled names of former students written above mine in the inside cover.

When I played war games with the other kids in my Baton Rouge neighborhood, I wasn't the general, or a regular infantryman—I was the medic. When I was growing up, I always pictured myself like Hawkeye from M*A*S*H, some cool ladies' man who also just happened to be a very gifted and caring surgeon. Thirty-odd years later, here I was, in the midst of the reality of the modern physician: the actual treatments and therapies; the cutthroat politics; the sometimes-frustrating patients and colleagues; and the mind-deadening reality of insurance, paperwork, and memos from the CEO basically written by hospital attorneys;

and bureaucratic legalese overtaking standards of care and other basic principles we should all be focused on.

Today the hospital attorney and CEO are at the top of my "unread" email list. I squint until I remember to put on my glasses (I'm still not used to them), and I scan the bold-faced unread subject lines that start with "PLEASE READ" and are full of precautions about reports to make and statements to read and policies to follow and updates about promotions and mergers and other stuff I don't give a rat's ass about.

There are two emails from my brother, asking if I'm leaving, if I want to come visit, what my plan is. I know I should respond, but I put it off, thinking I'll do it later, when everything's over and everything's fine.

I click away from my email and onto the NOAA website. I was checking it to the point of obsession when I was in here yesterday, waiting for the storm to turn to the right or the left. It always does.

My screen fills with capital letters shouting a breathless warning:

6:12 AM CDT, SUNDAY, AUG 28, 2005
DEVASTATING DAMAGE EXPECTED...A MOST POWERFUL HURRICANE WITH UNPRECEDENTED STRENGTH...MOST OF THE AREA WILL BE UNINHABITABLE FOR WEEKS... PERHAPS LONGER. AT LEAST ONE HALF OF WELL CONSTRUCTED HOMES WILL HAVE ROOF AND WALL FAILURE...THE MAJORITY OF INDUSTRIAL BUILDINGS WILL BECOME NONFUNCTIONAL.... ALL WOOD FRAMED LOW RISING APARTMENT BUILDINGS WILL BE DESTROYED... HIGH RISE APARTMENT AND OFFICE BUILDINGS WILL SWAY DANGEROUSLY...A FEW TO THE POINT OF TOTAL COLLAPSE. AIRBORNE DEBRIS WILL BE WIDESPREAD. THE BLOWN DEBRIS WILL CREATE ADDITIONAL DESTRUCTION. PERSONS...PETS...AND LIVESTOCK EXPOSED TO THE WINDS WILL FACE CERTAIN DEATH IF STRUCK. POWER OUTAGES WILL LAST FOR WEEKS. WATER SHORTAGES WILL MAKE HUMAN SUFFERING INCREDIBLE BY MODERN

STANDARDS. THE VAST MAJORITY OF NATIVE TREES
WILL BE SNAPPED OR UPROOTED...FREQUENT GUSTS AT
OR NEAR HURRICANE FORCE ARE CERTAIN WITHIN THE
NEXT 12 TO 24 HOURS...DO NOT VENTURE OUTSIDE!

I sit back in my chair. I turn to look out the window and see that there is a Wizard -of- Oz green to the darkness that has infused the sky; a day that was just starting seems to be ending already. Droplets of rain start to pelt the windows.

I think about the last time my family was here. I remember talking with Dad about how he was enjoying retirement. He had been a mathematician for forty years. He bought *The Good Life* two years before he got sick. He died at another hospital in the city, one with a better oncology program than ours. I used to wander over there after work, sitting with him at the oddest hours. They let me in past visiting hours because I'm a colleague. I would bring his newspaper and read an article or two to him before he fell asleep again or got too tired to pay attention. Then we would just talk about how we wished New Orleans had a baseball team or how Greg and the kids were doing.

That was my lowest point. I'm not an oncologist, of course, and Dr. Pelo is a great one. One of the best in the entire region. I knew Dad's cancer was too far gone for even the world's best oncologist to treat successfully. But we tried all the treatments, and some foolish part of me harbored hope. I prayed, which I hadn't done in a long, long time. But there was no miracle.

Dad, always thinking in numbers, asked for his odds on a regular basis. Dr. Pelo always gave him the most optimistic odds possible. But they still weren't great. Dad knew it too, although he never said it out loud.

We watched him slip away. It started with back pain, and four months later he was gone. He had injured his back several times playing football when he was younger. I had chalked it up to that and felt guilty. Who knew a doctor's visit for back pain would end up with a cancer diagnosis? Well, I should have known, for God's sake. His doctor son who had referred how many patients to oncologists couldn't tell his dad had cancer?

But I did tell him every year, several times a year, to get to his physician. To get checked out. To get tests he had never received and was long overdue for.

He hated to go. And when he finally did, it was too late.

I shut off the lights and lock up the office and make my way back over to the hospital in time for the 9:00 a.m. briefing. Chris, the kid at security, gives me a half-hearted wave as I leave. I nod in his direction. "Be careful," I say. I can't help it. He just looks so young, even younger than my interns.

As I walk back on to the ICU floor, I see Marius, one of our custodians, bringing a box of batteries and flashlights out of the janitorial closet.

"Great. Those are on the list," I say. The list of supplies we need to double-check again today. I realize Marius doesn't usually work on Sundays and wonder if he's up to speed.

"Have you seen the checklist? Did Teddy share it with you?" Teddy is the head of housekeeping. He was supposed to review the list with his team before he hightailed it out of here to stay with relatives in Texas.

"Yes, Doc, I have it right here," he says. He pulls a slightly crumpled piece of paper out of his pocket.

"How are we looking?"

"We've got most of this stuff. We're missing some portable radios. I'm working on that. And I need to get fuel for the portable generators."

I nod. In addition to the industrial-sized generators in the basement, we have two portable generators, one for each ICU. "Keep me posted. You got someone helping you? We don't have a lot of time left."

"I got some guys looking on the ground floor, out in the physical plant and the utility closets on every floor."

I nod my thanks and turn back toward the conference room. I nearly run into Natalie Harlan. Nat is one of the best and most experienced nurses on staff. She's on her way to the same meeting.

"Ready for an adventure?" she asks.

"Hope we don't have one," I reply. "Hey, Nat," I say, remembering one of the points we had talked about in our meeting on Friday. "Has everyone finalized with family members who's leaving and who's staying?"

She shakes her head. It's hard to ask family members of people who are critically ill to leave their sides, but we have a dilemma. We'll have limited resources and potentially a good deal of confusion if the power goes out and things get tough. In theory, we'll allow one family member per person, unless it's a minor who has both parents and/or younger siblings here; in that case, we allow the family to stay.

Natalie and I both know these rules will not be strictly enforced. People from the neighborhood always come here when a really bad storm is threatening. This is a low-lying part of the city. Contrary to the belief of all these idiot reporters, our whole city is not below sea level. Many neighborhoods are at or above sea level. But ours isn't one of them. The locals know they'll be safe here. If people lose power, they'll come here. If they get hurt during the storm, or get sick, they'll come here. They'll bring their ailing elderly or disabled relatives here. We are pretty much all they've got.

"Okay, let's get the conversations started. We'll need everyone who is leaving out of here by eleven a.m. I'll reiterate this in the meeting, but I want to make sure the message gets out to everybody."

When I get to the conference room, I see an early hurricane party—a tame, corporate hurricane party—already under way. My little bags of chips I dug up from *The Good Life* are a pathetic contribution compared to the big bowls of pretzels and Doritos and the plates of doughnuts and hot dogs and muffulettas. There are blue plastic plates overflowing with big stuffed po'boys. The sandwiches are all homemade. There is one bowl of salad—I bet a Northerner brought that—and then more homemade po'boys and more muffulettas that stretch across the table. And coffee...big boxes of coffee. An overflowing tray of pecan pralines from Southern Candymakers and a big bowl of peanut M&M's. If we weren't working, it would not be Barq's or Coke we'd be pouring into these rows of red plastic cups.

Nat appears in the doorway. "This should get us through the next couple of hours," she says and laughs.

As people file in, I check my agenda, which is basically a list of reminders scrawled on the back of a printout. This room is where we usually have our meetings with the CEO. They only happen, thankfully, once or twice a year; our CEO rarely graces us with his presence. On Friday night, he issued instructions to the chain's facilities in the endangered areas. The instructions were basically to do what local law enforcement tells us to do.

"Okay, guys, listen up," I say. I repeat myself while people talk over me. For a moment I look down at my jeans and Chuck Taylors and push my hands into the pockets of my coat. These white lab coats are so formal and sometimes unbearably hot. But they are big on official dress code around here.

I wait for my colleagues' voices to trail off. It's still laughable, even though I graduated from medical school nearly twenty years ago and have had positions of increasing responsibility since then, to see myself as one of the grown-ups in charge. That was one of the problems I had with my ex. She, quite reasonably, saw herself as a grown-up and wanted to move to the suburbs and buy a house and do all the things that grown-ups do.

The conference room is finally quiet except for the sounds of everyone eating. This meeting is like our senior-staff meeting, with nursing directors, senior therapists, and the chiefs of each department, except we also have housekeeping, security, and reps from other departments—the ER, the OR—in attendance. Everyone chomps on doughnuts, sandwiches, and candy, while I go through the agenda, which is basically a long checklist. We wrap up a few outstanding items: housekeeping has procured boards to secure broken windows; we get an estimate of our food stores and an update on supplies like portable radios and generators.

"Has everyone signed in?" I ask. "We need to have an accurate record of who's on call." I have already seen faces of some people who had today and tomorrow off. They came here because they knew they would probably be needed. Some of them have kids, and their spouses and children have evacuated without them.

"And does everyone have their evac bags?"

The evacuation bags contain rudimentary but critical supplies in the event of an emergency. Every staff member has one.

"And I need to make sure y'all have your bracelets too," I add.

I hold up my wrist to show the plastic bracelet dangling from it. "Didn't know you liked jewelry, Reid," says one of my partners, Dr. Jain.

"They're very fashionable, Dr. Jain," I say, waving my wrist. "So everyone? Get yourselves one. You won't be let into certain areas if you can't prove you are a member of the staff."

We try to get an accurate count of how many people are in the hospital: the admitted patients, their families, the staff who are on call and the staff who came because they wanted to help out or they thought their family would be safer inside these concrete walls. We come up with an estimate of 570, but people are still arriving.

"How many people do we have food for?" I ask as I turn to the hospital kitchen manager.

He hesitates. "I'd estimate we have enough to feed maybe seven hundred people for two days," he says. "We stocked up some before the storm, but we also won't get our regular Monday deliveries. We tried to get an extra delivery last week, but they couldn't fit us in." As he says this, I notice a few people around the table indiscreetly shoving extra doughnuts and candy in the pockets of their lab coats and scrubs.

Food will definitely be a concern if the roads are impassable, so I ask the kitchen manager to start rationing, and he suggests scrounging up anything canned that wasn't on the corporate menu. I tell him that as far as I'm concerned, he can get as creative as he likes.

We cover a few more outstanding questions. A few staff members have brought their dogs and cats. We decide that pets will be housed in two large waiting rooms on the third floor, not far from the parking garage entrance. That floor has only doctors' offices and no patient rooms or other areas that need to be as sterile as possible. Dog owners can use the garage for walks during the storm. This was not something that was addressed in our official instructions. In fact, I'm pretty sure our official guides and manuals for emergency situations (I confess I have not read them very carefully) don't allow for lifting the hospital's ban on pets. But I'm not going to tell any of my colleagues they can't bring their pets, unless they have a pet alligator.

"Anything else?" I ask. The NOAA warning I saw on my screen this morning has been rattling around in my head. But these things always turn away at the last minute.

"We need a cutoff time," says Judah Gainsboro, the head of security. "A deadline. Past that time, we won't let anyone in. But you need to tell us when that time is. I can tell you that the parking garage is already almost full. All these folks milling around is not..." he trails off, but we all know what he's saying. The more people arrive, the harder it is to contain any situation that might arise. Wherever you have a large group of people, you have at least 10 percent addicts, based on what I've seen. And if you're talking about a struggling neighborhood like ours, you can assume an even higher percentage of people are actively using.

"Well, we touched base on this earlier, but let's make sure our inventory assessments are up-to-date. Let's get a count on them right after this meeting and then double-check that we have put the lid on those supplies."

The nursing director, Susan Robertson, speaks up. She's been a nurse practitioner for decades; she came to St. Liberatus thirty years ago, right out of nursing school. "I've directed the head nurses to report the inventory for their respective units," she says. "Reports are due at eleven a.m. Only the nurse supervisors and their designated backup will have access to the pharma areas." She says this last part a little bit louder and looks around the room to make sure everyone heard this. We had a scandal a few years ago with a nurse who was caught stealing drugs from one of the supply closets. We had protocols in place, but they were obviously not followed. That nurse was fired, and Susan was aghast; she ran a tight ship and was determined it wouldn't happen again.

"Just to wrap up here, we need a cutoff point, Doc," Judah reminds me, because I have been hesitant to start shutting people out, and he knows it.

"Twelve noon," I finally say. "At that point, direct your staff not to let anyone else in unless they are arriving via ambulance or in obvious medical distress. Get the ER docs to help with any assessments—I don't want your guys trying to determine if someone's actually in trouble." Judah nodded.

There are a few more questions, and then I tell everyone to meet again at five o'clock this afternoon to review anything that has changed. As the meeting breaks up, I linger in the room a moment and go to the windows. I notice Susan standing next to me, doing the same thing. The sky is dark gray with a tinge of green.

"That's a tornado sky," she says. "We used to have those sometimes when I was growing up in Arkansas. This one's going to be really, really bad."

I go to each floor to check on preparations in person. I start with the NICU. Dr. Armstrong is the physician in charge. I go up to her where she is standing next to the nurses' station, issuing instructions to one of the veteran nurses there. I always thought this team had the hardest job in this hospital. There are seven tiny babies here now, in incubators; five are preemies, and two are term, but they need surgery to repair heart-valve defects.

"Do you need anything, Amanda?" I ask Dr. Armstrong. She is a short and round-shouldered woman, a strong woman and a no-nonsense colleague I have worked with for a long time.

"We're all set, Ray," she says. "Just hoping we get nothing more than a glancing blow."

I nod. This is what we're all hoping for and, probably, expecting.

I pop my head in to say hello to a few of the other nurses here I know, and then I'm anxious to get off the floor. I avoid NICU sometimes, yet these are our most vulnerable and precious charges, who are top of mind even more than usual with this storm coming.

Jane and I had a baby boy. He had a heart defect too, but he didn't make it. He was in the NICU at Tulane; they have a more preeminent staff than we do, and I didn't mind Jane saying so; when it came down to it, you want the best for your baby even before they are born. She wanted to deliver there and so she did, but he was nine weeks early, and his heart was already shutting down; hypoplastic left heart syndrome. We held his incredibly tiny hands as he left us.

She shut down after that, and so did I. You don't get over that. I could have ten more kids, yet I didn't want kids anymore; I had a son, and he was only here for two days.

I leave the NICU and continue my check-ins with each floor. As I walk down the hall, it seems that more and more people from the neighborhood have taken a spot on the floor, on the arm of a chair, in any open space. People line up at the windows. Elderly people, young people, whole families who did not trust the soundness of their own homes but trust that they will be safe at St. Liberatus.

I take the stairs, and it seems like each time I climb another step, the sky outside looks darker.

Chapter 6

Sunday Night
Gentilly
We're waiting.

I have a sheet of plywood in the garage left over from a long-ago project rebuilding the floor of our gardening shed. I take that and any spare boards I can find, put my elderly table saw to work, and do my best to board up the windows around the house. My back is screaming. It is so frustrating to work so slowly. I want to be back inside helping Penny. But then I think of my father's gnarled hands and just move as best as I can. After three hours, I have covered every window, except the small ones in the attic and the one over our front door.

The heat is stifling, so I open the garage door to let air in. It does little to alleviate this heat and the heavy air. There is a weight to it; that is the thing with the hot weather down here. It has a presence you can feel and touch. I watch as the garage door finishes its shakes and creaks; it has not been touched since I installed it sometime in the early '80s. It's likely to give out any day now. Since I retired, we had been able to finally organize this long-neglected part of the house. And now that we no longer have a car, it is even neater than before. We had held a yard sale but ended up keeping half the stuff we had meant to sell—mostly the girls' toys, old books, and old games we had played together as a family. We reasoned that the girls might want the stuff someday. I tried not to imagine the girls going through it after we are gone.

With the door open, I can survey half our street from here. I smell rain and wet vegetation in the air. You could feel her coming; the air is heavy, the birds silent. Our neighborhood, usually lively, is now a ghost town.

I don't know all the neighbors anymore. Our girls had grown up with the Robinsons, who had lived two houses down, and Stacy had babysat for the Pettingills, who had lived across the street. The Pettingills' kids had graduated college, and the parents had moved into a smaller home somewhere outside the city. The Robinsons were both in a nursing home, last I heard. Strokes.

The neighbors on both sides of us are gone. I still don't really know their names. They're both relatively new to the neighborhood. They had packed up their SUV and minivan and headed out Friday night and Saturday morning. The only neighbors I knew who had stayed lived catercorner from us, one street closer to the lake. The Schultzes, Emerson and Marie. Emerson is wheelchair-bound, and Marie and I help each other out sometimes. She takes good care of him. And she can barely go up the stairs herself. I had called on them before the storm—Penny reminded me to—and they insisted they didn't need anything and that their adult son was going to be staying with them to help if anything happened with the house.

I go back inside, where Penny is sitting on the couch. I sit down and put her feet on my lap and start to rub them. She is reading one of those large-print books. She has a special holder for it to help stabilize it. Reading has always been one of her favorite things to do, and she always had a book on the bedside table or in her purse or in the back of the car. Now she'll often put down a book because reading gives her a headache.

I strain to read the splotches of red letters blinking on the screen. Every once in a while Penny lowers her book and looks solemnly at the TV. The meteorologists are beside themselves, and we hear the same dire warnings over and over. Finally she puts her book down on her lap.

"Can't we listen to the radio instead?" she asks, her growing nervousness making her testy. I gently lower her legs to the couch and slowly get up. I switch off the TV and walk over to our old radio and switch it on. It was already tuned to the public radio station that Penny likes, because they play some good jazz. But, of course, they were talking about the storm like everyone else, so I kept changing stations until I found music. It was the oldies station, the one that played music we listened to when we were still young and we would go out sometimes in 8th Ward. The girls were so young then. I still think of oldies as my parents' music, but they don't even play their music on the radio anymore.

I hear a banging sound in front of the house. Penny flinches. I can't look out my boarded-up windows, so I open the front door a crack to watch light reflecting off pellets of water hitting the ground. The humidity hits me full force; it seems harder to take a breath than it was just a few minutes ago.

Penny was still this strong, tiny, wiry woman I had met when I was just a kid in basic training all those years ago. She was a Memphis girl, but when she moved to New Orleans, she embraced the city with her whole heart. She took on every tradition I had learned from my parents. When Penny became Catholic, it cemented the already sharp rift that had opened between her and her Methodist parents. Penny's parents believed that good girls did not leave their mothers, and Penny broke that rule when she moved away with me. They thought I should become Methodist, but Penny thought I was more Catholic than she was Methodist, and she wanted us to go to the same church together, especially after the children were born. She baked king cakes and bought the girls dolls that wore Mardi Gras costumes. She learned my mother's gumbo and cornbread and fried catfish recipes, and she eventually made all of them pretty damn well. She was an enthusiastic supporter of the Krewe of Zulu, to which my father, my brother, and I belonged. Many of my father's friends had been part of the krewe, and it was the one time of year that I saw my parents actually relax and enjoy themselves and even have a beer or two. I had many real and honorary uncles in the krewe; some were flambeaux, the torchbearers who would light the way for their parade on Mardi Gras. I still remember the feeling of danger and excitement that rose up along the street when those flame bearers approached; I can see them stalking the crowds now, their serious faces glowing behind the flames, spooking every child into an awed silence. In the '60s, it was not popular to belong to the Zulu. Their tongue-in-cheek use of blackface, coconuts, and other white stereotypes of blacks was not well tolerated by those fighting for equality. But my father never wavered in his support; he didn't see it as a contradiction.

My parents loved Penny. Some women do not like their mothers-in-law, but Penny loved hers. I think she respected the fact that they worked so hard. The loss of her family, and her parents' rejection of her, was so painful to Penny, but she rarely talked about it. We did pack up the girls every summer to spend a week with Penny's sister in Memphis, and the trips were never easy. For the first few years, Penny would put the word out through her sister that she was in town. Her parents never came by, not even to meet their granddaughters. They were a strange and unforgiving people. Penny, usually able to put on a brave face, was in tears by the end of the trip that first year or two. But after a while she reasoned that if they didn't want to meet her precious babies, they didn't deserve her guilt or her love.

Penny's sister Betty had died several years ago the year after she retired from teaching. Penny and I and the girls all went to the funeral. Betty's death closed the door on Memphis for Penny forever. I knew we would never be back.

She was closer to her big sister than I ever was to my little brother Charles. It wasn't that we didn't get along; it was that like Russell, Charles had joined the navy and traveled the world for a couple of decades. He was just the wrong age and got caught up in Vietnam; I had been old enough to miss it by a hair, and I never got called back in. We rarely saw each other from the day he shipped off except when he was home on leave from one place or another, new girl-friend in tow each time for years. Eventually he retired and came back home for good, and he lived in 9th Ward—the East New Orleans section—for ten years with his second wife. But years ago they had moved out to Florida, where they live a modest life off his pension and his part-time work at Home Depot. I never see my brother anymore. We talk rarely. We call on occasions like this, if a hurricane is aimed at him or me. We call at Christmas. We don't remember each other's birthdays. We are all that is left of our family, and I know I should make more of an effort. But neither of us has ever been very good at that. How is it that someone who knows you so well and who you spend such critical years with can recede, like a tide going out, into the background of your life? I should call him more often. I will call him more often—once we get through this storm.

As I turn from the front door, I hear a sound like open gates banging against their latches. Even normal sounds of the neighborhood are eerie and threaten-ing. Baron growls. The fur on his back stands up. He has been on edge all day, sniffing the perimeter of the house, asking to go outside over and over. He knows. Baron is looking at me now. His short, stout, brown-and-white body is tense; his wiry fur is on end.

"Buddy, it's going to be okay," I say, reaching down to give him a pat. He clearly doesn't believe me; his ears are down. But he wags his tail slightly, as if to placate me.

"I'm just going to go check the backyard again," I say to Penny as I pass back through the living room. Dusk is turning into dark, but it's an early dark for this time of year. It's the green-black-gray of the storm approaching. I turn on the light above our little deck and open the back door into our yard. Baron is nervous and flighty beside me. I don't let him out with me for fear he will run away. He is usually a solid and unflappable dog, but storms have always made him nervous, and more than once I have had to chase after him when he got out during a thunderstorm.

Our yard is neat, even if it isn't as well-tended as it used to be. Many nights in the summer when the girls were young, if it wasn't raining, we would sit out here before the bugs got too bad, in that magic hour when the girls had gone to sleep and we had a little time to ourselves. I would have an Abita or two, while Penny smoked a cigarette—that was before she quit when she had that cancer scare. We would pick up the girls' toys and put them in the old metal washtub by our little deck, and the girls would pull them out the next day and start all over again. Those were probably the happiest years of my life, looking back. It hurts to think that I rarely realized it at that time. We always think the best years are ahead of us, that if this one thing happens or doesn't happen, then we will finally be perfectly happy. I had a beautiful, healthy wife; a nice home; and two amazing daughters. I like to think I enjoyed some moments here and there, but through it all, I was always worried about my job at the oil company, about the girls' grades, my parent's finances, or some trifling thing that seemed monumental back then. Now I stand here with the ghosts of our life in this house—the memories that bubble up, the scenes I can still see in my mind's eye, where my sight is still perfect.

The rain is coming down harder. Everything in the past is a blur. The wind is starting to talk more too. I walk to the edge of darkness beyond where my porch light can reach, stumbling a bit along the way. I double-check the old shed door, feeling around for the big lock; I don't want anything flying out of it tomorrow. I had jammed our four rusty, old lawn chairs into the shed somehow, adding them to the pile of garden hoses that needed to be repaired and those old tiki torches that were popular in the '50s and '60s that we still used when we had backyard parties with our neighbors in the '70s and '80s, the new kiddie pool we had bought for the grandkids. I can see the dim outlines of what is left of Penny's garden. I've done my best, but I gave up the vegetables; I try to keep her flowers alive—amaranth and zinnias, mostly—because she loves them so much. They might get ravaged, so I think about replanting. Then I wonder if it makes sense to replant. How much longer will we be able to stay here?

I have just walked back in when I hear a loud scratching sound. The storm is scratching at the door like a dog asking to be let in.

"Branches on the roof," Penny says. I nod. She has Baron on her lap. He is curled up, trying to make himself as small as possible.

"I'm just going to get a few things together," I say. Just in case.

"Don't forget our meds, honey," Penny says.

I grab my portable radio off a shelf in the back of the pantry and dig up some batteries. I turn it on to make sure it still works; sure enough, it is barking frightening weather alerts…talk of taking cover, evacuating, catastrophic damage. I turn it off again. The oldies are still playing in the other room.

I pick up a gallon of spring water from the floor of the pantry and bring it up to the counter top. My back protests the whole way. I go back to the pantry to dig up some nonperishable food: peanut butter, crackers, a couple cans of tuna, and a jar of applesauce. I put them in a shopping bag along with our weekly medicine containers, some of Baron's canned dog food, a spoon, and a can opener. I root around in the junk drawer until I find our wobbly ancient flashlight. It takes the same-size batteries as the radio, which is lucky because I only have one size of batteries on hand. I add the flashlight and more batteries to the bag and heave that up onto the counter top too.

"I feel bad about the girls," Penny says from the next room. They had called again last night, and both got pretty upset when we told them we weren't evacuating.

"I told them we were all set," she says. "That everything will be fine."

"It will be," I say.

Later that night, I help Penny take a shower. In case the water gets turned off or they tell us not to use it for a while (every New Orleanian knows that you don't drink the water after a hurricane until they tell you that you can), we both wanted to get clean while we still could. I stand there to steady her and help her grab the handrail; she sits down on the little bench we bought for her. While she washes and rinses her hair, I fill up a few containers—some vases and our sweet tea pitcher—with water from the bathroom sink and set them to the side in case we need them for washing or using the toilet if the water gets turned off.

After Penny gets settled into bed with her book, I prepare her tea and put it on the nightstand next to her. I put a special cover, like the ones on the grand-kids' sippy cups, on her mug so it doesn't spill as she tries to handle it. I go take a quick shower, and I sit on the little bath stool that Penny was just using. My back and legs are aching from all the work I've done today. When I'm done, I turn off the water and sit back down for a moment while I towel myself off. I pull back the shower curtain to let in some cooler air and look over at the sink. On Penny's side of the counter is a bottle filled with sea glass and a little framed painting of a scenic ocean view. Penny got them both on our trip to Charleston. We went there when I first retired from the oil company. That was like being newlyweds again. I had also gone on a fishing trip with Russell. All day long, sitting in the sun on a boat on the Gulf, cool breezes, beautiful water as far as you could see in any direction. We didn't catch much, and we didn't talk much. But I know we were both thinking that we ended up having it pretty good and being pretty lucky. Things weren't perfect, and back on land we had some problems, but still we were luckier than our fathers ever were.

Penny and I had imagined many more trips like that—both together and with our friends—especially California, to see the girls. But it was about a week after I got back from that trip with Russell that Penny got her diagnosis.

In the painting she bought there is a bright white beach, and pink and green buildings on a hilltop behind the shore. White boats bob in the water.

It occurs to me that I forgot to fill up the bathtub. Just in case we need it for drinking or to flush the toilet if the water gets cut off. I put the drain plug in and turn on the tap.

Stacy and Michelle both called while I was in the shower. The phone lies on Penny's lap. "I just told them again not to worry," she says. Her eyes are shining. "I told them it's still our job to worry about them, not the other way around." I nod.

I take Baron out in the backyard one more time for the night. I put him on the leash because he is still skittish, and I don't want him finding his way out. He is taking too long, overcome with smells and anxiety. I see his eyes glowing in the reflected light of the kitchen behind me.

"Time to go to bed, buddy," I say. I gently tug on his leash and bring him back inside, locking the door behind me.

Soon I get into bed next to my beautiful hazel-eyed wife. She smiles; I smile. Everything will be okay. The branches thump against the roof, and the wind whistles like a passing train.

Chapter 7

Early Monday Morning
St. Liberatus

"Dr. Reid," says a soft voice near my ear. I wave it off as a weird anomaly in my dream, a dream in which I am on *The Good Life*, somewhere in Bayou Barataria. I am sitting back in my chair with a cold one, and it is a hot, sunny day with a cool breeze off the Gulf, and I am hooking some damn big fish.

It is fucking hot in here. I wake up and realize I had dozed off in front of the call-room computer.

"*Dr. Reid!*" says the voice, more urgently this time. It's Tennant, one of the interns. His face is perspiring.

"I need a consult," he says. "I paged you..."

"All right," I say, sitting up and straightening my aching neck. I shrug into my deteriorating lab coat that is hung over the chair and follow him down the hallway to a patient's room.

It is disorienting to see people sleeping in the hallway and near the nurses' station. But there they are, dozens of people, lying at awkward angles in an attempt to keep a pathway clear. They all look, not surprisingly, uncomfortable. Jackets and bags are shoved under their heads to serve as pillows. I nearly trip over a man who has fallen asleep with his legs sprawled out into the corridor.

I notice that there is a sound above the hum of machinery and beeping of equipment. The wind is roaring. She's on her way.

"How are you, sir?" I say to Emmett Bartlett and his wife, who is sitting by his bedside.

"Been better, Doc," Emmett says. He is clearly uncomfortable. His room-mate's television is on. The roommate, who is elderly like Mr. Bartlett, lies back in his bed and ignores us. I don't know his name since my practice didn't admit him. He is staring at the screen that shows a whirling mass sitting on southeastern Louisiana and southwestern Mississippi. I notice he has no family members with him, at least not at the moment. Maybe they are in the cafeteria.

The patient that Tennant has called me about has a swollen abdomen and lower extremities. He was admitted with severe heart failure. His vitals are weaker than they were over the past couple of days.

I refresh my memory by glancing over his chart. Like many of our patients, Bartlett is obese. He's also diabetic. No surprise there.

But the real reason he's here is because of the heart failure. He's been in failure twice in two years and is on a slew of medications. We don't have a separate cardiac ICU in this hospital, something that has, like the lack of a peds ICU, been a matter of discussion lately. NewCare wants us to expand, to bring in more patients, to bring in more money. Of course, they don't seem to realize that our patients, for the most part, have no money. Oh, but the government does. A huge percentage of our patients are on Medicaid and Medicare. At the same time, they have initiated some pretty extensive staff cutbacks, so I'm not clear on how we are going to staff those new departments. So here is Mr. Bartlett in our ICU, when he clearly would be better served in a CICU. We have been trying to get him stabilized, at which point he might, although I doubt it, be a candidate for a defibrillator and pacemaker implant.

"What did La Blanc say?" I ask Tennant. He looks at me and says nothing.

I excuse myself and motion for Tennant to follow me into the hallway. "What did La Blanc say?" I ask. "Did you page him?" La Blanc is the cardiologist on the case.

"He's on vacation," says Tennant.

Dix is intimidating. I'm sure no resident wants to bother him when he's on vacation. They don't even want to bother him when he's in the room with them. But this is about what's best for the patient. Tennant needs to put his own ego and fear aside.

"Page Dix," I say. "He's the cardiologist on call. You let him know the patient is in distress, right?" Tennant looks uncertain. "Well, I thought he wouldn't…"

"Code your page. So he knows it's an emergency and not just an intern with questions."

Tennant doesn't know what the code is. I wonder for a moment if Dix decided to bail. But that isn't like him. He should have told us if this was the case, but maybe the message didn't get to me.

"I did page him. He didn't respond."

"How many times did you page him?"

Tennant looks sheepish; he knows where I'm going. I don't care how senior Dix is—and he is senior. If he's on call and a patient in distress needs a consult, he needs to get his ass down here or at least return the call and find another cardiologist who will cover him. I won't say that, though. I understand the intern's reluctance, but I don't give a damn about ruffling feathers or "bothering somebody" when a patient might be at risk.

"Next time," I say, "page Dix with the proper code. And the nurses can help you get on his case. I am not a cardiologist, and just because I'm the guy in charge during this—" I gesture out at the blackening sky "—event…doesn't mean I should be calling the shots on this guy's cardiologic care."

I look at Tennant. "Your thoughts, doctor?" I say, challenging him rather than rescuing him. I remember others doing this to me. On my first couple of rotations as an intern, it made me incredibly nervous. But I grew to look forward to the challenges. I am not optimistic about Tennant's prospects; from what I've seen, he does not retain information, and he does not have the desire to solve these little medical mysteries that we spend our days trying to solve. Good physicians like to solve problems. We take it as a point of pride that we can outwit and defeat injury and disease. Tennant's long, pale face registers no self-confidence.

"I think we should increase the Lasix," he says.

I look at the patient. "You've been eating the low-sodium meals?" I ask. It's not going to save him or even help him at all at this stage. I ask out of habit more than anything else.

He nods.

I turn back to Tennant, raising my eyebrows, picturing how my father would give me a look pretty close to the one I am giving Tennant now. Expectant, impatient. It was like this when he would help me with my homework. He was forever testing my math abilities. I remember a strange feeling of safety at their

55

house when I became a physician, sitting at the Sunday dinner table in my co-coon, talking about things they didn't know about and Dad couldn't question me on. I felt important. I hoped they felt proud.

Even though it feels a bit futile, I tell Tennant to instruct the nurses to make sure Bartlett is getting the low-sodium meals instead of the regular meals. For the thousandth time I wonder why we don't just serve all our patients low-sodium meals, but that's a question for another day.

I page Dix myself; he better respond.

I go back to the darkened call room to check the computer, but it gives me nothing but the same dire NOAA warnings from earlier and the headline "GULF COAST BRACES FOR IMPACT; THOUSANDS FLEE NEW ORLEANS AS STORM TAKES AIM." I start to read the story: "Officials estimate as many as 100,000 remain in the city. At least 30,000 are in the Superdome, one of the city's designated shelters of 'last resort'." It occurs to me that we seem to be a shelter of last resort. Are we designated as such? Not technically.

I abandon the site. Nothing new to learn here. They're just ratcheting up the drama.

For the next two hours, I wander the halls instead, checking in at each floor and looking in on patients and staff members, just making myself visible in case someone might need my help. Few of our patients, except the sedated ones, are sleeping; the storm is getting too loud.

I stand at one of the nursing stations, listening to the nurses talking to each other. Under the sound of voices, the pelting rain and wind are a steady drum-beat getting louder; everyone eventually gets quiet and pensive. I go down to Susan's office and ask if she has instructed her staff to move patient beds as far back from the windows as they can just in case. I don't want anyone getting in-jured by flying glass. I double-check with housekeeping that they have plywood ready. Then I go back to my floor and walk to the end of the hallway to stare out the windows.

The first thing I notice is the near-total lack of visibility compared to what we could see an hour ago. The streetlights are dim, ghostly circles. Although the sun has risen, you can't really tell. Trashcans are rolling and crashing down the street, and I see some fallen branches on the tops of cars in the parking lot across from the hospital. From somewhere comes the faint bleating of a car alarm.

It is oddly exciting at first. But soon enough she is shaking the building like a pissed-off giant, and my excitement turns to fear. St. Liberatus is this old cement bunker of a building—it was a fallout shelter during the Cold War—yet still she is rattling the building's very bones. Bits of palm trees and sheet metal are blowing by the windows; they strike the building like demented metallic birds. Trees are bending near to horizontal, and street signs are battered by the wind.

It's a little after 6:45 a.m. when the power goes out. I am surprised it lasted as long as it did. We all stop midstep or midsentence and wait for a nervous second to hear the hospital generators shudder to life.

The lights flicker and then go out again.

But then there is a rumbling, and the very building seems to creak and groan. The generators have kicked in. The hallway and overhead lights do not come back on with their usual harsh brightness; the generators direct their power to the essentials—nursing stations and the bedside outlets—where critical machinery is humming in patients' rooms. The hallways are stripped of their usual bare fluorescent industrial high beams. They are replaced by pale green auxiliary lights that point the way, flickering like fireflies.

I check in with housekeeping and maintenance about the generators. Marius was unable to secure fuel yesterday, and I don't know how long we are going to need them to work. At 6:55 a.m., I walk the floor, eyeing the crowded waiting areas at the far end, where some families have camped out. I note that the vending machines are already nearly empty. I ask if there is any restock available in the food storage or maintenance closets—I haven't the faintest idea where they keep it—but maintenance tells me that a contractor comes and refills those once a week. On Mondays.

Downstairs in the cafeteria, the kitchen staff brings out fresh coffee and bagels and whatever breakfast food they have allotted for today. There is a television in the cafeteria that is powered by a portable generator on a twenty-four-hour news channel, and there is an idiot reporter leaning into the wind outside somebody's condo apartment. He is soaked, and he is yelling at the anchorperson that it is very windy now.

"Turn that thing off," I say. "Use the portable radios. Don't waste generator energy on this garbage." A cafeteria worker I don't know looks at me, annoyed. He switches it off.

Coffee is a good distraction, even though it's shitty coffee. I pick up a bagel—nobody is paying for any of this, since the cash registers are down—and start back upstairs. For the third time today, I will stop in at every floor and check in with the staff members in charge of each department, asking for updates.

I notice as I walk back through that our cafeteria is jammed with families disproportionately represented by the very old and the very young. This is not so unusual in a hospital, but it is more noticeable today. I can tell the relatives from the neighbors; the relatives are here to stay with people they love, and they are shadow-eyed, distracted, and quiet. The neighbors who came over here because they didn't trust their little houses are laughing, talking, playing cards, or eating breakfast as if they were at a camp or on a family trip. But when an unusually rough wind gust rattles the building, or the already dim lights flicker, everybody freezes, regardless of why they're here.

Back upstairs it is noticeably hotter. The generator powers the AC, but at a higher temperature, so it doesn't take up as much resources. The windows are shaking even harder in the waiting room. There are dozens of people sitting on the floor near the glass, mostly teenage boys from the neighborhood, who think they're invincible. They're sitting there playing video games and daring each other to go outside. I warn them to move away. I have warned them of this before, but it is crowded, and more and more people are curious and can't help but look outside.

Less than a minute after I've warned them, one of the windows shatters. I feel a wall of rain and glass hit my face. I jump back in surprise, and people around me scream. My heart starts pounding. I wipe my hand over my face and feel little shards of glass stuck to my cheek and palm.

"Get out! Get into the hallway!" I shout, which isn't really necessary, since people are running for the exit, pushing into each other, children crying, their parents picking them up and rushing to the door. I see two men who are injured by cut glass, and before I can go up to them, there are already a couple of nurses taking the men by the arms and leading them out of the room. I follow the last person out of the room, tripping over some bags that were left behind, and shout for housekeeping. I don't see anyone from housekeeping in the immediate vicinity, so I ask a nurse's aide if our internal call system is still working, and he confirms it is. I tell him to call housekeeping and have them come board up the windows.

I instruct people who were just in the waiting room, people who are now standing around dumbfounded, to spread out along the hallways and go to the cafeteria where there is more room. I hate to vacate them from the few pieces of comfortable furniture, but I don't want to be picking glass out of people's skin all day either.

I walk along the hall looking into the patients' rooms, expecting other windows to explode. And they do; I hear a few loud pops and the skittering sound of breaking glass hitting the floor, like a bomb bursting against the building, shrapnel splintering in every direction. I hear a scream, noise, and then two nurses running into the patients' room. I follow on their heels and am immediately hit by something sharp and hard. I look down on the floor and see rocks, white granite stones. For a moment I am confused and can't imagine where these came from. But then I realize they look like the rocks that cover the roof of my medical office building, which is diagonally across from us.

As I'm about to turn into the room, I skid on the watery floor and brace myself for a fall but manage to catch myself. There is glass all over the floor. I look over at the patients. Their beds had been turned away from the windows and pushed closer to the doors; they look frightened but okay. They are trapped and helpless, hooked up to their machines. Nancy Davis, who is recovering from her kidney surgery, gives me a thumbs-up to let me know she is okay. Michaela, the teenager who had been in a car accident, looks at me with wide eyes.

I work with the nurses to gently wheel the women and their myriad pieces of equipment—catheters, IVs, heart monitors—out into the hallway, against the outside wall of their room.

"Sorry, Michaela," I say as I help position her in her bed, while people move past us down the hallway. "You're in the middle of everything now." She nods. She says something, and I can't hear her over the noise of the wind and people milling about. I lean down, my ear close to her mouth.

"You're bleeding," she says, her voice a raspy whisper. I look at my hands; they're fine. I wipe my face and realize that what I thought was water was actually blood, probably from the glass in the waiting room. Since it is pretty much the worst protocol ever to be treating a patient while openly bleeding, I need to clean up.

"Don't worry about me. Do you need anything?" I ask. She shakes her head. I pat her on the arm and move quickly down the hall to check on other patients. I see Marius helping carry plywood toward us. I tell him to have housekeeping mark all the intact windows with duct tape in the shape of an "X." I kick myself, because we should have done this before. I really didn't think this damn storm would be that bad. I doubt any windows will be saved, but at least the glass won't disperse as widely if the windows are marked.

I quickly check in on Andy, hoping the windows in his room stay intact. So far they are. His mother is huddled near him, and his cot has been pushed as close to the door as it can be while still making room for the nurses to come and go and read his machines.

I take a quick break to wash up and check the weather on the radio. We are almost through the worst of this storm, they say. The Mississippi Gulf Coast is getting lashed pretty hard, but we don't know many details yet. I expect that *The Good Life* has been dashed to pieces against the docks by now. I try to remember what I had saved from her before I left but then decide it is a useless thing to think about. There is nothing I can do for her now.

For the next hour or so, windows are popping intermittently. The tape seems to help contain the glass, although it still spills out into the rooms along with rain and leaves and other storm debris. I tour the other floors, checking in with senior staff, and see it's the same everywhere else. I feel like we are under attack. The patients are stacked up in their rooms close to the doors, and in each room where the windows have completely given way, the patients have been moved into the hallways. Housekeeping tries to keep up with the slippery floors, all slicked up with rain. But it's getting dangerous to walk around. I ask them to focus on the hallways and any common rooms or waiting areas where most of the traffic is.

Some ceiling tiles have fallen in, soaked with water that is getting in from above and making some of the patient rooms that still have windows unusable.

Tiles that have not already fallen are sagging in places, saturating, crumbling, falling to the floor, and forming piles of yellow-gray slush. The wind shrieks through the gaping holes the windows leave behind.

The banshee screams of the storm are one of the most haunting sounds I have ever heard.

"Doc, we're running out of plywood," Marius says. He is sweating from running from one floor to another. I nod.

"Try to get all the common rooms at least," I say. "If you have enough. We need somewhere for all these people to sleep." He nods.

I stand at the nurses' station to check in with Natalie and Susan. We hear crying and look over to an elderly patient whose bed had been moved out to the hallway. Her face is wet with tears, and she is holding a crucifix. Her husband tries to comfort her. Looking at her and the pile of ceiling tiles in the room behind her, I think of the time my brother and I stopped to watch an apartment building that was getting demolished. We were still little kids then, cruising around our neighborhood on our bikes. We each sat with our hands on the handlebars, one leg on the ground, one leg dangling. There was a rope line we could not go past, and then on the other side of the street, there was this old apartment building, and the cops were keeping people away while the bulldozer started to chew at it and then punch it, making the bricks crumble in on themselves, breaking all the windows, folding and crumpling like a cardboard box. I remember an old woman standing there, held back from the police, crying. She was holding a crucifix tightly as the tears ran down her face.

Chapter 8

Early Monday Morning
Gentilly

Baron is whining and wants to go outside. He was awake for much of the night, barking at unfamiliar sounds, growling at an unseen enemy. All three of us were uneasy all night long. The wind was too loud and threatening to sleep through. Penny and I held on to each other, my arms around her, her hands on mine.

I did get up and pace the house a few times. Every once in a while there was a bang of debris—trash cans, branches—hitting a house or a parked car. The sounds grew louder as dawn approached. I sat in the darkness on the couch for an hour, listening for what I don't know, thinking about this house, about everything we experienced in this house, about how I used to come through that door when I was working at the oil company all those years. I thought about how Penny and I went through a phase where we thought we wanted to retire and open a bed-and-breakfast together—so not really retirement but a second career. We talked about how we would buy a little shotgun house in Treme or the Marigny, where the European and Japanese jazz fans like to stay, and we would fix it up, and it would be quaint and historically decorated (Penny and I were going to do some research and find out what the original colors of this pretend house were and paint it accordingly, we would have hurricane shutters, and we would plant palms there if there weren't palms already), and we would meet people from all over the world who would ask us about our home and about New Orleans and could point them to the right jazz clubs, the good ones, not the tourist traps. And Penny would make her famous crepes—she and the girls just loved to make crepes ever since the girls were in high school and taking French class. And Penny would make her perfect Eggs Benedict and that mouthwatering cornbread and sausage. My mouth starts to water at the thought of it. How fun that would have been.

Suddenly the sound of something slamming against the garage shocks me out of my thoughts. I sit up straight. Baron comes into the room, his ears back. Penny calls out to me, and I push myself to a standing position, ignoring the protests of my back and knees. I hurry as much as I can out to the family room and curse myself when I hit the corner of the door; that would be a bruise tomorrow. Damned depth perception.

I walk back out to the door that leads to the garage and open it to find that the garage door has been dented in. It hasn't broken completely, but it is warped off its track and bending in on itself. As I survey the damage, I hear glass breaking. I go back inside to where the sound came from. The family-room window has been busted. Glass lies over the couch, the rug, and the coffee table. I use up all the big pieces of plywood on the front windows and figure the south-facing windows are the most important to protect. But now wind and rain take over the whole house. Outside the bathroom window, I see trees bending at impossible angles.

"Rob! Are you all right?" Penny calls, her voice strained.

"I'm okay, honey, just a broken window. I'm going to take care of it." I hurry to the garage to scrounge up something to block the window with. I try to ignore the dented door. There is nothing I can do about it now anyway. But I do wonder if insurance would cover it. How much does a new garage door cost? It has been so long since I have had the automatic one installed that I have no clue what it would take to get it replaced. I look around the rest of the garage. Some left-over, odd-shaped pieces of wood still sit on my table seen from my preparations yesterday. I pull some of the bigger pieces out, finding a couple of boards that would block much of the gaping window. I walk as quickly as my back will let me around to the back door and go outside, quick to close the wind-whipped door on Baron so he does not try to get out. I stand there, lashed by the wind and rain, finding the window by the light coming from the family room, and clumsily but effectively nail the boards over the broken glass, squinting against the water and steeling myself against the wind. It pulls at me as though it is a living thing. This thing hasn't hit us with its worst yet, and it's already pretty bad.

Nervousness makes my chest flutter, but I stop myself: landfall is still a couple of hours away. There is still time for her to move. The city might be bruised. There might be other broken windows, the power may go out, and there may be many more branches down in the streets. Some roof damage here and there. But this is just the glancing blow of a hurricane. This is nothing for New Orleans and nothing for me. Just a broken window and a broken garage door.

As I finish putting the last piece of wood in place, I look up to see Penny's worried face in the window.

But now I am back in bed with my girl, and Baron is at our feet, and even though the storm is still lashing the house, there is already a hint of daylight behind all this darkness.

Chapter 9

Maine

Ava was at work when Remy called. She had been obsessively checking news sites and listening to the radio, monitoring the fate of the people in her father's home city and in the path of this monster storm. There was definitely damage, but in the last few hours, the storm had been downgraded to a category three, although a powerful one, just barely below the threshold for a four. But it had turned just enough. The city would be spared from a direct hit once again.

"I don't want to jinx us, but it looks like we dodged a bullet!" Remy said.

"Yes! Thank God for a slight turn to the right," Ava said. She thought of her father's ancestral home, how he would be relieved to know it was spared. "But the Gulf is getting pummeled."

"Yeah," Remy said. Then he was quiet for a moment. "Biloxi. Gulfport. And Plaquemines really got hit bad. I bet my uncle's camp is long gone. Thank the Lord Dad came to his senses and got the hell out of Port Sulphur."

Remy's father had decided to retreat on Sunday morning. For days he had stubbornly ignored the panicked pleas of his wife, son, and brothers. But then he realized there was no sound in the wetlands around him. The birds had disappeared. That was what finally convinced him to get the hell out.

"Where is he now?"

"He's at home. He didn't get back until last night. He was one of the last people out of the parish. And by then it was too late to try to drive and meet up with Mom, and he figured he could keep an eye on the house."

"Well, I'm glad he's okay. And now you can relax."

"Yeah, and besides, I felt much better after I ripped him a new one."

"You gonna celebrate?"

"Hell, yes. I'm going fishing."

Remy had taken the day off, since he was too distracted by the storm to work anyway. And he had a bass boat that his father had given him that sat in a marina in Annapolis, where Remy spent many of his weekends in the summer.

"Hope you catch a big one."

They hung up. Ava felt a tremendous weight lifted. She went back to work in a great mood. It was quiet at the office; most people, especially parents whose kids were about to go back to school, were taking the week off to maximize their vacation time with the upcoming Labor Day weekend.

It was only 1:00 p.m. when Ava finished everything she had aimed to get done for the day. She wandered over to the windows. The windows on her side of the old mansion looked out over Penobscot Bay. She usually walked by it without a glance; she rarely looked at it anymore even though it was everywhere she went.

It was getting cloudy; there was a possibility of rain this afternoon. She watched dozens of little white sailboats darting toward shore.

Chapter 10

Monday, 9:45 a.m.
Gentilly

At some point early this morning, the power went out. That was when Baron really started whining harder. He has been fussing for the past couple of hours. The wind is down enough to let him in the yard, so I put him on the leash and take him outside so he can do his business. He keeps circling as if he is looking for something, his beagle nose to the ground. His hair is standing up on end, and he keeps pulling at the leash as if he wants to bolt. I have never heard him whine so desperately. I take him back inside after only a few minutes.

I follow him around the house, trying to settle him down. As we pass the front door, I hear a squishing sound. I look down and see water coming up from the carpet beneath Baron's paws. The carpet feels like a sponge beneath my shoes.

At first I think it's just a little water that was blown under the door.

But it's wet by the porch door too.

And it's wet by the door that goes out to the garage.

I open the door to see that there is water in my house, at least five inches in the garage.

And the water is rising higher as I stand there, dumbfounded. Holy God, that water is rising fast!

Penny calls me from the bedroom.

"Hold on, honey," I say. I rush—as fast as an old man like me can—to the kitchen. I grab the bags with our radio, meds, batteries, food, and water. I drop them at the floor beneath the drop-down attic door. I chase Baron—he is frantic now—and put his leash back on. I go to the bedroom.

"Penny," I say as she starts to talk about the power being out. Then she notices a sound.

"That sound," she says.

I shift. She looks down at my feet. "Penny," I start again.

The water is rising above the rugs, and she can hear the swoosh, splash as I rush toward her.

"Oh my God!" she cries.

"Let's go to the attic, honey," I say. I reach for her. "Probably just a little street flooding, honey," I say. But this is not normal, and even as I say it, I know she doesn't believe me. We might get a little flooding in the garage and the yard when we get a lot of rain and the storm drains get blocked, but I can't remember ever seeing wet rugs all the way into the bedroom.

I hurry to get Penny out of bed. She looks around frantically for her glasses. I find them on the nightstand, and she shakily puts them on as I put an arm out for her. I have Baron's leash in my other hand. I can feel the water rising past my ankles.

As we head out to the hallway, I see that the walls of our house are weeping water. There is water coming through cracks in the windows; everything seems to be creaking and giving way.

"The levees!" Penny cries. "Oh God! No! Our house!"

She starts to go over to the front door, wanting to look, but I point her—more roughly than I meant to, but the fear is rising in me—toward the attic. I don't think we'll still be standing if we open the front door. Somewhere down there, through that door, beyond where my eyes can see, the street ends at the lake. It used to. But now Pontchartrain is coming for us.

She tries to go toward the front door again. I start to push her away, but she says, "No, Robert! The girls! The girls' pictures!"

The wall along the living room that leads to the front door is lined with photos. Kindergarten photos, high-school graduation, fourth-grade plays, weddings, college, babies. Our girls.

"There is no time, honey," I say as I pull her away and toward the attic trapdoor. I pull it down. I briefly glance at her. Her eyes are shining, but she is listening to me. Behind me, water seeps in beneath the windowsills.

The water is close to my knees now. I am wading in my own damn hallway.

I start to help her up the stepladder, but she says, "No! Get Baron up there first." I look next to me. The water is already up to Baron's neck.

"Okay, boy," I say. I pick him up with my right hand and use my left hand to haul myself up the ladder.

"Hold on to the ladder!" I say sternly to Penny. I am using my army voice. It is still there after all this time. Automatic.

I look down and see the emergency bags I had packed floating away from Penny. I say nothing since I don't want her to try to grab them. I'm already terrified she is going to lose her balance and slip away from me.

I push Baron up over the last step and into the attic. "It's okay, boy," I keep saying. "It's okay." He runs to the far corner of the attic, his leash trailing behind him.

I'm back at the bottom of the ladder, and the water is rising. It's getting close to my waist, and it's been maybe two minutes since I saw it coming through the walls. Penny is next. I help her up the stairs, and all the while the water seems to be rising quicker than we move. It is cold around my back. I feel something swimming in here with me. The thin screen between us and nature—and all its violence, apathy, and force—has been completely ripped away.

I steady Penny as she climbs, bracing for her to fall, but she scrapes along, and then she is on the attic floor.

"Come on, honey!" she says. But I have work to do.

Once I see she's safely off the ladder and sitting down on the attic floor, I run—well, I wade—to the living room where I last saw one of the bags bobbing along next to the furniture. Items are spilling out of the bags. I grab the bag. More spills out as I lift it out of the water, but I catch what I can. Penny is yelling my name. I have never heard her so frantic.

I can't respond as it takes everything I have to swim, banging up against my own living-room furniture that is now floating around me, to the wall next to the front door. The water is past my shoulders now. I grab a couple of the girls' photos that are still above the water and jam them into my bag. I turn for the ladder and feel the force of water coming in from outside. It is still rising.

I feel panic grip my gut and my throat as I splash toward the ladder. In just the last few seconds, the water has risen over my chin, my lips; I tilt my head back, straining to keep my mouth and nose free. I am going to drown.

Oh God, I am going to drown. I take a deep breath of air and try to push myself forward. Only a rung of the ladder is visible above the water now.

Water splashes over my face and head, and I can feel things—animals, fish, everything I own—bumping against me as I stretch out my arms toward the ladder.

I can hear Penny screaming and crying. I can't leave Penny. I have to help Penny.

I try to grab the ladder with my free hand and miss, panicking as the water is now over my head. My lungs are straining as I push around and struggle to see underwater; everything is black and green and stinging my eyes. I finally flail around in the area where I think the ladder is, and my hand slams into it, making contact. I pull myself up, coughing and gasping as my mouth hits air. I drag myself onto the attic floor and collapse. The bag and everything in it rolls away. Penny stumbles toward me, crawls, puts her arms around my neck, and kisses my cheek.

"Thank you, God," she says. "Thank you, God, thank you, God."

All I can do for a few minutes is heave and cough. My head is pounding. My chest is on fire; my lungs are screaming.

Finally I have enough air to say, "I'm okay, honey." She is still crying. I put my arms around her; she holds on to me, and I can feel her shaking.

I can't just lie here. How much higher is this water going to go? I sit up, with Penny's arm around my shoulders. I grab her hand and look down at the black sea in my family room. I hear thrashing around. Things are alive in there. I don't know and don't want to know what they are. Gators, I think. Possums. Deer. Snakes. Fish.

It's still rising. I struggle to stand up, steady myself, and look around for something to break a hole in the roof. I start tossing boxes aside, pushing old furniture out of the way.

"Do we have an ax or a bat?" I ask. Penny looks at me and then understands.

She thinks for a moment. "The girls' softball bats," she says. "They might be up here."

Baron is cowering in the corner, confused by all the activity.

Our eaves slope gently upward; they look impossible to cut through. I rifle through boxes looking for bats but don't find any. Finally I throw open a trunk of my old army gear and find my old rusty rifles, long parted from its ammunition. I grab it, holding onto the barrel, choose a spot within easy reach, and begin pounding at the roof with the butt of my old gun.

"Can you keep an eye on the water, sweetheart?" I say to Penny.

That is all she can look at. "It's still rising!" she cries.

It's dusty, hot, and musty up here; I'm still drenched from the water but can already feel myself starting to sweat from the heat. I glance out one of the two tiny attic windows and see cars floating down our street, bumping into each other and into the tops of houses.

There is black, black water everywhere, surrounding us, swallowing everything in sight.

Chapter 11

Ava went home at 1:30 p.m. She was gardening out back and watching Tiras stalk a chipmunk when her cell phone rang from the kitchen table just inside. She tore off her right glove and went in to answer it.

"Are you watching TV?" It was Remy. She froze when she heard the tone of his voice.

"No...why?"

"The levees broke."

Her heart surged and seemed to stop beating for a moment. "What? Which levees?" She remembered those summers long ago. Running along the levee with Ellis and other cousins whose faces she could barely remember. Running in the grass, watching for snakes. Running where her father ran when he was a boy.

"A bunch of them! Jesus. Industrial Canal. Seventeenth Street. People's Avenue. London Avenue. Fuck...St. Bernard Parish is probably completely under water."

"Oh my God! Are they getting people out?"

"I don't know. We don't know how many people are still in the city."

"Oh my God," Ava said again, feeling confused, numb.

"Industrial Canal. It's fucking MR-GO..."

"MR-GO?"

"Mississippi River Gulf Outlet—that shortcut they built years ago between the Gulf and the inner harbor. It brought the fucking water right into St.

Bernard's Parish, New Orleans East…" He knew the geography in a way that Ava did not. She just remembered green grass, the Mississippi River, and Lake Pontchartrain. She thought of her father's old hurricane book. The resort islands that had disappeared under the sea, eaten up forever by storms.

"How bad is it?"

"I don't know. I tried to call my dad, but he didn't answer."

"I'm sure he's fine," Ava said, although all she could think was they were all going to drown. This is it. The big one. She fought the urge to cry. Losing her father's city was like losing her father all over again.

But crying didn't help things—her mother taught her that.

She thought of her cousin Ellis, and her heart sank. She had never heard back from him. She could only hope he had decided to evacuate.

"I don't know," Remy said. "I don't know if Dad's fine. Fuck. Fuck, fuck, fuck."

"Remy, I'm so sorry," she said.

"I gotta go," he said. "I gotta make some calls. Talk to you later."

Ava ran upstairs, whistling for Tiras to come back in with her. He banged through the swinging screen door and trotted behind her upstairs to her dad's office. The big mutt sat in the doorway, startled at her rushed activity. Ava hit the refresh button on the news site she had been checking before she had left for work many hours before.

BREAKING: Multiple Levee Breaches in New Orleans. Details to Come

There was frustratingly little information. Remy was getting his intel from people who still lived and worked there. Ava went back downstairs and sat in front of the TV with her laptop on her lap. She would be there for hours, watching the nightmare unfold with millions of other Americans.

Later that night, Ava watched a woman being interviewed outside the Superdome: "My neighbor, he's dead. The boy who cuts my lawn, he's dead too. I saw him floating…" The woman was dead-eyed, and her face looked swollen. She was stifling sobs throughout the interview. She described how the walls of her house collapsed in on her when the water rushed in and how she floated out on a door, clinging to her two granddaughters and her daughter. Four souls, surrounded by floodwaters, hanging on to nothing but a door.

Her voice turned hoarse from shouting for help. The Coast Guard rescued her and her family. The Coasties brought them to the I-10 overpass on Claiborne Ave. They told her to go to the Superdome.

One of the woman's little granddaughters said, "I had to keep jumping on my toes so I could keep my face out of the water."

As the night wore on, Ava flipped between channels, looking for new information, trying to avoid the same interviews. She remembered doing this nearly four years before, watching horrific scenes over and over until she couldn't take it anymore and stopped watching the news for a month.

With daylight, the news helicopters showed the devastation: a city underwater.

"An area of the city known as the Ninth Ward…"

"Nearly all this area, called New Orleans East, is submerged this morning…"

"Nine one one system is overwhelmed…"

"FEMA response is slow…"

"We are getting additional reports of problems inside the Superdome…"

Reporters asked about levees, about the mayor, about the senators and the governor, about FEMA, about the president. They reported from the outskirts of obliterated towns and devastated cities like Waveland, Gulfport, and Biloxi, places relief services could not yet get close to because so much debris blocked the roads.

The nation watched, transfixed and horrified.

Ava called in a personal day on Tuesday. She had nobody to call in to, but she left a message on her boss's voice mail.

As the news crawlers advanced across the screen, Ava thought about the night of the accident. She could not remember how she had gotten home. Later, much later, her uncle told her a nearby boat had reported the rogue wave, and they had called the Coast Guard, concerned because they had seen some kayakers in the area. A Coast Guard boat had been sent out from Portland, and they found her, sitting in the kayak, crying hysterically.

As the morning wore on, the news choppers showed 80 percent of the city underwater. People on roofs, asking for help; some of them had written it in paint or rocks on the tarpaper shingles or with wood torn and scrounged from their attics. No sign of the National Guard. The White House claimed that FEMA was doing everything they could. The Superdome and Convention Center were surrounded by miserable, thirsty, frightened people with nowhere to go. Crying women and angry men with babies. Old people. An old woman dead in a wheelchair out in the street. Just sitting there until someone finally put a sheet over her.

Sometime in the morning on Tuesday, Ava picked up the phone and called Remy.

"It just keeps getting shittier and shittier, doesn't it?" he said by way of greeting.

"Any word from your dad?"

"Can't get through. My mom can't get through. Too many people trying to call, and Lord knows how all this is affecting communications down there."

At that moment, Ava surprised herself with a wild idea. She blurted it out before she could change her mind.

"I think we should go down there."

"To NOLA…?"

"Yes. We can take your boat. We can do something instead of just sitting here."

Remy was usually fast with a quip or a joke. But she had surprised him into silence.

"Rem?"

"Shit, yes, we should." He paused. "And the boat. Yes." The bass boat he kept in Annapolis, the one his father had given to him.

"Of course, I also have a twenty-year-old Volvo. I don't know if it can handle pulling a fifteen-foot vessel." He thought for a moment. "One of my buddies at work, Nelson, has a truck, and he owes me one. Actually he owes me three. One, I helped him move a couple weeks ago. In ninety-five-degree heat. That fucker. Two, I basically wrestled his keys from him when he was going to drive home drunk from a party, and three, I introduced him to his girlfriend."

"Wow. You own that guy," Ava said.

"I do. Nelson is my bitch. Which is good, because it may be a little tough to convince him to let me take his truck into a flood zone."

"You can use your Volvo as collateral."

"Don't even suggest that I would not get my Volvo back."

"Why don't I pack up some stuff, fly down to DC, and you can get the boat ready, and we go?" Ava suggested.

"Fly into Baltimore. I'll be coming from Annapolis." He paused. "You really want to go all the way down to Louisiana? You don't even like to cross the state line."

"Come on. Before I chicken out."

"Will they let us in? They want everyone out, right?"

"They'll let in volunteers who have a boat and want to help, won't they?"

Remy considered this. "Hmm. I would hope so. But what if by the time we get down there they don't need us anymore?"

"Then maybe we can help with the cleanup." Ava's determination suddenly felt like a thin thread that might unravel. She wanted Remy to stop pulling at it.

"Can you get off work?"

"Yes. I have worked ahead, since it's been quiet the past couple of weeks with so many people away. Besides, I haven't taken vacation since…I don't even remember. My boss will be amazed. What about you?" She knew a little thing like no vacation time would not stop Remy. He had a knack for convincing people. She was sure he would find a way.

"I have some time. Maybe not a lot. I'll have to check. I have been on a bit of a vacation spree this year. But I'll talk to my boss. She'll let me work something out. Maybe I can work weekends next month or something."

"Then you're in?"

"I'm in."

"Okay." Ava took a deep breath. "Let me look at flights right now. I'll call you back." She poked around and found a flight from Portland to Providence to Baltimore. It left in two hours. She bought a ticket and gave Remy the information. She wondered if he could hear the fear in her voice. She was shaking.

"I don't know what you did with Ava, but I like this new girl," Remy said. "She's feisty."

"Okay. I gotta pack and take Tiras over to my uncle's house." She looked at the dog. He wagged his tail, happy with the attention. But his demeanor soon changed from happy to stressed as he saw her start to pack her bags.

Adrenaline helped. In less than thirty minutes, Ava had taken a shower and packed. She had grabbed her backpack and stuffed it with basic hygiene items, bottles of water, and a couple of changes of clothes. On the rare occasions she went anywhere—even to her aunt and uncle's to house-sit when they were traveling—she would make a list, but she didn't have time for that now. She packed up some of Tiras's food and toys for her aunt and uncle to give him. She threw her cell phone charger, a flashlight, cleaning wipes, granola bars, and more bottles of water into a second bag. She basically tossed in whatever she thought might be useful in a flood zone.

At the last minute, after throwing her bags in the truck, she remembered her press pass. In case they did have any trouble getting into the city, she thought a press pass might be enough to finagle something. The last one the staff had made for her was from the previous year, when she helped represent Eastland at an event called "Best of Maine." She dug it out of her desk drawer and looked at it. The "2004" was small enough. Hopefully nobody would notice.

Her heart was thumping as she locked up and shooed Tiras into the truck. She left a message on her boss's voice mail, saying she was going to be out of the office for a few more days. As she drove through town, looking at the sun glistening off white clapboard houses and the gray-blue bay, she listened to the radio.

"The city of New Orleans is in a state of devastation…"

"There are bodies floating in the floodwaters…"

"Both airports are under water…"

As she walked up to the side door, Ava saw her uncle coming to greet her. He looked haggard, still walking slow because of his knee surgery, and surprised.

"Ava!" he said. "Everything okay?" He opened the door. Tiras ran in ahead.

"Yeah. This is very last minute, and I'm sorry about that, but can you take care of Tiras for a few days?"

"Of course. What's going on?"

"Can you drive me to the airport?"

He raised an eyebrow. "Why?"

She wasn't sure how he was going to take this. "I'm going down to New Orleans."

"No," he said, without hesitation. Sounding firm. Sounding like a father.

Ava paused and then steeled herself. "I'll take a cab if I have to," she said.

"No," he said again. But then Ava's aunt, Rosa, came into the room.

"What's going on?" she asked. She was in pajama pants and a wraparound cardigan and her ancient L.L.Bean slippers, her gray hair up in a bun.

"It's not safe down there, Ava," Uncle Keenan said.

"I'm not going alone. Rem's coming with me."

Rosa quickly figured out what was going on and started trying to back Ava up.

"Remy's still got family in the city, right?" she said. "Are they home? Are they okay?"

"Yes. Well, his father is in Uptown. And we hope he's okay." And then Ava sort of lied, saying, "We're going to meet up with Ellis. He's a Louisiana State Trooper now; I don't know if you remember him." She hoped they would meet up with him.

"Oh, of course! I remember Ellis," Rosa said, turning to her husband. "We met him at your dad's...after your dad passed away." Rosa bent down to pat Tiras on the head. "And we'll take care of Mr. T. And Ava, you'll be careful." She turned to Ava, as if asking her niece not to make her regret lobbying for her in this moment. "Right? You'll be careful, honey? You're always so careful."

Ava nodded.

"I'll go with you," Keenan said.

Rosa seemed to consider this.

"No, no," Ava said. "You can barely walk, for God's sake." He couldn't dispute that as he hobbled across the kitchen.

Rosa poured Ava some coffee, while Keenan tried to wrap his mind around the concept. "When I said you should go on vacation, this isn't really what I was envisioning," he said.

"I think it's great. They could use the help, I'm sure," Rosa said, in a tone that suggested the time to debate this decision was over. "Just be careful, honey, like I said. There will be some desperate people around. Don't go anywhere alone. Now. How can we help? What's your plan?"

"Remy has a boat. We'll meet up in Baltimore and drive from there," Ava said. She followed her aunt out to the back porch.

"It's not a sailboat, is it?" Keenan asked. He was half-kidding, adjusting to the idea.

Ava shook her head. "Fishing boat. Remy's been on fishing boats since he was a kid." Keenan's face was tight; he looked older this morning. He turned abruptly and headed out to the garage. Tiras trailed after him.

Ava and her aunt stood on the porch. It overlooked the backyard. The Beals' garden was the only tamed part of a rolling hill of wildflowers that overlooked the harbor.

"You won't go out with just the two of you. You'll bring that trooper—your cousin—with you? There will be looters. Or other trouble." Ava had heard plenty of news reporters talking about looters and people shooting at cops, but she pushed them out of her mind.

"Well, they might have things under control by the time we get there, and they might not need us at all."

"It doesn't look that way, but maybe," Rosa said. "What will you do then?" she asked.

Ava shrugged. "Rescue pets? Help with cleanup?" She just knew she had to do something.

Rosa nodded.

"Beautiful day, huh?" Rosa said, looking out at Tamarack Harbor. A replica of an eighteenth-century ship was anchored out there, in front of a straight-on view of the breakers and the bright white, green-roofed lighthouse that rose up at the harbor's edge. From the porch it looked as if the old ship, its sails snapping in the breeze, was about to set sail.

Keenan emerged from the garage with a first-aid kit and a full tool belt in his hands.

"I figured these might come in handy."

"When's your plane?" Rosa asked.

"Soon. I need to go in a few minutes."

Ava said good-bye to Tiras and handed her aunt the bag with Tiras's things. An hour later when they pulled up at the airport, her uncle handed her a wad of cash. "When you get there, duct tape it to your body," he said. "The duct tape is in your duffel. I also put a knife in there. You better check it. Don't carry it on the plane with you. I want you to, first thing now, before you get into New Orleans, I want you to go to the ladies room somewhere and tape that knife to your belly, okay? It has a sheath and everything. It's very sharp, so be very, very careful with it."

The fact that he clearly was sure she would need a knife made Ava nervous all over again. Time to get going…before she lost her nerve.

He got out of the truck to get in the driver's seat. But first he hugged her. "Just please be careful, honey," he said. "Be very careful."

Chapter 12

Monday Night

Gentilly

I am watching for the next rat. At first I was focused on the roof, pounding away with all my strength, watching slivers of wood splinter away from the beams above, but I could not for the life of me bust it open. I did, however, manage to do a lot of damage without actually punching through to sunlight. I wonder what it will take to fix it, but then I think, of course, it can't be fixed. This whole house can't be fixed, and I feel a fresh wave of sadness and dread wash over me.

Earlier we had been watching the water. It crept up and over the ladder, through the opening. It started to pool on the floor. But when it seemed to settle and the pool did not get any bigger, I turned my attention from the stubbornly solid roof to one of the windows, thinking I could bust away at the sills and break out the frame, creating a bigger opening that we could escape through to get to the roof. I got pretty far along.

But around then the water seemed to stop rising. So now we have a busted window, which lets hot air into our hot attic, but at least there was the tiny promise of a breeze, so we leaned out of it, looking for rescue boats or neighbors on their roofs. We listened for shouts, and we shouted ourselves hoarse. Right now we don't have the energy to move to the roof. We'll wait and do it later, or maybe we won't even have to. Someone will come along soon.

I heard screams earlier, but they didn't last long.

Now I look down and see just a pool of blackness that has swept animals and objects before it with the power of Noah's flood.

The water has brought us rats too.

The rats are everywhere now. They're in every corner of the attic, behind us, scraping at the edges of the stairs, desperately trying to escape the water below. Baron has already killed two of them, and I'm afraid he's going to get bit, so I've called him off.

Penny cried at first, but now we're getting used to them, and as long as they don't touch us, I think we'll be okay. I hate rats. It reminds me of when we had a rat problem in our military housing in Texas. There's something primal about our hatred of them, like we are protecting our cave and it's either they get to survive or we do. Or maybe it's a collective imprint of plague memories, of bodies stacked in the dooryards of abandoned villages, populations wiped out.

"Rob," Penny says, "it's so hot." She has said that many times now, because it is so hard not to say it. I can only nod in agreement. For a moment I foolishly look around for our old box fan, but, of course, we don't have electricity. I rip a piece of cardboard off of a box and use it to fan Penny. I look out the window and see nothing but the same black lake I have been looking at for hours now.

The sky is impressively blue.

I had rummaged through the old trunks and bags and boxes up here and found an old blanket for Penny to lie on. I found an old tablecloth and rolled it up for her to put under her head, although she's been afraid to lie down because of the rats. Earlier I had just sat next to her, near one of the windows, and when she got tired of sitting at the window, I described to her everything I saw: the waste of houses floating, clothes stuck on lamp posts, mailboxes, the stop sign at the end of our street covered over, cars bobbing down the street and ramming into porches, and dead animals. We hear desperate dogs barking, and it is a heartbreaking sound. Terrified barks from these miserably abandoned descendants of wolves, companions who came to the campfire and made a deal with mankind: protection for food. And all their human friends had broken the bargain, leaving them to die.

At first I am surprised; I am sure all the other dogs in the neighborhood, if left behind, must have drowned by now. But clearly some of them have made it to rooftops or higher ground or have clawed their way to survival on the top of floating furniture.

I bring Baron closer to us.

"We'll get out of here soon," I say. To Penny, to Baron, to myself. I imagine airboats, state police, fireboats, and firemen with ladders on their way.

I try not to think about downstairs. I try not to curse myself for not bringing more of our precious belongings up here, but I can't stop thinking about it. I open the bag I had managed to drag up here with me, and two of the girls' photos—elementary school—have survived. I put their pictures on top of a box in a far corner of the floor, where they can't get wet.

So many other treasures are lost below us, within agonizingly close reach. Our wedding album. All the other photos of our girls and grandkids. My parents' wedding rings. The box of tokens and trinkets marking every Mardi Gras this family had celebrated, fake doubloons and chips with Rex's faces on them, and cups with our krewe's symbols. The joyous and tongue-in-cheek themes of more than three decades of parades.

"Rob," Penny says, "can I have a little water?"

"Yes, honey," I say. I look at her. She is covered with a light sheen of sweat; it dampens her hair, her face. That beautiful face. She wipes her eyes with unsteady hands.

I help her drink; she is shakier than she should be by this time of day. I look at my watch. We didn't take our meds this morning. Of course, we didn't. We are on so many meds now, to lower blood pressure and cholesterol, to help manage my pain and her symptoms.

I go to the bag. I reach in and feel around for our pillboxes. There is a jumble of items in the bag; besides the two photos I saved, there is the radio and some batteries, peanut butter and crackers, tuna fish, a bottle of water, and a can of Baron's dog food. I feel around again and start to get worried.

"Are they in there?" Penny asks. I don't respond. After fishing around some more, I finally take out all of the bag's contents on top of a box and start to look through them. I starting panicking when I look at what is in the bag and think, *This is all we have left.* But then I stop myself. We have each other.

I sort through the items. Our medicines are not there.

"It's okay, sweetheart," Penny says. "Someone will be along soon. They must know our whole neighborhood is like this. We'll get out of here, and we can get new prescriptions right away."

I nod. I wonder how long it will take them to get to us. I wonder how many people are in the same position we are in. It might take a few hours for them— them? Police? Firemen?—to arrive, so I was glad we had saved at least one plastic water bottle to get us through the rest of the afternoon.

Penny leans back and closes her eyes. I resume fanning her with the torn cardboard. I look around the attic, scanning for rats and occasionally telling Baron no when he starts to go after one.

We hadn't been up here in a while. Well, not since Penny got sick. She used to come up here once a year and go through things, giving away some items and sending a few things to the girls if they wanted them, things she thought the grandkids might like. But Penny had not been able to come up here in a long time.

I look around at a few items that are stacked alongside boxes, perhaps things Penny was thinking of giving away. There is a pitcher with purple and yellow flowers on it that we received as a wedding gift. Neither of us are big fans of purple, so we didn't use it much over the years. I no longer remember who gave it to us; it might have been some army buddy and his wife we long ago lost touch with. I can still picture that day and the look on Penny's face.

I got such a great girl.

I sit down beside her. Baron is panting heavily, his eyes still on the rats. This heat is not good. I think about trying again to bust a hole in the roof to get more air through here—hell, the house is a total loss now anyway—but decide to hold off awhile.

I laugh. Penny looks at me as if I'm crazy, and I say, "I thought I was being so...meticulous. I checked everything in the yard, made sure everything was secure, got the candles ready as a backup for the flashlight, and then I thought I better fill the tub. Fill the tub! The tub is ten feet underwater." I laugh again.

"That's what you're supposed to do," Penny says. "You always told me, you grow up in New Orleans, you learn three things about hurricanes. One is to fill the tub before the storm. Two is you don't drink water from the tap after a hurricane. And three is you don't buy dead crabs."

"Yeah. And if the water drowns your bathroom, number one isn't too useful." I chuckle.

"But remember Betsy," Penny says. It wasn't a question but an admonition. We have every reason to take every precaution, but sometimes a storm comes along that knocks you off your feet. They do unpredictable things, and all we can do is try to take cover or sway with the wind. Or evacuate. How I wish we had taken Russell up on his offer again this time.

"Yes. I remember," I say.

"Rob, this might be it for us," she says. Penny has a way of being right, so this statement chills me.

"No!" I say sharply. "Honey, we'll get out of this. We just need to sit tight for a little while."

We sit and listen as dogs wail outside. We hear a thump. Our furniture downstairs is still floating, bumping against the walls.

Chapter 13

Monday, Early Evening
St. Liberatus

We did not see much of the sun yesterday, and certainly not today, but already it promises to make a return. It will shine down, no doubt, on a collection of broken glass, overflowing storm drains, and fallen trees, the same sights we saw this afternoon after the storm started to move out.

After we were sure that the rain had slowed to a trickle and the wind had died down enough to stop throwing debris, we moved the patients back into their rooms. I went to every floor to check in with the staff members in charge of each department and get a report on patients and staff and anything I needed to know. We talked to visitors and families about when they might leave. We suggested they wait until first light so they could clearly view any obstructions in the streets like downed electrical wire that could send them right back here or worse, but many opted to leave now. They were anxious to check on their homes.

Housekeeping had continued to board up some of the broken windows during the storm, which was not an easy task, but now we are taking the boards down, because without air conditioning—lost hours ago when we lost city power and the generators took over—it is getting very hot in here. Even with open windows, everybody, including the patients lying in their beds, is soon covered with a light sheen of sweat.

We still have Internet, so I fire an e-mail off to my brother to let him know I'm okay. Most of us have little to no cell reception.

But the tension is dissipating. I walk along the halls and see visitors who have just woken up talking and laughing. Nurses and nurses' aides and physicians are joking around. Hours before, all we heard was praying and the sounds of the storm.

I go visit Michaela. She is in pain but in a good mood. Before and during the storm, we have been conservative with the painkillers in case we need to ration them. Now I update her orders so she can have more relief. She is joking with her nurse. That is usually a good sign.

The staffs distribute food to the patients who are awake. I finish my rounds and compare notes with the other department heads. On the OR floor, I see Dr. Osgood. He's one of the physicians we brought into our practice. He's a talented family doctor, a throwback to the types of doctors we all think our grandfathers had. He's also, in a most contradictory way and to my frequent annoyance, the guy who seems to do the most ass-kissing at our administrative meetings. He's always serving on some board or another, and he's been known to go out of his way to schmooze with our CEO who was noticeably absent this weekend. In our last administrative meeting, he held forth about the importance of following protocol, specifically not going against the judgment of your fellow physicians. It was a thinly veiled attack on me for ordering a procedure on a patient that one of the CEO's other henchmen deemed unnecessary. She was elderly and had a terminal illness as well as a bowel obstruction. They said to leave the obstruction alone; I thought the risk of the procedure was worth relieving the woman's pain. The surgeon who performed the procedure agreed with me. I was chastised, in my opinion, because I was supposed to follow the herd, patient's interest be damned.

But on the other hand, Dr. Osgood was supposed to be on vacation this week; instead, he drove back to New Orleans, leaving his family behind in some beach house outside of Charleston, because he thought the hospital might need him. This is why I find him somewhat infuriating; as much as I want to dislike him, I think he's a good physician, and I can't help but respect him for that.

"We dodged a bullet," he says.

"We sure did," I say.

I am in the men's room—which stinks worse than I have ever experienced, thanks to this overcrowded floor—washing my hands and staring at my gray temples, which seem grayer than they were yesterday; just then I realize the water is coming out of the faucet in a trickle. This happens sometimes after a storm. These storms wreak havoc with city water in so many ways. I try to keep it quiet so there isn't a rush to the bathrooms, but at the next check-in meeting, I let all the department supervisors know they should probably tell their staff to use the toilets and have the ambulatory patients use theirs while they still can.

I try to call Jane, to let her know I made it through okay. We rarely talk, but she had tried to call during the storm, so I want to let her know I'm still alive. Even though I should maintain a cordial distance now, I refuse to pretend I don't know her incredibly well, and I know she's awake because she was always an early bird. But it doesn't matter, because I still can't get a good signal; only one shaky little bar shows on my cell screen. I can see my voice mails and the fact that I have missed four messages—one from my brother, one from Jane, and two from friends who live out of state and doubtless have been watching the news. Even within the hospital, we are having a hard time communicating. The intercom is now dead. The emergency call signals from the patients' rooms are down, but the critical patients' machines are all still working because the bedside outlets are the number-one priority for our generators.

As I walk down the hall back toward the meeting room, one of the nurses tells me that the Internet is down now too. Our portable radio has been temperamental; it was working during the storm, but now all we have is static, as if all the radio stations have gone off the air.

It has grown more unbearably sticky and muggy. We are all moving slowly, yet sweat droplets quickly turn to rivulets. With the fear and excitement gone, we are all becoming hot and impatient. But the city made it through, and we know they'll get the roads cleared and power restored soon enough. We'd get to change shifts, and tomorrow I can go see what became of *The Good Life*.

"Looks like we all made it out alive," Natalie says to me as she joins me in my walk down the hall. The window at the end of the hall still shows a dark-gray sky. It is unusually dark, since the streetlights are out, and the lights across the city are out too. It feels prehistoric to rely on the sun for light.

"Yep. Dodged a bullet again," I say. That's what they were saying after the storm passed through yesterday—New Orleans was once again spared a direct hit. Sometimes it felt like a direct hit with glass crashing around our ears and this old building shaking to its core, but other than the windows and some concerns about the roof, I doubt there was any extensive structural damage to St. Lib.

"Not so the Gulf Coast," Natalie says, her face somber.

"Don't you have relatives up there?" I ask, praying I am not confusing her with someone else on the staff. It's not that I don't listen, but…well, sometimes I try to listen, and I'm really thinking about my cases.

She nods. "My brother and sister-in-law live in Biloxi."

"Any word?"

She shook her head.

I start to say something, but Natalie turns and goes to the nurses' station.

I remember a news report we heard last night about the Gulf Coast; there was an old Mississippi town known for its four-hundred-year-old oak trees. They had all been blown away, bent like kindling from the force of the storm surge.

I think about everything those trees saw, all that had happened in the region as they grew to maturity and stood tall along the coast for four centuries. They were here when Bienville arrived and when he decided he needed slaves to drain this swamp. They were here when the French gave us up to Napoleon's war-mongering. They stood watch as Butler and his men swept in to help tighten the Union's vise grip around the South. They were here when Homer Plessy lost his court case and when Huey Long reigned over the state of Louisiana.

They were here through one hundred hurricanes before this one.

I look around me as I reach the end of the floor. Housekeeping and some of the staffs have straightened up a bit, pushing some of the rotting ceiling tiles into piles in the corners, putting up caution signs, and emptying overflowing trashcans. But there are still broken windows, smelly bathrooms, and crumbling ceilings. The gray-green hallway walls are wet with sweat and humidity, and the smiling photographs of patients and staffs that hang on the walls look out at dozens of people congregated outside every room. The halls are awash in patient beds, catheters, heart monitors, ventilators, tubes, and instruments. Crumpled-up paper towels and empty bottles of water are piled in the corners at the ends of the hall, next to the recycling bins and medical-waste containers. It has been less than forty-eight hours since the visitors started arriving, and this place is already looking like a disaster area.

Cleanup will get easier when more people leave. The windows will be fixed and the rooms cleaned and the trash emptied, and everything will be put back in its proper place. In a few days, we'll be back to normal.

I am standing at the podium in the corner of the conference room, jotting a few notes down to make sure I don't forget any announcements at the next meeting, when I hear Natalie and Dr. Osgood gasping at the window.

"Oh my God."

"Holy shit!"

"What?" I ask. They continue to stare, not responding. I walk over and look out the window with them. I stand dumbstruck as my brain struggles to register what I am looking at.

Gasps rise along the window as the staff all crowd in to look.

Water is rushing up from a side street; it is streaming over the storm drains, and the street is rapidly flooding, like a pan filling with oil.

It is rising too fast. It is flowing over car tires; it is engulfing the curbs and climbing up the trees and bubbling up through manhole covers, splashing through sewer grates.

"Oh my God," Natalie says again when we see water start to stream in from the other side of the hospital. The two rivers grow to meet each other.

Water is invading from every direction.

Branches, cars, street signs are starting to float.

One of the nurses, Arlene, who has worked here only a couple of years, comes to the window. She had been on the phone with Jerry, her husband, who is an NOPD officer. Her face is distant and afraid. She tells us what we all have already figured out.

"The levees broke," she says.

"Which ones?" I ask.

She looks confused. "I don't know…all of them."

There are no levees near here. They are all in other neighborhoods of the city and in the distant reaches of the neighborhood that borders us. Those areas must have been underwater for hours now. I wonder how many people have already died.

Other staff members have gathered. I hear murmurs and gasps in the hallway.

And then I hear call buzzers going off—alarms. Crash-cart alarms.

"The basement!" I exclaim, realizing what is happening. "The generators!"

As I'm saying it, more alarms start going off up and down the floor.

We start sprinting to the ventilated patients. As I run down the hallway, I shout to the staff, "Bag teams!"

We have trained for this; we practiced this in our emergency drills. Every resident and nurse knows who is on a respirator. Each respirator has a battery backup, but sometimes they don't work. You have to bag the patients by hand.

We spread out to patient rooms and quickly ascertain that the batteries have failed on four machines. The teams set up in each of those four rooms, while nurses watch and listen for other machines failing.

My heart sinks when I realize that the batteries on Andy's ventilator are among those that have failed. Like this kid needs another challenge.

"The portable generators!" I shout at Tennant and Marius when they come over to find out how they can help. These are industrial sized like the ones in the basement; there is supposed to be one on every floor.

Marius shakes his head. "We did not find any gas for the portable ones," he says.

My skin, in all this prickling heat, grows cold. We can't bag people by hand forever. It takes a considerable amount of forearm strength to work a bag. Andy, and the NICU patients...how long do they have? Mr. Bartlett?

But I can't think about it right now. We'll get rescued soon, and in the meantime, we'll keep the ventilated patients alive. But there is another problem we need to solve.

"The water's still rising!" shouts a nurse looking out of the patient windows.

I hear a chorus of "Oh my God" rising along the floor once again.

The ventilators are not our biggest problem.

"Marius, come with me," I say. "Tennant! Ferguson! Jain! Let's go!" I shout to the physicians and able-bodied men nearest me. We may have to carry people up here.

"Downstairs!" I say as I start to run down the hall. "The ER!"

We run first toward the elevator out of habit, but before we pull up, we collectively remember we can't use it without power, and it would be safer to use the stairs anyway given the situation. Marius reaches the stairway first. He flings the door open. It clangs, metal on cement.

We run like hell down the stairs. Each step is a blur. On the floors below us, the stairwell doors bang open as others rush to help. We can hear yelling, shouting, and water sloshing as we get closer to the first floor.

We land in water as we hit the first-floor stairwell. People rushing down the stairs in front of us open the door, and more water rushes in; it is up to our knees and rising. I tell half the team to go to one side of the floor and the rest to go the other. We fan out across the floor, water splashing up to our knees.

At first, the wide lobby doors are opening and closing, opening and closing; a malfunctioning robot; a ghost. Then they stop dead, stuck half-open as water rushes through them.

I find the doctor who is in charge of the floor. "Let's bring them up to the OR floor," I say. We've kept if off-limits, but it has the most room; since most operations were rescheduled before the storm, there is only a skeleton staff up there. It means two more flights of stairs, but it also means the patients won't have to be moved again.

I look around for any OR staff and find Dr. Osgood, who came downstairs behind us.

"Let's bring 'em up, but keep two ORs closed and sterile in case we need them," he says. "Let's say nine and ten. Off-limits."

Jain and I repeat this instruction through the chain as people make their way to the stairs and off the floor. "Everyone, listen up!" Jain says. "Take them to the OR—anywhere up to OR eight. *Do not* enter nine and ten."

The water is rising. People are screaming and crying.

"Use both stairwells—make sure you get the patient charts, grab the evac bags!" I shout to the staff.

Hip deep in rising water, we try to guide all the ambulatory patients off the floor.

"Everyone who can't help carry a patient needs to be carrying supplies!" I shout.

The water is relentless. We push each other toward the stairs.

We carry patients who cannot walk. We do it fire-bucket-brigade style; we get a group of immobile patients out and off the floor; staff members get them to the next floor, and then another group takes over. Several of the patients are morbidly obese, so it takes six or eight men to lift them.

The water is up to our waists now, and I see rats swimming alongside us—they are fighting for survival too. The air is thick with sweat and humidity. The air we breathe seems to condense along the walls. The waiting-room furniture starts to float and bump into us.

As the patients are evacuated up the stairs, Osgood and I are splashing through the corridor, looking for anyone who might be trapped. People are crying, screaming; there are waves now, lapping over stretchers.

"Doc, a little help here!" shouts Marius. He and two burly male nurses are trying to lift a morbidly obese man through the stairway doors. I wade over to help shoulder the patient's weight. He is embarrassed and clearly suffering. We are all gasping; it is hard to find each step as we make our way up; the shouting around us and the rising water distract us from the focus we need to shift his bulk as we round corners and slowly move upward. The water is soaking our clothes, trying to drag us under.

"My...chest..." the man says, "feels like a truck is sitting on me." He is gasping for breath; his pale white skin is turning gray.

"Does the pain radiate?" I ask as we continue our awkward journey.

"Yes," he gasps.

This is clearly the most stressful patient interview I've ever conducted. "What else hurts?" I ask.

"My..." He holds his jaw as if he has a terrible toothache.

"I need an evac kit!" I shout into the stairwell, at anyone near or with me who might have one. I should have mine on me too, but it's sitting on the conference-room table upstairs.

We are at the door to the OR floor. I wait until we bring the patient out of the way of the other evacuees before I open the kit that someone has shoved under my arm. I take out aspirin and nitroglycerin, and I administer them to the patient. A nurse carrying supplies hands him a bottle of water. I gesture to the nurse to keep an eye on the patient as he is carried upstairs; then Jain and I head back down the stairs to make sure everyone got out. But it is too late. The water is halfway up the stairs to the second floor.

Thinking someone might have made it to the stairwell and is treading water down there, we shout, "Is anybody else here? Is anybody else here?"

We don't hear anything except the lapping of the water. I pray to God that everyone has made it out.

Chapter 14

Tuesday, Late Afternoon
On the Road

Welcome to Baltimore—the sign sat above the escalator, that strange Maryland flag with its coat-of-arms and taxicab colors at the diagonals. Standing in the airport baggage claim, waiting for Remy to call, Ava watched CNN. It was clear within minutes that not much had changed in the past couple of hours since she had been waiting at the airport gate in Portland. She watched an interview with a man who had been staying at his house a half mile inland on the coast of Mississippi, a sturdy house he had built with his own hands, a house his whole family had taken refuge in.

His voice was otherworldly and ragged. "The water rushed in like a freight train. I never heard a noise like that. It was roaring, like a wild animal." A twenty-foot-high storm surge—a tsunami—had obliterated the landscape, and it took his daughter, his wife, and his mother-in-law. It left him, clinging to the remains of his porch, a broken man.

Ava thought, *I hope it's not too late for all of them.*

By the time Remy called her to let her know he had pulled up outside baggage claim, it was past 4:00 p.m. She walked through the sliding doors into the enveloping heat. Remy was parked at the edge of the terminal, next to a dogwood tree that had lost half of its white-pink petals. He held a cigarette in one hand and wore jeans and a navy T-shirt. His sandy-blond hair was mostly hidden under a brand spanking-new Nationals cap.

Ava couldn't help but grin at the sight of him despite the circumstances. They hugged. "You smell good," he said. "And you look skinny."

"Thank you and thank you. You look good too." At six feet four, Remy towered over her; she was a foot shorter. Remy threw Ava's bags into the truck.

"Called in that favor, huh?" she asked.

"It was a few favors. And he still put up a bit of a fight." Ava couldn't blame him.

The truck was one of the more heavy-duty types of pickups, one that looked like a handyman might drive it. It was red with a black interior.

Ava walked to the back and looked at the boat. It was sleek and white and new.

"Have you ever used this thing?" Ava asked.

"Of course I have," Remy said defensively. "I take good care of her."

Ava looked at the stern. "I can't believe you gave it such a cliché name," she said. "I'm disappointed."

Remy rolled his eyes. "Uh, my dad had that put on there. Do you think in a million years I would choose '*Rajun' Cajun*'?"

Ava laughed. "No, but your dad would." They climbed into the truck.

"The Nationals, huh?" Ava said, flicking at his cap. For just a moment, she wanted to pretend they were just visiting and catching up and not talk about anything but what they were about to do.

"Yes. So ten years from now when they are a real team, I can be smug about it. I don't want to jump on the bandwagon. This way, I am pretty much the only occupant of the bandwagon. Driving it, if you will."

"Should've gone with the Orioles."

Remy shrugged. "I live in DC." He started the engine.

Ava forced herself to get on task. "Have you heard from your dad yet?" she asked.

Remy shook his head. "Nope."

"From everything I've heard, he should be okay. Not a lot of flooding in Uptown compared to everywhere else."

Remy nodded, but his gray eyes betrayed a hint of worry. "Ready to go?"

Ava's stomach flipped. "Ready," she said.

Rain hit them in Virginia and Tennessee. They switched off every couple of hours; one shift of bleary-eyed driving blended into another. They stopped at crappy gas stations. Their eyes and minds were tired, and they each tried to steal some sleep when the other was driving. But it was hard to stop thinking about what they were going to confront and how they might be able to help.

They descended into Alabama. Green land in the dark. By now they had listened to all the reporters repeat themselves. "They've been through this before," one reporter droned. "The year was 1965. Hurricane Betsy devastated New Orleans, flooding the Lower Ninth Ward..." Somewhere the sun came up, and the stories started changing, getting more local.

Occasionally emergency vehicles roared past them, out of place and heading south, their shining chassis bearing names from Kentucky and Tennessee, New York and Pennsylvania. The farther south they got, the more vehicles they saw.

In Southern Mississippi, the little they could see from the roads that were open was bad enough to hint at the wreckage that lay beyond the downed trees and roadblocks. At this point, they were frequently stopped in traffic because of debris still in the road. It was on Mississippi public radio that they heard the story of the girl whose family climbed to the rafters as the waters rose and how she and her family listened in the darkness as an alligator killed a deer in their living room.

The storm surge broke everything in its path, a pulverizing bomb, an invading army that wrought devastation and slipped away, leaving behind the cement footprint of homes and ruined trees, boats thrown two miles inland, bloated bodies, the wreckage of lives hanging shredded in bare branches.

"Maybe we should just stop here," Remy said, because by now they had some firsthand experience of the extent of the devastation. But they both knew they wouldn't do that.

Ava said, "The storm surge is over. They need food, shelter, and medical help. Cleanup. But in New Orleans, there are still people on their roofs. And we still haven't heard from your dad or Ellis. I'm worried; I'll admit it."

Remy nodded.

As they got closer, they began to discuss plans for getting into the city. Remy had gotten through to one of his uncles who was an EMT in Lake Charles. He asked around and called Remy with advice on which roads they should take and which ones were completely blocked off.

They tuned into local radio somewhere near the Louisiana border, and they heard Garland Robinette, a New Orleans radio host, reporting from Baton Rouge. He had been forced to leave when his studio flooded Monday night. He was railing against the lack of preparedness, talking about people who had been forced to gather at the elevated highway, I-10 West, because they had no-where else to go. His callers were telegraphing every rumor. There was a nurse who was gangraped on the roof of a hospital. Armed gangs shooting it out with the few remaining NOPD officers. The Convention Center was as bad as the Superdome. Coast Guard choppers shot down. Explosives had blown up the levees in Lower 9.

It was early in the afternoon on Wednesday, August 31, when they stopped at a gas station to fill up one more time before they descended into New Orleans. The two of them went in to grab a few more supplies and stood there under the buzz of a broken fluorescent light, and then Remy wolfed down a shriveled hot dog that looked as if it had been sitting under a heat lamp for far too long.

"Any luck?" Remy asked. Ava had just tried to call Ellis again as they were walking in. She had tried a couple of times every few hours, but his phone just kept ringing.

The shelves of the gas-station convenience store had been pretty well picked over. A tiny TV sat above the freezers opposite the cashier. They glanced at it and saw video clips of the head of FEMA and the mayor, the governor, and the president.

"They're sure as fuck going to have hearings because of these incompetent shitheads," Remy said. "I feel as if we are in a developing country right now."

Ava was scouring the shelves for anything she might have forgotten. She settled on some pain reliever and more water.

As they paid for their purchases, Remy said, "We should probably clear a few things up before we get in there."

"Okay. Like what?" Ava asked. The cashier looked at them. This was a conversation they had both been avoiding. But they knew from the radio reports that it was a necessary one.

"There are undoubtedly going to be some not-so-nice…uh…people we're going to run into," Remy said. "So other than obviously not splitting up, we need to figure out how we'll protect ourselves if we need to. I have a knife…" He lowered his voice, even though they were now walking out the door. "And a pistol. You should carry one. Probably the knife, since I guess you don't know how to use the pistol."

"What?" Ava said, not sure she heard him right but then almost immediately realized she did.

Remy arched an eyebrow at her. "I'm from the South. There is no way I am going to go into a situation like this unarmed."

"How many guns do you have?" Ava asked. She had never really seen this side of him before.

"I'm not a collector. I just have this to protect myself. We always brought guns out to the camp. There are gators, you know."

"Do you have a permit?" she asked.

"Of course I do," Remy said. "Although I don't really think that's important at a time like this."

"The NOPD might disagree," Ava said.

Remy shrugged. "I think they are a little preoccupied."

Ava had never handled a pistol before. She knew people who had guns—lots of Mainers hunted, including her uncle and her grandfather—but they usually had rifles, not handguns. Suddenly it occurred to her that she probably knew people who had handguns but never talked about it. She felt incredibly naïve. A bit defensive, she said, "Well, it just so happens I have a knife." She had been feeling the weight of it every time she shifted in her seat.

"Oh, okay," Remy said, eyebrows raised.

"No, really, I do," Ava said. "My uncle gave it to me. I had it in my checked luggage, and when I landed, I taped it on in the bathroom." She pulled up her shirt just enough to show him.

"Wow. Okay, I'm impressed. You're prepared," Remy said.

"Well, I don't know about that."

The sun rose with them as they drove in the flat Louisiana heat. Soon they were crossing the Crescent City Connection, a pair of cantilevered bridges that lead over the Mississippi into New Orleans from Jefferson Parish.

The city came into view.

"Holy Jesus," Remy said.

There was smoke and fire and helicopters circling. But most of all, there was the water. The sickening shine of oil-stained black water.

Black water everywhere.

Chapter 15

Tuesday Night
Gentilly

Last night, we heard the cries of our neighbors, Emerson and Marie. I had been so consumed with saving my wife and dog that I forgot about them. I forgot they were staying home too.

I imagined how they felt, holding hands, screaming for help until they couldn't scream anymore. We had not heard their voices in hours, and I feared the worst. And I couldn't get out of my own damn house to save them. I was too afraid of drowning, and I couldn't break a hole in the damn attic ceiling. If I make it out of this attic, I fear I will hear their screams every night for the rest of my life.

Yesterday we managed to hang an SOS sign out of the window with the help of some nearly dried-up paint and an old sheet covered with a faded rose print pattern. It was one of Stacy's bedsheets when she was a little girl. I didn't realize Penny had saved it, but seeing it brought the memory back of those little hands trying to learn to tie her shoes; red ribbons and ponies. She loved ponies! We were able to give her lessons for a couple of years when she was in elementary school. When I was laid off, we had to stop the lessons for a while; by the time I was back at work, and we were back on track, she told us she wasn't interested anymore. I never really believed her; the girls rarely asked for anything. I know they are trying to get ahold of us now. I wish we had bought a cell phone when they told us to.

The first night was hard. Before it got dark, I doled out a little water and food to Baron and then water and food—tuna fish—to me and Penny. It was still unbearably hot, although at least the setting sun, while bringing an unwel-come and eerie darkness to our powerless city, also brought some relief from the heat.

We could hear the rats scurrying around. Occasionally during the night we heard shouts, but they sounded far away; the water distorted everything. Sometimes we would hear splashing. At one point we heard the whir of helicop-ters and sirens in the distance. Occasionally Baron would growl or whine pite-ously. I thought he would beg to go out, but he hasn't; he seems to understand that we have no control over this situation. I think about how he was pacing before the water came. It reminds me of a story I read about a dog in California who warned his owner that an earthquake was coming. Or tried to. The dog went crazy and acted completely unlike himself the night of the earthquake, and the owner didn't understand why until after it happened.

I am starting to think that there will be no boats motoring by tonight and no rescuers to find us. From what we can see out of our attic window, these rescuers have a lot of work ahead of them. For the first time, I think we might need to get ourselves out of here. I lean against the wall next to the window and think through my plan for tomorrow: search throughout the attic for anything that might float, and break one of the windows. Hopefully we will fit through; if not, I will hack away at the frame until we can. I need to get Penny and Baron out of here.

Now I am staring into the inky darkness, when Penny, who I thought was asleep, says, "Hear that?"

"What?" I strain to listen.

"It's so quiet out there."

No cars, no voices, no splashing; no frogs bellowing down by the London Avenue canal. Not even crickets. I'm sure they've all drowned. Quiet as death.

In the early morning hours, I attempt to sleep, but I only doze off for short periods of time. I am so afraid that I might miss a passing boat or a helicopter overhead. But they likely won't search at night. I don't want to give up hope that someone will get us out of this, even though I am now prepared with my plan B. As I lean against the wall near the window, Penny is lying near me on the blanket I found yesterday.

As soon as it is light enough to see around the attic and dodge the rats, I start going through boxes and trunks I hadn't opened yet, looking for something we can get the hell out of here on. An hour or so later, I have not found a damn thing that would float.

I go back to hacking away with my limited tools—the rifle and a chair leg—to widen the space by the window. At least we—well, I—could climb to the roof and maybe get someone's attention. I might have to get Penny up there, too, although I'm not sure how I'll do that. Even though the water has stopped rising, this attic is too hot, and we won't survive in here for long.

Chapter 16

Tuesday Night

St. Liberatus

Staffs, patients, and visitors: everyone with a working cell phone has been trying to call 911 for hours. But we get nothing, not even a busy signal. There must be 911 calls flooding the city, and given our location on the edges of the city, a good distance from any levee, I guess the rest of the low-lying areas in New Orleans have been flooded for hours, and emergency services are completely overwhelmed.

We are on our own.

I look for the portable radio that was in the meeting room the day before; its batteries have run out. There was another one at the nurses' station, but that one has disappeared.

"Did we get everyone?" I ask Dr. Jain as she stands next to me, dripping wet, outside the conference room.

Jain gives me an uncertain look.

"I don't know," she says.

If anyone was left down there, they are already dead.

The water kept rising after we got back onto the upper floors. I posted a couple of housekeeping staff members in the stairwell to take turns monitoring the progress. It's now well into the second-floor stairwell, but it hasn't risen past that. Yet.

Now I need to focus on getting everyone the hell out of this ship that is going down.

I seek out Marius and find he has been dispatched on a mission from Susan, looking for batteries for the in-room generators so we can relieve the bag teams.

"Anything?" I ask.

He shakes his head. "Unfortunately it looks as if they were on back order."

"Shit."

"Yeah."

"Has your team checked the roof recently? Is it cleared for medevacs?" We have a helipad, but Lord knows what kind of debris might be up there.

"I don't know. I'll go check," Marius says. His face, like all our faces, is dotted with drops of sweat. It is crowded, it is hotter than Hades, and it is starting to stink like shit. The relief that I saw on everyone yesterday after the storm passed has disappeared; there is fear and tension and weariness spreading through the staff, patients, and visitors like a virus.

While Jain's staff members are still assessing everyone on the OR floor, I track down a couple of nurses and interns to help relieve our bag teams back in the ICU. I knew that batteries for the in-room generators were on our emergency checklist. We did a run-through months ago—a pretend emergency that included a pretend hurricane and subsequent power outage. We hadn't figured on flooding in that scenario but more a short-term power loss due to downed power lines. There were a number of things the team did right during that drill. But a few things we missed, and this was one of them: we didn't have enough batteries to ensure all the portable generators would be up and running in case of a long-term power failure.

But it looks like nobody—including me—remembered to check to see if it was actually followed up on. Fear squeezes my chest. If patients die because of this, I am at least partially at fault. I was supposed to review the recommendations again thirty days after our trial run to make sure that progress was being made on the items we failed on.

I call a quick meeting with the nurses and interns and ask the teams that have gone the longest without relief to hand off their patients.

Two hours later, I'm behind on my rounds because of everything that happened this morning. The one piece of good news is that Marius confirmed the roof was cleared for medevacs. If only they'll come soon.

I track down Susan. I feel eyes on my back as I walk down the hall. People counting on me. Another problem to solve. I can do this. I can get us out of here.

"We need to get back into a routine with these patients," I say. "Rounds. Keep everything as normal as possible."

"Already on it."

"Of course you are," I say. I love Susan and all the staff members here who are like her. That is how we are going to get through this thing—by doing our jobs.

On my way over to Andy's room, I try for what seems like the thousandth time to call 911 on my cell. Nothing.

The landlines, not surprisingly, are down. We can't get online. We have been meeting every two hours today, and at each meeting, many of us have updated the team on our attempts to call not only 911 but also the fire department, the mayor's office, the governor's office, the National Guard, and the State Police. Nobody has been able to get through.

I walk into Andy's room and nod at his mother. She is leaning against his bed, her face gray in spite of the heat. I am relieved to see that his ventilator is still working.

"How's our young man?" I say, trying to sound upbeat. We all know the situation is beyond bad. She looks at me.

"What are we going to do?" she asks. "We can't keep this up forever."

"We'll keep it up until we can get him out of here," I say, thinking, *I'll be damned if I'm going to watch this kid die...*Fuck. Am I going to watch this kid die? "We're calling all the authorities but haven't gotten through yet. But we will."

I check with the nurse administering Andy's IV drips; I instruct her to adjust his dosage. I look at him lying there, just a kid, covered in tubes and smaller than he should be, just a rail-thin, awkward preteen in a hospital gown. They have pulled the sheets back to try to cool him off, but his black hair is dark with sweat.

The humidity is worse than ever with this water all around us. It is suffocating, and we have no real way to cool down our patients.

An hour later, after helping to bag one of the patients whose ventilator failed, I step aside as the next bag team steps in. I walk out of the patient's room, fingers and wrists aching, into the hallway to watch the battery life start to drain from my phone. I have tried all the emergency numbers again but to no avail. I flip the phone shut and shove it back into the pocket of my jeans.

I go to the conference room for our next check-in. As usual, the heads of every floor and department are sitting and standing around the conference table: OR, emergency, housekeeping, security. I thought we would be done with these meetings twenty-four hours ago and all home sleeping in our beds, postcall and recovering from one of the longest, hardest shifts any of us had ever worked.

I ask for updates. A knot of people gathers at the windows not only to look out at the flood but also to get some air. For whatever reason, the windows in this room are bolted shut. I ask housekeeping to find something to open them and break one if they have to. Even though it's just the conference room, any air getting into this hospital is a good thing.

I ask if anyone has heard anything from the outside world. It seems strange to say that when I can look out the window and see my city. Arlene, the nurse whose husband works for the NOPD, said she was able to get through to him, and he said nearly the whole city is flooded and that the NOPD has fallen apart; the officers who are still on duty are fully aware that the hospitals—all of them—are swamped and need rescue. But the NOPD doesn't have the resources to come rescue us. Somebody got through to someone at the mayor's office, but they got the same message, that we are on our own and that they can't do anything to help us. Somebody—not me—had the presence of mind to try to reach the National Guard at Jackson Barracks, but they got nothing but a busy signal.

"One guy I haven't tried to call is our CEO," I say. "Let's all add him and anyone at corporate to our phone lists." I'd love to see how he handles this. I don't care if he's the worst CEO on earth, but he must know we are in trouble and have some sort of resources to bring to bear in this situation.

I get an update from the bag teams. Nobody complains of sore wrists and numb hands, but I know it's hard work, and it will be difficult to keep it up. This morning I would have guessed that we would only have had to do this for a few hours at the most. But now, hours have passed, and we are still cut off from the world with no hint or promise of rescue.

"We'll need to train the nonmedical staff to assist," I say. "You've all done tremendous work, but this is unsustainable." Susan identifies some nurses' aides she feels would be good candidates to learn; they will be trained after the meeting.

Osgood and Jain give their updates; security reports issues with crowd control, especially after the flood, and problems with people breaking open vending machines and subsequently not only stealing part of our now much-limited food supply but also injuring themselves. I order stricter food rationing, because our cafeteria is now under water, and the staff was only able to escape with a small portion of what was left. I tell Judah and his security team to double the guards on the pharmaceutical storage areas on every floor.

"Phones," Susan Robertson suddenly says, raising hers in the air. "They're dying. We need working phones. And with no working generators, I don't know how we're going to charge them."

There is a tense silence for a moment, and then Dr. Jain exclaims, "Our cars! Anyone have a car charger?"

"And a car that's not under water?" Marius adds.

I don't have one, but a couple of nurses and docs do. Marius gathers car keys and descriptions and grabs a few dead phones to go charge them up on the car batteries.

We wrap up our meeting; the senior team will meet again in an hour. God, I hope something does change. There must be other emergency personnel streaming toward this city. There must be some military that can be activated or cops from surrounding parishes or somebody who can get us the hell out of here.

Someone in housekeeping found batteries for the portable radio that had given up the ghost, so at the end of the meeting, we sit and listen to incredibly disturbing rumors, broadcast from one of the few radio stations we can find, out of Metairie, about panicking police officers, drowned firemen, murdering, looting gangs at the Superdome, and would-be rescuers getting shot at. Everyone gasps or shakes their heads at each new and disturbing story.

"Guys, remember, we have to take all this with a huge grain of salt," I say. "This is just a guy in Metairie relaying stories he's heard from God knows who."

"I don't know, Doctor," says Arlene. "From what Jerry could tell me, things are pretty bad."

"It would explain why we haven't heard a peep from anyone we thought would be rescuing us by now," Natalie says. Hospitals and schools are always at the top of the list, for obvious reasons. It is bewildering that no authorities have arrived yet.

Dr. Osgood sits down beside me with a sigh. I can smell his sweat, but I am sure I stink just as much. We all do.

I realize I am still wearing my wet, dirty lab coat. I rip it off and feel cooler for a brief few seconds.

At 8:00 p.m. I lean against the nurses' station, writing a few notes on patient records. It seems like a low priority, but it's habit, and eventually we will have to transfer these patients, God willing, and I want to make sure their records are up-to-date. I've just finished training two aides on how to work the bags. I've checked in on our most serious cases. The one I'm most worried about, besides Andy, is Mr. Bartlett with his heart failure as well as the man who had the heart attack on his way up the stairs. But we have NICU patients who are even more vulnerable, and many elderly patients who won't last long in this heat. We have twenty-three patients here in the ICU right now, and a few more have come down from other floors because the heat and overall conditions have put them at increased risk. And all the elderly patients are particularly vulnerable to de-hydration. All we can do is keep giving them small amounts of water; we have absolutely nothing to cool them with. The nurses try to fan them with manila folders and pieces of cardboard ripped from medical supply boxes.

Jain, Osgood, and I have started taking turns trying to reach our CEO in his far-off office in Atlanta. Jain and I both got through, which amazes and encourages us, because we have been hearing busy signals and static on every other call. Both of us leave desperate messages, one with his admin and one on his voice mail. I feel a sense of hope, and some anxiety dissipates; surely they must be making preparations to evac everyone here, or maybe they are already on their way.

Natalie comes up to me and leans against the nurses' station. "I bet you never would have guessed just how bad your turn at this thankless job was going to be," she says. I shake my head.

"Have you gotten through to your kids?" I ask her.

"No," she says, her brow creased with worry. "Thank God they're with their father," she says. "I was going to keep them here, thinking, you know, the storm would turn at the last minute like it usually does. But if they were here...anyway, I know they must be worried sick, and I wish I could just let them know that I'm okay."

I want to say, are you okay? Are we going to be? But then I remember the CEO's admin. She certainly seemed to understand the gravity of the situation. And besides, all the authorities, whether we can reach them or not, must know now that the hospital is cut off. It must be one of their priorities to evac the hospitals. The city's most vulnerable citizens are in our care.

"They're in Baton Rouge then?" I ask. I can never remember where her ex lives. She's probably told me one hundred times when we've chatted about vacations, holidays, and schedules.

She shakes her head, frowns at me. "Shreveport," she says.

Shit. "Right." I nod.

We both fall silent for a moment in the wake of my gaffe. A voice gets louder on the portable radio; it's a woman calling in to the station. Her husband is sick, and they are both trapped in their attic. She is crying, her voice becoming a wail. She can't get through to 911. What all of us know is that even if she could, it's unlikely anyone would come.

Around us a couple of the nurses stir from where they were sitting and stand up to hear better.

The radio host asks her address, and she gives it. He sounds defeated, almost embarrassed, as he repeats her address in hopes that somebody out there will go and help her.

"I just don't understand why nobody will help us," the woman cries. "Isn't there someone who can help us?"

Chapter 17

Wednesday Afternoon
Entering New Orleans

New Orleans had drowned. The city looked like an ancient, crumbling capital in a long-forgotten land, one that archaeologists would one day dredge up and uncover, layer by layer. Ava cried and thought of how her father would look upon this scene—how much he had loved this place in all its rambling, historic southern glory.

As they crawled over the bridge, watching state troopers in front of them wave trucks on or pull them over, Ava and Remy looked over to the bridge on the other side of them, the one that led out of the city. It was empty except for a knot of cops standing guard and milling about.

"That doesn't look right," Ava said.

"What?" Remy said. But then, looking out over the ruins of his city, he clarified, saying, "I mean...what specifically?"

"Shouldn't people be streaming out of this place?" Ava asked. "That bridge is swarming with cops. Shouldn't there be vehicles on it taking people out of here?"

"Oh, shit. What the fuck?" Remy said. "Looks like they're not letting anyone cross the bridge."

"Are those NOPD?" Ava asked. Their uniforms looked brown.

"No, those are..." Remy squinted. "Those are Jefferson Parish Sheriff's deputies." He snorted. "Fucking rednecks—no, wait. Correction. Those are sheriff's deputies and NOPD. Fucking rednecks and fucking corrupt bastards."

Ava cringed. "I'm sure they're not all like that." But in this hellscape, who knew?

Remy wanted to say "Any New Orleanian knows otherwise," but the truth was, he had a few friends on the NOPD. Some of them were great people, but he knew they would admit the same about the police force: corruption was rampant. Corruption had been a part of the Crescent City's public service and political culture for a long, long time. He stared at the bridge and wondered what was going on there. Jefferson Parish was notorious in the black community for racial discrimination. African Americans who lived in the city didn't go over there. And yet—wouldn't they be headed there now, out of desperation?

Ava took a closer look at some of the helicopters hovering above the city. It was tough to identify them all, but there were definitely some media and some Coast Guard helicopters up there.

They found themselves behind a Louisiana Department of Wildlife and Fisheries truck that was quickly waved through the checkpoint. As they followed behind it, Remy briefly hoped the state trooper would just wave them on, but the trooper put up his hand with the command to stop. Remy rolled down both their windows. The heat hit their faces. He showed the trooper Ava's press pass. Ava heard some other cop asking about the boat, although she couldn't see his face from where she was sitting.

Remy lied, saying, "We're here to report on this for *Eastland* magazine. We figured the best way to really see what was happening would be by boat."

The trooper nodded. He waved them onward. "Move, go. Put that boat to good use while you're out there, but don't get in anyone's way." Remy nodded and waved.

Ava heard snippets of conversations between the cops around them as they slowly drove on.

"Bunch of fire ants at the bottom of the bridge."

"Fucking stubborn…"

"Hey, what about Jimmy P? Where's he at?"

"He ain't shown up."

"He lives over in Pines Village. They got hit hard, you know."

"I heard. Shit."

"How the fuck they gonna get all this water outta here? Duncan Pumping station is still offline."

"Bonnabel Pumping stations are kaput too."

"There are no working pumping stations in Orleans Parish."

As she looked over the drowned city, Ava remembered flying down with her mom to meet her dad for one of their summer vacations many years ago. He had gone down early to give a talk at Tulane; Ava's mother had to wrap up her school year and attend teachers' meetings. Up north, the school years always started and ended later. By the time they came down, it was Fourth of July weekend. Ava remembered looking down from the plane window at bright, shocking swaths of green lining the edges of the vast, brown, churning Mississippi. It was a striking landscape, so different from Maine. The vastness of the river was amazing to Ava; it seemed as wide as a Great Lake. From the plane you could see how New Orleans is where the Mississippi starts to say her fare-thee-well to the continent before spilling out into the open reaches of the Gulf of Mexico.

Now Ava looked down on a stretch of gray smoke and dingy black water with the tops of buildings poking miserably out of it. It seemed to blend into the river, nearly; but the truth was, none of the river levees failed that they had heard. As far as she knew, all the failed levees were on Lake Pontchartrain and along MR-GO, as Remy had said. The city was drowning in ocean and lake water; the Mississippi wound her way as usual, unmoved.

"I can't even tell what anything is," Ava said, "except the Superdome." It stood there in the distance, its ripped roof exposed, gray and yellow. According to the radio, people there were still waiting for buses; only a handful had arrived so far.

Remy pointed at different neighborhoods, marking the geography, getting his bearings in this new New Orleans while simultaneously helping Ava remember where everything was. His voice started to get shaky.

"Lower Nine." He extended his arm farther out. "Chalmette." Then he pointed toward the lake. "Gentilly. Lakeview." He pointed along the length of Canal Street. "There's CBD—Central Business District, if you don't remember. That fire burning? That looks like it's in the Warehouse District." The freeway, I-10, that ran through the city was dry where it was elevated and underwater in many of the places where it was at street level. Remy rested his hand back on the steering wheel for a moment as they continued to follow the Fish and Wildlife officers across the bridge.

"They've been saying for years that the levees were leaking in Lakeview," he said. "Just weeping water, you know? Even when the sun was shining." He raised his hand again and pointed. "Da East—that whole area is New Orleans East— that's where Ellis lives now. A lot of law-enforcement folks live over there." It was a gigantic lake with tiny buildings sticking out of it. In the other direction, Remy pointed at Uptown and the upper Garden District. They were mostly dry, but there was some flooding and significant wind damage, he had heard. He still hadn't heard from his father, and neither had his mother. And they still hadn't heard from Ellis either. Ava looked at New Orleans East and prayed her cousin wasn't dead in there somewhere. She thought of his kind face, and that summer after her father died, his was the only face in that family that didn't hurt her to look at.

As they drove off the bridge and into the city, Remy tried to envision how New Orleans should have looked now as it had looked every summer since he could remember: the gleaming riverboats, kids playing by the levees and swinging on the swing sets in Audubon Park, the neighborhood crowds drawn to fried food at Dooky Chase, the tourists and old-timers drawn to fancy food at Galatoire's, and the trumpets punctuating the steps of every street band in Treme.

There was none of that here. Just the clouds occasionally parting to reveal the sun beating down on all that oily, stinking water. Trash on the street, where the street could be seen. A telephone pole snapped in two, lying like a broken matchstick in the grass of the neutral ground. Cars sitting in water up to their rooftops.

With the windows down, as the bridge gave way to the streets of New Orleans, they smelled it. The air was noxious. As the stench hit their nostrils, they both grimaced. "Jesus," Remy said. Ava's eyes started to sting.

"It's only going to get worse," Ava said as they made their way into the Lower Garden District. It did.

"Still no army trucks," Ava said, a bit incredulous despite everything they had heard on the radio on the way down.

Ava thought of her father's family house, that old Victorian in Uptown. Such a short drive from here. Maybe they could check on it later, when the crisis had passed and there were no more people to be rescued.

They drove past a few cleared blocks, past sagging medical tents, Louisiana Fish and Wildlife and fire trucks parked in clusters and groups of people huddled on the side of the street. There were crowds on the sidewalks (banquettes, locals called them), and throngs of sweating people spilling into the street, some men shirtless, crying babies, and women fanning themselves with ripped pieces of cardboard. All of them waited. For buses, for water, for food, for some kind of medical care and a way out. In the background of this surreal scene were the familiar palms, the nineteenth-century buildings, brick painted yellow and green and white and pink, painted shutters, star-shaped bolts in old brick walls, low-slung shotguns, and Creole cottages, slumping in the heat.

Looking out at the crowds, Remy thought, *My poor city.*

Ava thought, *It's too late.* They were driving so slowly that one man walked up to Ava's window, having noticed the boat and the out-of-state license plate. He had a little girl by the hand and a trash bag over his shoulder.

"Do you folks need directions?"

"Yes, sir," Remy said, before Ava could answer. He had snapped back into his southern self. "Where are the emergency responders congregating? Or is there some sort of headquarters?" he asked.

Before the man could respond, a wailing siren cut him off. He closed his mouth, waiting for it to pass by. He wore jeans and a polo shirt, and his face was slick with sweat. A gold chain with a Celtic-style cross was hanging from his neck. It was gold-on-gold, with a crosshatching of lighter metal.

As the sirens faded, the man pointed and said, "Go down that way. Just park on the neutral ground up there where you can find a spot. Then follow the water. Folks still out there. I'd be out there looking too. But I have my little girl here to look after."

Remy thanked the man. Ava looked at the little girl. She had wide brown eyes, and she wore a purple T-shirt with a picture of a butterfly on it. She started to cry, and the man moved away. He looked at Ava, and she held up her hand in silent thanks.

As they moved toward Central City, Ava and Remy soon saw that emergency responders—those who were here—were using the freeway on- and off-ramps as staging areas, launching boats and receiving survivors. At one intersection there were several men in black uniforms and wraparound sunglasses getting out of a Hummer. Their uniforms were not from any recognizable branch of the American military.

"Holy shit," Remy said. "Are those Mossad?"

"What?" Ava turned and looked. "No. What would they be doing here?"

Remy shrugged. "If CNN and NBC Nightly News can get here, I think Mossad can." Then he laughed. "Hell, we got here."

"I think you have been reading too many conspiracy theories. I bet they are private contractors." She watched them shoulder their weapons and move down the street. "You know, I really thought that by the time we got here, the National Guard would be all over the place."

"They're all in fucking Iraq. You know, I bet you're right. Those guys are private security. Like uber-security or contractors like Blackwater or some shit." They watched the phalanx of men, in bulletproof vests, file in a single line down the street.

Ava felt a twinge of bitterness at the thought of those men working to protect manicured lawns and antiques. The goddamn antiques will be safe, but there are people huddled on a freeway overpass with their little kids and people sitting on rooftops above stories-high toxic water, waiting for someone to evacuate them.

They passed a line of cops, in uniform but pushing grocery carts, kids in tow. They were either looting (on Robinette's show, callers breathlessly spread rumors that everyone, including NOPD, was looting; there was looting on the Gulf Coast too) or carrying all their worldly possessions.

"Where are they going?" Ava asked.

"I guess to the overpasses," Remy said. Where everyone was congregating, waiting for a ride out of here.

"Even cops?" Ava asked.

Remy shrugged. "They've got kids too."

"Shouldn't some of them be out here helping people?"

"Who's going to help their kids?"

They kept following the directions the man with the gold cross gave them. Finally they found themselves at the edge of a vast black lake. At the water's edge was an impromptu command center, just off St. Claude Avenue. Dozens of people who looked like private citizens, as well as a few officials in an array of uniforms, were launching boats of every type into the water. There was a motley fleet of private and public vehicles: beat-up and brand-new trucks with boat hitches and Louisiana plates, the Fish and Wildlife truck they had followed over the bridge, an NOPD car, a local fire chief's SUV, and a state trooper's car, all parked at right angles on the neutral ground.

Men in stained T-shirts clutching garbage bags full of their families' belongings waded up to the makeshift command center.

Remy and Ava squeezed the truck into an empty spot next to the state trooper's vehicle and hopped out. They glanced around at the pirogues, airboats, blow-up rafts, skiffs, and baiters. Some of them were going out, and some were coming back with people aboard. Men and women were handing water bottles to people who had been rescued. Remy and Ava approached the group of volunteers and rescuers and looked for someone who might be in charge. A petite red-haired woman near them, who was wearing jeans; a UL Lafayette cap; a white T-shirt; and a fishing vest with pockets overflowing with rubber gloves, tools, and a walkie-talkie, looked their way and headed over.

"What outfit are y'all from?" the red-haired woman asked, walking up to Ava. She was all business, and Ava liked her immediately.

"Uh, we're our own outfit," Ava said. "Where do you need us?"

"Do you know this area?" the woman asked, looking at Ava skeptically. She clearly didn't want to waste her time on someone who needed a lot of handholding.

"I do," Remy said, "Uptown, born and raised." The woman's facial expression relaxed a bit; his accent reassured her. She introduced herself as Irish Broussard, said there wasn't time for conversation but that basically she and her husband, Van, and some like-minded fellow citizens were part of a volunteer rescue operation from Acadiana, a bunch of Cajun shrimpers, fishermen, business people, and pleasure boaters from southwestern Louisiana, who had organized a caravan to come down to New Orleans and start rescuing people. They called themselves the Cajun Navy. They had arrived the day before.

"We're dividing up the neighborhoods so we can get the best coverage possible," Irish said. "Right now we need more help in Gentilly, Lakeview, most of Da East. We got a few people down in Lower Nine, Creoleville." She pulled out a map that had marks all over it to show where people had searched. "Northern part of Gentilly hasn't even been looked at yet," she said, "at least not by us. Eighth Ward needs more coverage—that's closer by."

"What's the latest? I mean, news on the army coming, or FEMA?" Ava asked.

"Who the hell knows?" Irish said. "Last I heard there would be buses to evacuate everyone yesterday. Those buses ain't showed up yet. I heard the army was coming, but I ain't seen them either, and I've been hearing that rumor since before we got here. The army that is here is busy dropping sandbags on the canals at the levee breaches or at least the breach at Seventeenth Street."

Remy and Ava nodded dumbly.

Now that they were here, it was a bit overwhelming. "Now there are a few things you need to watch out for," Irish continued. "Because we don't want you to get stuck out there, and then your asses need to be rescued too." She pushed back her cap and pulled it forward again absentmindedly. The rim was stained with salt and sweat. "Some people say there's sharks in the water, but I don't know 'bout that. But you still need to stay out of the water if you can. There's lake water, and there's Gulf water, and there's definitely gators and shit and piss, and God knows what nasty-ass chemicals and snakes. Just try to stay out of it, and try not to get it on your skin," she repeated.

"Anything else we should look out for?" Ava asked. *Or anyone.*

"There's tons of people down here who can't swim, so be careful nobody drags you down with them if they're struggling. You got an oar or something in that boat?" she said, gesturing at their vehicle.

"Fishing rods," Remy said.

Irish nodded. "Use something like that if you got to."

"What about first aid?" Remy asked. "Anything we should be prepared for?"

"If you have a first-aid kit in your boat, you'll run out in no time, so be stingy," Irish said. "We've already run through a lot of the supplies we brought, so we are trying to ration. Just do the best you can with what you've got. All the hospitals are cut off, so we can't send them somewhere local as you know."

Ava said, "When is the cavalry coming? Isn't there local National Guard at least?"

"They're all in fucking Iraq and Afghanistan," Remy said again, angrier this time.

Irish ignored Remy's comment. "From what I heard, Jackson Barracks got swamped. They were swimming for it like a lot of the folks out here." She paused to hand surgical gloves to a tall couple on their way to load up an airboat.

A broad-shouldered man with a sunburned face walked up behind Irish, listening to what she was saying. He was wearing a stained T-shirt, and his curly hair was wet with sweat and tucked into a UL Lafayette cap that looked exactly like his wife's.

"This is my husband, Van," Irish said.

He nodded at Ava and Remy. But there wasn't much time for pleasantries. "Irish, we need your help over here, hon," he said to her and tapped her on the shoulder on his way to greet a pair of Cajuns steering their baiter in. Sitting on the starboard side was a woman who appeared to be injured.

"I gotta go," Irish said as she started to jog after her husband. She called over her shoulder, "You can leave your truck right there after you get the boat out. You gonna go over to the Eighth Ward or Gentilly or what? I gotta mark the map."

"Eighth Ward," Remy said. It was closer; he wanted to start right then. Irish nodded and yelled out two cross streets they should aim for. Then she offered a piece of advice: "Oh, and don't drink the water! You'll be shitting for days."

As Ava and Remy turned back toward the truck, a man striding toward the water with a state trooper, a tall, light-skinned black man wearing a T-shirt and jeans, glanced at them and then stopped and did a double take. He shouted, "Remy!" and then, seemingly confused, he shouted, "Ava?"

Ava looked over, and her mouth broke open in surprise.

"Ellis!"

She hadn't seen him in so long, she might have walked right by him. But looking at him straight on, she knew who he was right away. He was taller, older, and more filled out, walking with the bearing of someone trained to be a cop. Remy's face registered surprise and then relief. He flashed that familiar wide smile that Ava hadn't seen since she got into the car two days before.

They took turns hugging. A solidly built guy, with hair so blond it was almost white, stood next to Ellis.

"What the heck are you doing here?" Ellis asked Ava.

"I figured now would be a great time to visit," she said.

Ellis laughed. "God, I haven't seen you in years. What a total shitshow, huh? Welcome back to New Orleans."

"We've been so worried about you, man," Remy said. "We were calling you every hour like a couple of stalkers."

Ellis introduced the blond guy as Erick, his patrol partner. Erick was wearing the deep-blue uniform and the broad-rimmed hat of the state trooper. Erick said he was off duty on vacation visiting his wife's family in Tennessee, so he left his wife and daughters up there in Memphis and came back to help before the storm hit.

"I was also off duty and decided to stay to keep an eye on my house and Mom and Pop's house," Ellis said. "Monday I was checking on their place, when I found out my house was sitting in ten feet of water." He shook his head. For a moment, he looked ten years older.

"Monday morning I was at headquarters, and by around nine a.m. we were getting calls that the levees were breaking. By nine thirty a.m. we were out there in a boat that we basically stole from a guy's front yard near us. We heard over the radio that London Avenue broke; it was breached on the west bank, and there was Industrial and Seventeenth Street...and then to hear that we did not have one working pumping station left in Orleans Parish."

"And we still don't," Erick said.

"I went out with my sergeant, and we rescued as many people as we could," Ellis went on. "One guy. I'll never forget. He had water up to his goddamn chin. He was standing on top of his bathtub. We saved that guy. We saved a bunch of people on Monday. But I know for every person we saved..."

He shook his head.

"This is a goddamn shame," Erick said. "A goddamn thing to see."

"Yeah, and my house is in ten feet of water now, so I got nothing else to do," Ellis said and laughed.

"I'm so sorry. Where are you living now? Are you still in East?" Ava asked.

"Yes," Ellis said. "Well, I was." He had moved to New Orleans East a few years after he became a trooper. He still lived a bachelor's life, although there had been a fiancée at one point who had precipitated the move out of his Bywater apartment and into a solid middle-class family home in Da East. This was the type of information Ava knew from Christmas cards, Remy's news from home, and the annual e-mail or two that she and Ellis exchanged.

"Ellis," Remy said, "any word from our old neighborhood? My dad is over there, but I haven't been able to get in touch with him. I was thinking of going over tonight to see if he's okay."

"I know my folks' street"—Ellis looked at Ava too—"had mostly wind damage, not much flooding. They're more worried about looting over there."

"Where are your parents?" Ava asked. She hadn't seen her aunt and uncle in more than a decade. She remembered they had been kind to her when she was a little girl.

"They got out," Ellis said. "I told them they had better." He laughed. "They listen to me more now that I am a cop."

"How many people are still out here?" Remy asked.

"We've heard a bunch of estimates. Latest was several thousand," Erick said. "But we really don't know. They estimate maybe one hundred thousand stayed in the city, and there's forty thousand or so at the Convention Center and the Superdome. Maybe sixty thousand left total? And maybe half of those folks are in areas that are not flooded, and another ten thousand got out themselves?" He shrugged. He had what looked like three days of blond-white stubble. "It's really just a guess at this point."

"Where do we take people after we pick them up?" Ava asked.

Erick pointed back in the direction of the freeway ramp. "We thought we'd bring folks we rescued to the Convention Center, but that's no longer an option. So we just drop them off at the causeway ramp. Give them whatever basic first aid you can, and water, if you can scrounge some up. That's really all we can do right now."

Ellis nodded. "Yep. Convention Center can't take any more residents. They want to evacuate the ones they have. Here—" he gestured at the ramps "—they're supposed to be taking people to the airport…at least when they can commandeer buses. Haven't been many, but there are supposed to be more coming. Any minute now." He laughed grimly. "They were supposed to be here yesterday morning, but who the hell knows. From the airport, I don't know where they're going. But our priority is to keep getting people out of these neighborhoods."

"Anyway, man," Ellis said, "it's so good to see you guys, even in all this. Sorry you worried about me. I kept meaning to call y'all, but then everything went to shit." He hugged Ava again and slapped Remy on the back. "But we gotta get going. Where are you guys headed?"

Ava said, "Eighth Ward and maybe Upper Nine. That's where the Cajuns said they needed the most coverage right now."

"Great," Ellis said. "We're going on nearly twenty-four hours in that neck of the woods now, so we can tell you exactly where you need to go. Can you guys get your boat in quick and follow us?"

Remy nodded and trotted back up to the truck. Ava thought of her aunt's seemingly Pollyannaish belief that somehow Ava would be meeting up with her cousin, the state trooper. And here he was. Remy, Erick, and Ellis hauled the *Rajun' Cajun* into the water, and Ava loaded it up with supplies from the truck.

Erick and Ellis headed over to the flat-bottomed boat they had commandeered.

"We just borrowed it from our brothers in Baton Rouge who had come down here, and now they're doing crowd control, and we're doing rescues, since we know the neighborhood much better than they do," Erick explained as the two boats pulled out into the neighborhood, motors sputtering. "At least, we *used* to know the neighborhood. It looks pretty damn strange now. Anyway, we're doing this organized-like, you know, a grid, but be forewarned you might have a hell of a time recognizing some of the streets when you're scraping over the tops of the signs."

"A few things to keep in mind," Erick shouted over the motors. "Cut your engine every few minutes to listen. People are getting hoarse, so listen carefully. Also, whatever you do, don't get this nasty water in your mouths. You'll get the runs, rashes, fever…you name it, you'll get it. Oh, and watch out for downed light poles. A number of folks have been electrocuted already. Oh, and snakes. Water mocs."

"Yep," Remy said mildly as if this was the most banal conversation he had ever had. Ava just stared at Erick and then stared into the black slick of water.

They headed off, Erick and Ellis leading the way.

Chapter 18

Wednesday

St. Liberatus

We lost our first patient early this morning.

He was elderly and had presented with several serious issues when he was admitted: heart failure, Alzheimer's, and liver problems. The heat sent him into cardiac arrest despite our desperate attempts to cool him.

We put the patients near the windows, we carried them to the roof, we wet cloths with bottled water and laid those on them. But even the bottled water we have is hot; everything is swollen with heat. It is over 100 degrees in here. This is what people in this city are dying from now.

I hold yet another emergency meeting with senior staff members, and we determine that, because the hospital morgue is unreachable—it's in the basement, of course—we will use our small chapel as a morgue.

Slowly the staffs wheel the patient down the hall and then carry the gurney down one flight of stairs to the chapel. Many of the staffs trail behind, mourners at a strange and joyless jazz funeral.

We put sheets over him and then say a prayer and hold hands around him. His family members are numb and mute with grief. There are never the right words to help console the patient's family at times like this; you can only try to be kind so you do not add to the pain. The family is in a haze of grief and cannot fully understand what is happening. It is never easy. But this is not how it should have happened. But putting their dead relative alone in this chapel to rot is not helping, to say the least.

Maybe he would have died in our care despite our best efforts, regardless of the circumstances. But I am sorry for the suffering they should not have had to endure.

There is a tremendous stench coming from the now-overflowing bathrooms. We hunt down everything we can find to clean patients. Antiseptic wipes, antiseptic gel, disposable alcohol swabs. There is no water, and we are out of paper towels. I ask two members of the housekeeping staff to search for paper towels and tissues on other floors, but it's the same everywhere.

With Jain and other senior staff members, I review the oxygen tanks and other emergency supplies so we can pool our resources as best as we can and make sure the most vulnerable patients continue to be prioritized.

We try to make the patients comfortable, but in this suffocating heat, it is an impossible task. Any windows that were not broken in the storm are broken now. We repeatedly run at them with chairs until they give, and we fling our arms up to protect our faces from broken glass. It's hot outside, of course, but at least it lets in some bit of a breeze and the cooler night air.

The floors and walls are sticky with sweat and tracked-in floodwater and the typical humidity of New Orleans in late summer. The bagging teams can keep our patients breathing. But there are other machines that were working on battery power that are failing, and we can't replace those with human hands. Infusion pumps that drip medicine into patients' veins stop working. We can give shots, and we can deliver medicine, but now the nurses have to be even more careful than usual to make sure the patients get the proper amount of medication.

Defibrillators, monitors, and nursing-station equipment start to die too. As the hours pass, a wailing crescendo of beeping fills the floor. I go upstairs to the NICU floor and survey a very similar scene up there. Dr. Armstrong is in charge of that floor, and her nurses and fellow physicians are struggling to keep preemies and sick infants alive.

But I've just been told that FEMA is on its way. One of the nurses got through to her state representative's office, and that's what they told her. I work with the staff to determine which patients are the sickest. Theoretically, as the ICU, we should be the first to evacuate, as our patients, along with the NICU patients, are the most critical. But we must triage each floor. Some patients' conditions have worsened considerably over the past couple of days. Everyone who needs a respirator or a dialysis machine is a priority. We work with our NICU and labor and delivery colleagues to put the babies and at-risk pregnant mothers at the top of the hospital's overall list. We start packing things up, writing or updating records, taping them to patients' limbs in case doctors' orders get lost in the confusion. We lift many of the sickest patients onto neck boards, securing them so they will be ready for a helicopter ride.

FEMA will be here soon.

This morning, that's what they told us. Well, that's what they told Osborne. He got ahold of someone in our state senator's office.

After our preparations, I make quick rounds to reassess and make adjustments to my evacuation list if needed.

"How are you holdin' up, Mr. Bartlett?"

I know the answer. We now have him on oxygen, as he has seemed to stabilize, although his infusion pump is failing. I call a nurse over and ask her to start counting drops so he isn't overmedicated.

Osgood has been keeping an eye on Mr. Bartlett. We are sitting at the end of the hallway, leaning on a ledge outside the window. This window didn't break during the storm, but it has been broken since then to get some air coming in the hallway. Osgood has something on his mind; he keeps drumming his fingers on the windowsill. Finally he gestures for me to go into the meeting room. He follows me in, checks to make sure we are alone, and closes the door behind us.

"You know, if FEMA doesn't come, we might have to do something about Mr. Bartlett," Osgood says. He is speaking very slowly. I think I understand what he is saying, but then, as he continues, I think I must be misunderstanding him. *First do no harm.*

"I can't imagine hauling all these patients to the roof, especially if some of them aren't going to make it anyway," Osgood says. "It's torture for them and for no reason."

"I'm going to pretend that we didn't have this conversation," I say. "Our goal is to get all these patients out alive."

"I'm not saying…look, as you well know, we're in desperate straits here. Mr. Bartlett, the heart-failure patient in room five…they're not going to make it. We're prolonging the inevitable," Osgood says.

I stand up. "That's Mrs. Lawrence," I say. "And yes, she probably doesn't have long. The meds haven't been working for some time, and she's clearly not a candidate for an implantable device."

"This is what I mean. She's going to die. Why are we making her suffer in this heat?"

"This is why we need to get the patients the fuck out of here, Dr. Osgood," I say. My voice is rising. I'm surprised and disappointed at what he is suggesting. Yet I understand that on some level, he is trying to be humane.

"We might not have a choice soon," he says. "The bag teams are pretty worn down."

"We will keep doing what we need to do until help arrives," I say. "And that's the end of this conversation."

"Dr. Reid! Dr. Reid!" One of the nurses is frantically gesturing at me from down the hall. I hear that sickening beeping that tells us another ventilator has failed.

I sprint down the hall, nearly wiping out on the damp floor, and realize as I get closer that the nurse is outside Andy's room.

"Get a bag! Get a bag!" I shout, but the nurse has already done this. Andy's mother is crying, but I have to ignore her right now. I lean over him, stripping off the useless ventilator's wires as the nurse puts the bag in place. I check his heart rate. It is irregular, not surprisingly, but it is still beating. He is hot as hell. I watch for an anxious second as the nurse compresses the bag and see with relief that it is working. He is breathing. But this boy cannot survive much longer in these conditions.

I line up another bag team to take over, and only then will I allow myself to focus on Andy's mother. She is standing silently over her son, eyes fixated on the bag as the nurse compresses it.

She sees me looking at her and says, "I can't let my son die like this." She has stopped crying.

"When we get medevac'd, he will be at the top of my list along with the NICU babies," I say. "I will do everything I can. We are doing everything we can. All I can say is I'm sorry we're in this situation."

She doesn't want to hear my lame response, and I don't blame her. I feel helpless, and I feel what every doctor dreads: that I'm losing to Death. The enemy. I am here to solve problems, and I can't solve this one.

Hours later, we have reached 4:00 p.m. FEMA still isn't here. Osgood has tried to call back the man on the senator's staff who called him yesterday, but nobody is answering. We had debated among the staff whether or not they would come at daybreak or 7:00 a.m. or 8:00 a.m. or 9:00 a.m. And now we have all finally realized they might not come.

We have another meeting at 6:00 p.m. We discuss our dwindling water and food supply; the horrible morale; the security problem of angry, uncomfortable people camping out in our hallways; the growing body count—we lost another elderly patient today to this goddamn heat—and how we are turning people away from this hospital. *They are floating here on God knows what or wading up to the second-floor windows, but I cannot let them in. I cannot let them in. Can't all of you damn people see we can't even take care of the people who are already here?*

After the meeting, I walk out to the hallway. It is a dark, dank dungeon as the sun is getting lower in the sky outside. It is hot with sweat and the murmur of voices. Hundreds crowded into this hospital, along this floor, and the floors above and below us. Several times we have watched as able-bodied guests of St. Lib have tried to swim their way out of here. Some have swam off into the distance; we don't know how far they got and whether they are okay. Some struggled, and we sent people out to rescue them. Some have come back with chemical burns, and now they are throwing up and have diarrhea from whatever they swallowed in that putrid water.

I lean against the wall for a moment; for a fleeting second it feels cool against my forehead. Then it is hot like my skin and wet with condensation and, now, my sweat.

The stairwell door opens near me, and one of the nurses' assistants emerges. She looks sheepish and avoids my gaze. We have designated one of the stairwells, down at the edge of the flood downstairs, as the new bathroom area now that our bathrooms, after hundreds of people tried to use them when the water pressure died, were declared off-limits, a health hazard. Two brave souls in housekeeping went off in search of bathroom "alternatives." We had a wealth of bedpans, but they have all been commandeered at this point.

I run into Marius. He is hunting for more of the industrial-sized containers of antibacterial gel. It's all we have now to try to keep ourselves clean when we examine our patients. We are quickly running out of it.

"Find anything?" I ask.

He shakes his head. "Not much. Just two more containers. At the rate we're going, that'll last us through today."

I tell staff to stop using it to clean their faces and armpits. The cat's out of the bag: we all stink. Save it for hands that touch patients.

As I am walking back to the nurses' station to update an order for one of my cases, I hear laughing. Tired, half-hearted laughing.

"Doctor Reid! Get this! We've been rescued!" says Natalie and laughs.

"What?" I ask, stupidly hopeful for a moment despite the laughter.

"That's what they're reporting," Susan says. "They've rescued us."

"Always the last to know," I say.

Some of the nurses heard it on the ancient little portable radio that emits unintelligible crackling a good bit of the time. It is that Metairie station that we get intermittently; it has been the source of many frightening rumors since we were submerged in this flood.

Rescued.

"Anybody have a recently charged phone? Might want to try calling that station again. Get the word out that we are not fucking rescued. Pardon my French."

We have been taking turns charging our phones in people's cars out in the garage. Only a handful of people have chargers, and they only fit certain phones, but we've got enough working that we can keep attempting to make calls out to try to get someone to come help us.

After the meeting, I go to check on Michaela. She has worsened. The heat and these damn unsanitary conditions. She has developed an infection. It's a complication that I know would not have happened if it were a normal week here.

After updating Michaela's orders, I go up to the roof. The sun is dipping low in the sky. There are branches, roofing tiles from other buildings, rocks, metal siding, and unrecognizable debris up here. The custodians had worked to pile the debris to one side so there will be room for medevac landings. I stare at the cleared space, hoping it will be used soon.

I look out over the campus of our hospital and all the adjoining buildings. The landscape is so changed, submerged in black water. I look at the building where my medical practice is based, just a block away, and wonder how Chris, the young guy who works security for us, is doing. I hope he's all right, but there's no way I can get over there to check on him. Not with all these patients in my charge.

The roof has been our only respite. In the early hours, we would try to signal passing Coasties. But now we know that they know we are here; for some reason, we have not been made a priority. I'll never understand this.

We've learned that to get cool, when we take our breaks, the best thing to do is to climb up to the hospital roof. From here you can see the stars. It's as high as we can get in this neighborhood in this swamped city, and from here we see ourselves floating, an island in the sea; the nearest sirens, the nearest lights far away. If I lean and look over the edge, I can see the hospital sign, half-torn, hanging off the bottom of the roof, over the cement ceiling that marks the top of the top floor. The E has been blown away, so now it reads, "NewCar Medical Center."

I'm just about to leave and go back down, when I hear someone walk up behind me. I turn to see Natalie. Like the rest of us, she looks terrible. She's a beautiful woman; she reminds me of my Jane, who I usually try not to think about. Jane and her new life with the man who is actually home a lot of the time. But Natalie is tougher than my ex, God bless her, ever was; she has been one of the few who always advocates for patients regardless of what the insurance company or Waters and his cronies or our hospital colleagues, well-meaning or not, might tell her.

All this makes it more shocking when she comes up to me with her eyes red. She had been bolstering the rest of the staff, including me, but she is breaking down. She looks out at the stars hanging over our poor wounded city. Starlight is starting to glow in the darkening sky. Below us the floodwaters have an oily shine.

"It looks beautiful, actually," she says. She laughs.

"Yeah," I say. "It looks peaceful."

There are no lights anywhere around us. Our building is dark, buildings on our street, in our block, for as far as we can see—they are all dark. There is only the faint glow of our flashlights and the stars and the last rays of a burning sunset. I ignore the Superdome and the high rises in the CBD and try to imagine what New Orleans looked like before we had electricity, with candles glowing in windows and oil burning in street lamps. I lean back on my hands. A helicopter's lights glow in the distance. I wonder what the people on board are seeing. What do they know that we don't know as we sit here, cut off from the world?

"They forgot about us," Natalie says.

My first instinct is to disagree, to comfort her, to tell her it will be all right. But I do none of those things. Instead, I nod.

"Sure seems like it," I say.

At that moment, we hear a roar, and the building shakes. I stumble to maintain balance, and we both gasp as a bright-red flash snaps across the horizon. For a horrible moment, I think they have given up on us; they have decided to level the whole city. To nuke us and start over.

Later we learn from the Metairie radio station that it is an oil-refinery plant that has exploded on the waterfront. Our city is drowning in water and fire.

Chapter 19

Wednesday, Late Afternoon
8th Ward

As they made their way out into the neighborhood, they saw a ragged navy: rowboats, fishing boats, canoes, one lone NOPD vessel, and boats with far-flung origins spelled out on their sides: TENNESSEE HIGHWAY PATROL, AUSTIN POLICE, ALAMEDA COUNTY FIRE. The city's new landmarks were the tops of ruined houses, drowned vehicles, and broken second-floor and attic windows. There was a slick on top of everything and a suffocating odor of oil, gas, mold, and putrefaction. They passed a white cottage with a Mardi Gras Indian costume nailed to the roof, its vibrant red-and-white feathers fluttering in the breeze. Ava looked down to see a purple shirt bobbing in the water near the edge of the boat. She jumped back when she realized it was on a man's back. His bloated body rocked in the small wake of their boats, his mouth an agonized O.

"Oh my God," she said. Dumbstruck, she could think of nothing else to say or do. It was one thing to see or hear about this on television, but here it was, the death this flood had wrought, right in front of her. The faces of her father and grandfather. She turned away and tried to focus on keeping track of Ellis and Erick as they motored ahead.

Remy barely recognized the city he had known all his life. Overturned cars, refrigerators bobbing like bathtub toys, power lines splayed across the oily water, a green car resting against the roof of a swamped house. Everything had been submerged and flipped and ruined. And it wasn't just the peculiarly southern, uniquely New Orleanian strain of ruin or the usual careworn veneer of the City That Care Forgot. It seemed like the end of all things.

Ellis signaled to them to turn off their motors. At intervals, this is what they did, to listen for cries for help. For a moment they glided in the water, boats propelled forward until the propellers stopped completely.

Ava thought about what everyone on the radio, during that drive they had taken that seemed so long ago now, had been saying about all these levees breaking—Industrial Canal, Seventeenth Street Canal, London Avenue Canal. Now, in their wake, she could more sharply imagine them all bursting through, twenty feet of Pontchartrain water and Gulf storm surge pulsing through all these neighborhoods, silent, terrible, relentless, brutal nature engulfing everything. Ava imagined movement and chaos, the land around Noah's escaping ark turned end over end by God's punishing wrath.

But this was the aftermath: horrible stillness. The only noise came from the purring of boat motors, the whirring of helicopter blades, and the occasional desperate bark of a dog. Those barks ripped at their hearts; they could not see where they were coming from, and all agreed they had to keep looking for people first. But Ava silently resolved that she would come back for the dogs. Their barks were shrill with desperation and fear. Ava thought of Tiras, safe at home with her aunt and uncle. Just as she thought of him, she saw a dead dog, what looked like a pit bull or boxer mix, chained to a fence and floating nearby. He didn't stand a chance, left like that. All these animals betrayed by their guardians. Some of their guardians might be dead now too.

Remy thought of the sounds that they should be hearing, the sounds that mark every neighborhood like this: people talking, laughing, the beat of music blasting from cars passing by, church bells, lawn mowers, phones ringing. He too noticed the terrible silence and over it the menacing smell. They wished they had masks or handkerchiefs to block out some of the smell. They hadn't thought to bring any.

After a couple of minutes, and Ellis's periodic calls of "Is anyone out here? Anyone need help? Hello?" they turned their motors back on and headed deeper into the neighborhood. The sweat was already running down all their backs.

Their tiny two-boat flotilla was several streets deep into the Eighth Ward, when Ellis again cut his motor, and Remy followed suit. "This is about where we left off," Erick explained. They were trying to make sure they covered every part of the area.

They drifted for only a moment when they heard it.

"Hey! Help!"

They all turned to the sound of the voice, a woman's voice, and the first thing they saw was a dead man on a floating cooler. Next to him, his wife was shouting. The woman was red-eyed, hoarse; her gray hair was matted with sweat and dirt. She was struggling to push the cooler along, trying to keep the man on top of it. "It's my husband!" she cried.

"He's sick, he's real sick; please help. I was trying to get to the hospital, and I..." Her voice trailed off.

"Okay, ma'am, hold tight," Ellis said as Erick steered the boat toward her. She didn't understand and kept crying as though she couldn't hear them. She hung on to the cooler and to her husband's body.

"Hold on, ma'am, we're coming," Ellis said. He gave the engine a few short bursts to get closer and then cut it. He pulled an oar up off the floor of the boat and used it to steer the rest of the way. Ellis looked closely at her husband and said what everyone but this distraught wife would know:

"I'm so sorry, ma'am. I'm sorry, but he's gone." The man was elderly and his wife was too; it was amazing she hadn't drowned. Ava and Remy hung back, bracing themselves for the woman's screams, but she just nodded as her eyes narrowed, slits of grief and exhaustion, and tears spilled down her cheeks.

"Please climb in the boat, ma'am," Ellis said in his gentle but firm state-trooper voice.

"I can't leave him," she said, softly, defeated.

"I understand, ma'am, but we can't take him right now because...we don't have a place for him." And he reached out for her arm.

"He'll be picked up, ma'am," Ellis said. "They'll come back for him." He didn't know when this would happen, and he didn't exactly know who "they" were, but eventually he would be picked up. At least Ellis hoped so.

He and Erick pulled her up into their little boat. And then she did start crying, crying that she could not leave him, and that she was going to leave him. She collapsed, sliding out of the men's arms into a wet heap in the boat, her chest heaving.

Ellis started up his boat again, and Remy followed suit. As they motored away, Ava stared at the man's body. A dragonfly hovered over it, iridescent wings blinking, a streak of light soon joined by several others.

A Coast Guard helicopter swept above and past them, toward downtown, away from the lake. Remy looked up to see a man leaning partway out of the helicopter doors, looking down at the wreckage below.

They wound their way deeper into the 8th Ward.

Chapter 20

Wednesday Night
Gentilly

I point the flashlight in front of me as I take one, two, three steps over to the edge of the attic door, where the water stopped, and lean down to scoop some up with the vase with the purple and yellow flowers. I can't imagine and don't want to know what is in this filthy water, but it cools her off. So I pour it on her arms and legs. I get more for her chest, wrists, and ankles. I won't put it on her face because I don't want her accidentally drinking any of it. Every time I have done this, I say, "Be careful not to drink it, honey." We old married people do these things. We tell each other things we already know, because repeating the warning feels like some sort of talisman. If I remind her, it won't happen. If we are wary, nothing bad will happen. Yes, here we are; but maybe we won't be here much longer and things won't get worse.

"It smells," Penny says, her nose wrinkling slightly. "But it feels good. Thank you, sweetheart."

We've stripped down to our underwear. At first the thought of being rescued in this state was embarrassing, but it is so unbearably hot that we can't care about that anymore. I've dragged another sheet out of the other window, where it waves like a faded white flag of surrender. Hopefully someone will spot it. I've taken to pouring the foul but cool water on Penny and Baron every hour, trying to lower their temperatures. I'm trying to ration the clean water, but we're all so thirsty.

Every few minutes, I stick my head out of one of the windows and bellow like a fool: "Help! Help!" We heard helicopters all night and have heard more today, but nobody seems to have noticed the sheets, my flags of distress.

I have pounded the damn ceiling with the old rifle butt for what seems like hours. I've made more progress and see cracks of sunlight, but it's not enough for us to escape through there.

I used to be a strong man. Not as strong as Dad but strong. Certainly strong enough to split this roof open. I take a few more whacks at it.

"Honey," Penny says, "please rest. I can shout for help for a while. That's one thing I can do to help you, and someone is bound to hear me at some point." She starts to get up, unsteady; I offer her my arm. Our bodies are slick with sweat. She is stooped, the skin hangs around her elbows and knees; they are ashy like the heels of her bare feet. But when I look at her, she is the young bright-eyed waitress who swept me away in that diner so many years ago.

"We're going to make it," she says. She is trying to change her attitude. Penny does this sometimes. She is usually pretty strong, but sometimes a little bit of darkness creeps in. She is moody for an hour or two, but then she shakes it off. I wonder where her mind goes in those moments. I remember the darkness in the early years of our marriage. I always thought it was her parents and their rejection of her that she was thinking about, but over the years I realized that most people have a dark side, but some of us have better control over it than others. Right now, I see the darkness so clearly in her eyes that I don't believe her optimism for a second. Sometimes long-married spouses forget how well one knows the other.

"Remember when you thought you were going to be drafted? And that horrible year when you were laid off?" she asks, reviving memories in me that I don't want to think about right now.

I nod.

"I was so scared to lose you," she said. "I prayed to God every night that you would be discharged and never called back. And my prayer was answered. And then when you lost your job, I was so afraid we would lose this house…" She pauses for a second, and we both grimly chuckle at the irony of the situation. Then she continued.

"I didn't think we could make it. But I went out there, and I got a job, and you know, it all worked out. We got out of that hole. I think right now we're in trouble, no doubt. But I also think we'll get out of this, honey."

"Yes, we will," I say. I don't feel that way right now. I want my father's power of denial. I want his strength. For the past few days, ever since it became clear that this storm might hit us, I have been trying to fake it. But the truth is, I have not gotten over the shock of that water rising. I know we are in very serious trouble.

Penny reaches down and pulls off her socks. She was so afraid of the rats that she would not take off her socks for hours, even though she's in her underwear at this point. She was convinced they would bite her bare feet. But the heat has changed her mind. I have noticed that today the heat has kept the rats quiet too. Baron pants unrelentingly; I am worried for him. Like most middle-aged beagles, he has a few extra pounds, although now I am glad we put him on a diet last year. He isn't as fat as he used to be.

I pray he makes it.

Penny goes to the window and, when she settles herself, turns around to urge—no, order, with those eyes—me to sit down. She turns back to the window, yells for help. I wonder how far her weakened voice will carry; I wonder why I haven't heard a boat near us yet or seen any sign of anyone in this neighborhood. I sit down, and Baron comes over, moving slowly. I pat him on the head.

"Good boy," I say. "Good boy."

Chapter 21

Thursday, Early Morning Hours
St. Liberatus

They airdropped some food to us. A few staff members who were on break started yelling and jumping up and down when they saw the chopper, but it didn't land; it just rained packages down on our roof and the roofs around us. Food and water bounced and crashed; many of the bottles exploded when they hit, but we retrieved what we could and brought them downstairs and gave them to the most vulnerable and dehydrated patients. The packages of food contained MREs and cans of Spam. We were civilians in a war zone, getting humanitarian aid from some friendly Western nation.

This is the fourth day. Four fucking days of this. Two-hour team check-ins. Bag teams whose hands had cramped up from hours of squeezing, who could barely hold anything, whose wrists were on fire from the exertion of keeping the breath of life in their patients. Security problems: looting in the cafeteria, fights in the hallways. People still shitting in the stairwells. Dying cell phones. Dying car batteries, overly dependent upon to charge said cell phones.

Andy is hanging in there, by the virtue of the bag teams and his youth, but he will not last much longer. I look into that youthful face and see the pale strain of last days, and it is something I can never get used to. Unnatural. The young dying. I cannot look his mother in the eye. She watches the bag teams do their work and watches her son's chest rise and fall.

During rounds, I discover that Mr. Bartlett, my heart-failure patient, has gone into respiratory failure. Dr. Tennant, the nervous intern, is currently bagging him and has been for over an hour.

"We're ready to relieve you," I say, with Natalie, my bag-team partner for today, standing next to me. As Tennant takes his hands off the bag, I put mine on, an orchestrated movement we have all executed many times now. I can see the panic in Mrs. Bartlett's eyes. Like Andy's mother, she will not take her eyes off us except to check her husband's chest rising and falling, rising and falling, a metronome of life.

As a physician, I occasionally feel completely outmatched by Death. Those are the times when you either know it is inevitable, no matter what course of action, surgical or medical, that you might decide on with a patient. And then there are the times when Death strikes out of the blue—accidents and sudden massive coronaries. When that is the case, I feel like I missed a chance to battle my adversary, but no physician would have been able to stop what happened, and while it may be terrible, it is nothing to feel guilty about.

This situation is new. It's nothing close to a fair fight, but it's not because of the whims of Death, but because I don't have working equipment. I don't have the ability to give my patients the basics—cool air, fresh water. In 2005. In America. I walk down these familiar hospital hallways, stepping over the legs of my fellow abandoned citizens, who are lying in the heat, waiting for someone to get them out of here so they can find out what happened to their houses.

People are getting more violent. The young men are particularly restless, as young men tend to be, feeling helpless and physically uncomfortable, trapped in a bad situation. There are more arguments and fights with every passing hour. Exhausted mothers try to rein in their angry teenagers and soothe their tired babies. Frustrated fathers and uncles try to lay down the law or distract kids with cards or just sit there exhausted, staring at nothing, waiting for more news. Some take initiative to try to help out around here, but there is little they can do except help keep unruly visitors in check. More and more people leave on their own and take their chances with the floodwaters.

I remember arguing with Tennant during some political moment of tension in the last administration meeting. Arguing about protocol and procedures and our new parent company's bureaucracy. It is all so meaningless now. We are all focused on one thing. It is like practicing medicine in centuries past. Our profession stripped bare.

A few hours later, I'm back in Mr. Bartlett's room, monitoring his deteriorating vitals and standing by as relief for Natalie, when I hear someone shout, "The National Guard's coming!" I turn to see Arlene. Voices rise up in relief behind her. She is hanging on to the doorway, smiling, the first real smile I'd seen on anyone in three days. Dr. Jain follows close behind her, immediately registers the doubt on my face, and says, "It's true—I got a call." I motion for both of them to move out of the room as Mr. Bartlett's wife looks up. Her eyes brighten. I glance over to Natalie, and she nods that she is okay for now. "I'll have Susan send someone in," I say. I look at Arlene and Jain.

"Not another word for one moment," I say, holding up my index finger. I find Susan at the end of the hallway, discussing an unruly visitor's addiction issues with security.

"Sorry to interrupt, Susan," I say, "but I need someone to stand ready to relieve Natalie in Mr. Bartlett's room." Susan nods. "I'll do it," she says, wrapping up her conversation and heading down the hallway. She turns and looks at me. "By the way, I heard the cavalry is finally coming!"

I sigh and go back to where Arlene and Jain are waiting for me and steer them over to the closest nurses' station. I don't want to get anyone's hopes up until I have more information, for there have been way too many rumors in the past couple of days. In all my aborted and failed attempts to secure rescue for St. Lib, I had placed or tried to place countless calls to government contacts in emergency management—the city, the state—including the National Guard. This is the third time we hear that somebody is coming to rescue us. First it was FEMA. Then it was the fire department. And now the National Guard.

"Who contacted you?" I ask.

"Some guy named Larsen."

"What's his position? Is he in DC, or is he in the region?"

"I don't know," Jain said. "It was a short conversation. And I was kind of focused on the fact that they're getting us the hell out of here. He said first thing in the morning. It sounded much more detailed and...prepared than last time."

"What time are they coming?" I ask.

Jain hesitates.

Tomorrow morning is very far off under these conditions. I want to know if they promised 5:00 a.m. or 11:59 a.m.

"Can we get anybody medevac'd out before then?" I ask. I think about Andy, Mr. Bartlett, the NICU babies on the floor above us, our lung cancer patient, and even Michaela, who is one of the many patients I would not be very worried about if we had our usual resources at hand. "Maybe to another hospital? Did he have any details on the situation at Charity? Tulane? LSU? Memorial?" I ask. We had all been trying to get in touch with sister hospitals in the city, to see if anyone was in better shape and had a boat or other means to take some of our patients. Many of us have colleagues, friends, and relatives who worked at these other facilities. But the only communication we had had thus far was when a nurse at Charity, married to a nurse who worked here, said their situation was basically as nightmarish as ours and that they had not been able to get help either.

Jain gets short with me. I don't blame her. I'm asking her questions I know she doesn't have the answer to, because I'm so fucking frustrated and don't want any more false hope. I want reality, as grim as it is.

"I'm not an intern, so stop talking to me like one," Jain says. "I told you it was a brief conversation. It's not like the guy wanted to chat, and all I wanted to know was if they were coming to get us the hell out of here."

I nod. But then I just had to ask one more question. "Did he say where we would evac our patients to?"

"No," she says.

"Can you call him back and ask him some of these questions?"

"Fine." Jain turns on her heel, a bit deflated. Arlene looks at me as if I'm an asshole. Maybe I am, but as I walk down this hallway and look at all these patients and their family members, hot and tired and miserable, and my colleagues, hot and tired and miserable, I don't want to tell them rescue is nigh until I know for sure that it is. But they are already talking excitedly, showing hope.

I spent a lot of time, when I was younger, worrying what other people thought of me. Maybe because I'm vain, maybe because my father was very judicious about doling out any kind of praise. It doesn't matter, but one of the joys of getting older is not giving a shit to what other people think. I wasted so much time in the past worrying about that.

At the 6:00 p.m. meeting, I ask what the food situation is. Our supply is dwindling. We have enough to give out some sort of rations for one more day. I suggest that we cut rations in half again. Judah tells us he's had to separate people who were fighting and put them on different floors, and he's had people swimming up to the windows of the second floor of the hospital, looking for help. Osgood went down to the second floor with Jain and a couple of other docs to examine the people who came. They turned most of them away, since they only had minor injuries, but they did take in a woman whose husband had pushed her here on a cooler. She was clearly in severe distress as she was listless, her breathing slow and shallow, her pulse weak.

The biggest problem from a security standpoint is the drug users. Withdrawal has made for several attempted robberies, and we have nowhere to put people who are dangerous, and there are no police to come and help us. For now there is a waiting room off the second floor with three miserable drug addicts inside. Pairs of nurses and doctors, accompanied by security, have administered methadone to the heroin addicts. We also have several alcoholics going through withdrawal. They did not bring enough booze because they never thought they would be here this long; consequently some of them are getting only the most basic of DT treatments.

Our meeting is broken up by a cascade of shouts down the hall. Battery backups are dying on some of the last working respirators. The four-person teams are split up, and in this sweltering stink of a hallway, they post themselves in the rooms of more patients who now also need to be bagged by hand. Those who are not posted or on relief duty stand near their patients, rotating between cots, between rooms.

When I am preparing for the next staff meeting, the full reality of our situation hits me so hard I have to sit on the floor for a few minutes. No diagnostic tests—no x-rays, no MRIs—no working lab. We've got operating rooms with no lights. No working pharmacy, just a hoarded, guarded, dwindling collection of medications. We've got a nurse covered by three security guards as she parses out the remaining meds on doctor's orders. The guards have their guns drawn.

About a half hour later, a nurse's aide is able to get through to a cousin who is a member of the Louisiana National Guard. The cousin contacts an officer, and soon we hear a report confirming the first report that Arlene and Jain were excited about. The National Guard will be sending trucks to evacuate us.

"Where are they going to take the evacuees?" I ask the aide who made the call.

"To higher ground," she says.

"When are they coming?" I ask.

"They said soon, early in the morning," she says.

"They specifically named St. Lib?" I ask. She nods, smiles a thin, cautious smile.

"Where do they propose they take our patients?" I ask.

"He's not sure, but he knows there is a plan. They can't send them to another hospital here," she says.

This doesn't surprise me. She gives me the commander's name and the name of the unit. She has more information than Jain and Arlene; I start to allow myself to feel somewhat hopeful. But this also means we must work quickly over the next few hours.

"We can't evac patients, at least not until we know they will be transferred to another facility for medical attention," I say. The aide, whose name I should know but cannot remember, looks at me much like Jain and Arlene looked at me a few hours before.

"I can't release my patients when I don't know where they will be taken and whether they will get the care they need," I say. I admit I don't usually bother to explain myself to nurses' aides. I'm like most other doctors; we can be pretty shitty and hierarchical sometimes. But I'm tired and explaining things to myself, really, to bolster my resolve; it feels insane not to agree to hand off my patients. I can do so little for them here. But it's still my responsibility to ensure that they will be in good hands.

"But we can get the locals out of here," I add. That will take some of the pressure off at least.

We determine which ambulatory nonpatients, neighbors who came to the hospital for shelter but don't need medical care, would be prioritized for the truck rescue. The water has not dropped much, but we know the Guard has some massive, tall vehicles that may be able to reach us.

I sit down for just a few minutes in between meetings and preparations and immediately and unintentionally fall asleep. but am soon awoken by Tennant tapping my shoulder. "It's Mr. Bartlett," he says. I stagger out of the chair and jog in a daze behind Tennant down to Mr. Bartlett's room. Outside the door is Mr. Bartlett's roommate on his bed, lying blinking and confused in the hallway where they have removed him to give the staff more room to work.

Mr. Bartlett has coded. They have used the defib on him, but he is not responding. Not even a flicker is registering after Jain has used the paddles twice. Bartlett is gone. His wife is crying, that soul-piercing crying, and one of the nurses tries to comfort her, but she wrenches free in order to stand closer to her husband.

"Stand clear!" Dr. Jain says again before using the paddles one last time. She and I both know the patient is gone; the nurses know the patient is gone. At this point everything we are doing is futile. But we always try three times; that is the protocol. I ask the bag team what happened. They say his heart just stopped. They had shouted out to the nurse standing by in the hallway that they needed the crash cart.

In the best of circumstances, this patient would have had an implantable device if he were stable enough for one. But all our plans for him were put on hold with this damn storm and flood. Now he's dead, and his wife's keening is a sound I try to block out, but I will hear it later. They think we are so cold sometimes, the families, and I understand why they think so, but you have to block it out in order to walk through these doors every day. You block it out, and you make bad and ghoulish jokes. If you don't, you'll end up like some of the doctors who either get addicted to pain meds or, like a young resident years ago, drive out into the bayous and are never seen or heard from again.

We give Mrs. Bartlett time to say good-bye. And then we must contemplate when and how to get Mr. Bartlett, a very large man, down to the chapel. We wait for a few minutes and try to escort Mrs. Bartlett out of the room, but she does not want to leave. I tell her again I am sorry and whisper to one of the nurses on my way out to try to escort her out again in a little while.

Outside the patient's room, I lean against the wall. My body wants to collapse from the heat. I want to sleep for days. I look over at Mr. Bartlett's roommate, still lying dazed in his bed outside the door. He will soon have this room to himself.

Osgood, Susan Robertson, and I have a brief powwow in the meeting room.

"We lost Mr. Bartlett," I say to Susan, but she already knows.

"We'll need to get him down to the chapel when she's ready to leave the room," I say.

I go upstairs to see how the NICU babies are doing. The sanitary issues are of the gravest concern here. I pray the Guard can tell me this morning that they have a hospital to take these little ones to. I don't want to evacuate the visitors. I want to get my most at-risk patients to a safe and secure facility that can give them the care they need to survive.

I stop by Andy and Michaela's rooms.

Andy's condition is still deteriorating. He was already in rough shape when he was admitted, and my goal was to get him stable enough for a transplant. Now he is nowhere near strong enough for that; we are struggling to keep him alive. I have kept him heavily medicated over the past couple of days, to help his body focus on keeping his viable organs operational. I don't know how much longer his dialysis machine will be working. I pray the batteries last until we can get him out of here.

Michaela is stable but still fighting an infection that I am convinced would likely not have happened if we were able to follow all our usual protocols. Infections do happen, of course. I can't blame them all on the flood. But she is young and strong, and Death is threatening to take her too, when all of us here, those who are trying to save her, have one hand tied behind our backs.

I can't bring myself to look at Andy's mother or Michaela's parents.

By 8:00 a.m., we've started to gather the locals and the ambulatory, ready-for-discharge patients into the second-floor waiting room. From there, they can be lowered onto the army trucks. The water is right at the sills of the mostly shattered second-floor windows.

Word has spread throughout the hospital by now. People are humming, smiling despite the stench of sweat and shit, despite the site of a corpse being wheeled out to the stairwell, and despite the exhaustion of the bag teams and the fact that everyone is hungry and thirsty after going on our fourth full day of being rationed.

Then finally we spot them. Standing by the hallway windows, two nurses' aides start to shout and clap when they see four National Guard vehicles approaching. Many of us, staff and visitors alike, flock to the now-broken windows to get a better look. It feels like a movie, happening in slow motion. The cavalry appearing over the horizon. They are amphib vehicles, designed for wartime, meant for invading other countries. At first we cheer, and everyone is excited. But when they seem to take forever to advance, we realize the vehicles have actually stopped. And then they start to turn down a cross street.

We shout, as if they can hear us. "No! No!"

At first we think they are lost or have made a wrong turn.

One nurse hangs out the window a little too far; we pull her back. She looks like she is contemplating jumping into the water and swimming for it. She is crying.

In vain I wait a couple of minutes, listening to the wrenching disappointment around me; I keep thinking they will turn around.

"They'll be back," I say, with more confidence than I feel.

But they disappear out of sight. And they don't come back.

Nobody contacted Jain this morning. She tried returning the call she had received yesterday, but it just kept ringing. Were they given conflicting orders? Told to withdraw? Directed to some other hospital? Jain and Arlene keep trying to get more information. My cell phone ran out of batteries hours ago—days ago, it seems—so I can be of no help because currently the car batteries that are still working enough to power the chargers are charging other people's cell phones. We don't know what happened. But we do know that there will be no rescue today.

I sink to the floor in the waiting room, looking at the anxious faces of the locals and patients who thought they were about to be freed from this hellhole. This hospital, where I have worked for so many years, is unrecognizable right now. Are we going to die here?

As if reading my melodramatic thoughts, Natalie comes up to me. She has pulled her dark hair back into a bun; strands of it fall in front of her eyes. She crosses her arms in front of her scrubs. She is one of those nurses who always wears the standard-issue light-yellow scrubs. She doesn't buy cutesy scrubs with animals or floral prints on them. Always the uniform look.

"Perk up, Doc," she says. She lowers her voice and bends down close to me. "Don't let them see you like this," she says. Like many people in our field of work, she doesn't let herself stay down for very long. Her job is to support others. She hides the despair and hopelessness she was feeling when we were on the roof, and I am sure she still feels.

I nod and rub my temple. I think of how gray my hair looked in the bathroom mirror the other day. I feel fifty years older than that now. I get up.

"Okay, everyone," I say. I repeat it; I stare down at my sneakers again, take a deep breath, and think for a moment about what needs to be done now that our rescuers have failed us.

"Let's regroup," I say. "We'll get ourselves out of here."

After the meeting breaks up, I am walking down the corridor, checking in with nurses, when Marius comes up to me smiling.

"Got a present for you, Doc," he says. He is holding our two portable generators.

"But we don't have fuel," I say, not understanding.

"We do after I used my Mississippi credit card to open gas tanks in the parking garage," he says, holding up a screwdriver.

I laugh. "How'd you siphon it?" I ask.

He puts the screwdriver in his pocket and fishes out a length of respiratory tubing.

"You are a genius," I say.

One generator goes to the NICU. The other goes to Andy and one of our critical elderly patients. Of course, this is a relief. But it doesn't solve the problem that we have no therapies and no food and hardly any medicine and completely abysmal hygiene that will eventually kill any patient who isn't felled by the heat.

But if it will keep Andy alive, the babies alive, for a few more hours? Then it is more than what I could have hoped for five minutes ago.

Just then Susan appears at my side. "Dr. Reid?" she says. "There's someone here to see you."

This seems an odd thing to say, since people aren't exactly dropping by for visits. I turn around to see Chris, the security-guard kid from my office. He is carrying two bulging black trash bags in his hands. He looks down at one and opens it for me; inside he has crammed first-aid supplies, antibacterial gel, bottles of water, and apparently everything from the vending machines in our office building.

"I went through all the offices," he says. He is wet from head to toe. "I knew you guys were stuck here, so I thought you could use these," he said.

"We sure as hell can," I say.

Chapter 22

Thursday Morning
Somewhere Deep In the 8th Ward
They had slept in the truck that night, fitfully. It is difficult to sleep when you are envisioning people out there, waiting for you to help them; people who might die before you could reach them.

Every once in a while one of them would hear things and then wait to hear them again, more awake than ever. According to many, but not all, of the news, Coast Guard and navy choppers had stopped their night flights due to continuing rumors about snipers. So the city alternated between noise and an eerie quiet. There was the scream of sirens where the few functioning fire-department units were fighting a blaze at the edge of the warehouse district, right in front of the floodwaters. There was crying and talking and laughter from fellow rescuers and the recently rescued talking around them in the middle of the night.

Sometime around `2:00 a.m. they realized they were both still awake.

"This is even worse than I thought it would be," Ava said.

"Much worse," Remy said.

"Do you think they're going to make it?"

Remy paused. They. We. *The City That Care Forgot.* Outside there was a sound of someone starting an engine. Down the street there was the sound of splashing.

"This damn beautiful crazy city," he said, finally. He sat up and lit a cigarette, leaning against the window and dangling it outside so the smoke didn't bother Ava. She waited, listening to the *tap tap* of his hands on the pack. She thought of all the unnamed storms in her father's old hurricane book. People washed away. Islands sunken and forgotten.

"All these places I have been going to since I was a kid...ruined," Remy said. He took another drag of the cigarette. "I know you think I'm a conspiracy theorist," he continued, "but if this happened in Greenwich, Connecticut, do you think a damn soul would have been lost?"

"But look, we're here...the Cajun Navy is here..." Ava said. They both laughed at the name.

"And the Homeboys," Ava added. They hadn't met those guys yet, but it was a local crew of guys from the 9th Ward, who were out there in scavenged boats, rescuing friends, family, neighbors, and strangers. The Cajuns talked of them admiringly.

"Yes. So maybe things will be okay in the end."

"Maybe they will," Ava said.

It was too dark to see him very clearly, but Ava knew Remy was shaking his head by the glow of his cigarette moving back and forth. "Goddamn Army Corps of Engineers."

Remy wasn't convinced anything was ever going to be okay here. But then, had it ever been? It was New Orleans. They were a unique culture down here. People just accepted things and didn't necessarily try to fix them. People knew the levees would break despite what the Corps had been telling them for decades. Locals just knew. But most New Orleanians never really raised a big stink about it. They were too busy living their lives, feeding their kids, playing their music, going to their office or construction, or waitressing jobs. They just accepted it.

Remy thought about a story he had heard from his mother once. She was no great civil-rights champion, but she mentioned how the walls of Charity Hospital used to have two entrances: one for "Colored" and one for "White." After the civil rights movement got underway, somebody was contracted to chisel those words off the entryway. Now he thought about all the old buildings that were underwater, flood lines painting marks in time that would take a lot of chipping, sanding, painting to blast away. But they would still be there, under everything.

He started thinking about Mardi Gras. What would that look like next year? Could they even have it in 2006? Would this city still be underwater? Abandoned? He imagined ghostly parades, Fat Tuesdays of years past. Floats underwater, mildewed feathers and beads. Ruined Indian costumes nailed to the doors of submerged houses.

As they sat in the cramped, hot truck, Ava thought of her father's discomfort with his home city and its racial past. A historian, he did not forget such things and saw their legacy in the walking around of life; it affected everything and everyone in the city, whether they knew it or not. That was how he introduced his daughter to the city: through the layers. To him, they were transparent, present laid over past, but both still there. Easy enough to see if you knew what to look for.

It was like his hurricane books. He had not been alive for much of what he read in them, but those were the legacy of New Orleans and its relationship with Mother Nature, and every New Orleanian knew what she was capable of, as if they had all ridden out every storm together.

Ava remembered how her father used to prepare for storms with such a paranoid and almost childish fear and how her grandfather would mock him for it. He did not respect the water enough.

Ava drew herself out of her reverie and said, "You say it was the Corps. But whether it happened during the storm itself or afterward, does it matter? This is the result either way."

"Of course it matters," Remy said. "If the Corps built levees that actually performed as promised, these people—and these bodies we're seeing—wouldn't be out there. They'd be in their homes on a regular fucking night right now."

They were quiet again for a while. They both wanted the sun to just come up already so they could get back to work. Eventually the first few dim rays threw a reddish light on the black stink of floodwaters that stretched out before them. They walked out of the truck around five o'clock in the morning and shared a quick protein-bar breakfast. This morning a couple of New Orleans firefighters, who had been rescuing people in a boat they hotwired after they saw one of the levees break from their station on Monday morning, had joined up with the Cajun Navy.

Before they left, Ava retrieved her phone from the charger in Remy's truck. It had died somewhere along the way on Wednesday, and she had been so distracted by everything going on that she forgot to give her aunt and uncle an update. She knew they were worried sick. She flipped it open to see that she had missed calls from her uncle and her boss. Reception was terrible, so she didn't even bother to try to call them back, but she had heard that people were having more luck with texting, so she did that. She never used the phone for texting and barely knew how. She imagined that since she had no texting plan, it was costing her a fortune. But she couldn't have Keenan and Rosa lying awake at night worrying about her. Although they would anyway.

Doing OK. Found Ellis. Don't worry. How is T?

It took her uncle an hour to get back to her. Ava suspected he didn't know how to text either. *T. is ok. Misses you. Be careful. Keep us posted. Need anything?*

Meanwhile, Remy had tried for what seemed like the millionth time to get in touch with his father. He had heard rumors about Uptown since they had arrived that made him blanch: gangs of men from the projects were breaking into houses all along St. Charles. Ellis insisted that this wasn't true, from what he had heard from other troopers. But it was true that the hardware store near Mr. Devereaux's neighborhood had been looted. But was it a full-on race war, old white guys armed on porches and black men coming to get them? Ellis doubted it. Remy had already heard a number of rumors that didn't turn out to be true, but he was still nervous. Nothing about this was normal, and if the whole city was cracking open, maybe some long pent-up hostilities were about to blow up into something even more terrible than a hurricane and a flood.

This morning, Irish was handing out assignments, since more volunteers had arrived, and she didn't want any duplicated or wasted efforts. Thanks to her, the Cajun Navy ran like a pretty professional outfit. Irish asked Erick and Ellis, who were back after reporting to their commanding officer early in the morning, to go where the need seemed to be the most desperate—and conditions the most dangerous—Lower 9. She asked Remy and Ava to continue where they left off the night before in the 8th Ward. They would be deep into the neighborhood by now if they started where they left off yesterday.

They pushed off as soon as it was light enough to see.

They could tell by now, as they had mostly adjusted to the surreal landscape, where one street ended and another began. Now they knew to look for the peaks of rooftops and the occasional top of a street sign. Some roofs were completely under water, but there were enough attic windows poking out that you could make out a rough terrain. Until you got closer to the levees. Then truly nothing was where it should be.

As they had yesterday, they cut the engine every few minutes. Then they waited and listened like Erick had told them. About fifteen minutes after they left camp, as they were passing a pink Creole cottage on one side and the top of a white-painted brick house on the other, they saw a man sitting at the apex of a pitched rooftop covered with asphalt shingles, hands around his knees, a six-pack perched awkwardly over the angle of the roof.

"You need help?"

The man shook his head at Remy's question.

"You okay, guy?" Remy asked, wary.

The man stared and then nodded slowly.

"C'mon, man, you need to get down from there. It's not safe here," Remy said.

"I ain't going in that water," the man said. "I'm going to wait for it to go down."

"I don't know how long you'll have to wait," Ava said.

"Don't care."

Remy shook his head, irritated, and then gunned the motor; they blew past the man on the roof.

"What the hell?" Ava asked.

"Who knows. He might be out of it. In shock. Or he might just be fucking stupid."

"We can't just leave him there," Ava said.

"Oh yes, we can. Screw that fucker. There's more people down this street who want to get the hell outta here," Remy said.

They left him to his fate. As they continued down the flooded street, they passed the bloated body of a woman who had gotten caught in a pile of debris. It bobbed up and down. Ava stifled an urge to retch as she looked at the dead woman's arms. They were straight out, swollen, puffed up, and stretched out with gas. Dragonflies hovered above the body, but they didn't touch it, just like with the dead man she saw the day before. The woman's skin was marbled with patches that have been ripped off.

They wondered who this woman was and if she was alone when she died.

At the next intersection, two men in a rowboat emerged from the cross street. At first Ava thought they were would-be rescuers like her, and she raised her hand in greeting. But then she saw the pile in the back of the boat: TVs and brand-new sneakers. When they saw Ava staring at their loot, the man in front raised a shotgun in warning. Remy waved a hand as if to say, "Don't mind us, and we won't mind you," and then he and Ava both pointedly looked away.

"You better give me that pistol," Remy said. "In case they come back."

"Let's just get the hell away from them," Ava said.

"It may not be up to us," Remy said. "We're still gonna be searching this street, and they might come back."

Ava took Remy's gun out of the inside pocket of his backpack where he had stowed it, but before she could hand it to him, he said "I need to load it" and gestured at the backpack.

"Oh," Ava said, feeling stupid. She scrounged around the zipped pockets of the backpack, and sure enough, there was a box of ammunition wrapped with a rubber band in the inside pocket. She handed it to Remy, and he loaded his pistol and tucked it into the waistband of his jeans.

He laughed a half-hearted laugh and said, "This is fucked up. But at the same time, I can't believe I hadn't had to load it before this."

"You probably should have," Ava said, thinking of how that encounter could have gone very differently.

Ava imagined her coworkers seeing her now. She was the quiet one who had worked there for too long. The one who brought in leftover homemade dinners and baked goods on a fairly predictable basis. The dependable one who knew all the mistakes to look for in every article after working there for nearly twenty years. And here she was, handing her friend a gun so they might have something to shoot marauding looters with as they navigated a boat through the ravaged landscape of America's great cities.

A couple of years after they had graduated college, Remy came up for a long weekend in Maine and went hunting with Ava's uncle. It wasn't so much that they went hunting, but the fact was that they came back to Ava's uncle's house with a 12-point buck on the back of the truck and proceeded to hang it up in the garage. Ava didn't like it, and neither did her aunt, Rosa. But they didn't question it. It was tradition both in rural Maine and in the South.

Armed and nervous, they continued on their way. The water seemed deeper here. Some houses were submerged completely as they got farther and farther from where they started at I-10 and closer and closer to the broken levees. They started to see houses that had been blown apart by the rush of water. There was no rooftop, no frame, no porch, no second-floor windows. Just discarded bits and pieces of lumber, plastic, and wood. When they stopped and drifted, and cried out to see if anyone responded, they would stare at the floating detritus of human life: baseball trophies and bookshelves, cans of food and school-graduation photos, pajamas, and stuffed animals caught in the remains of chain-link fences. It was as if the landscape had been bombed and then sunk in a bathtub. Every time a helicopter would hover overhead, with an advancing and retreating roar, it felt even more like a warzone.

The piercing, haunting barking of abandoned dogs echoed sharply off the water as it had the previous day.

"The dogs," Ava said. The sound still ripped her heart open even though she had been hearing it for the better part of twenty-four hours now.

"I know," Remy said. "Maybe we can pick some up." At one point, they had seen a humane society rescue team, but it might have been the only one in the whole city for all they knew.

They had gone ten minutes without seeing another soul when they heard the shouting.

"Help!"

They both turned to the sound of the voices.

"Hey! Hey! Up here! We need help up here!"

They were one street over, at a diagonal from the boat. There was a woman, middle-aged, coffee-colored skin, with a young girl and a much older woman next to her. They were half-standing and half-sitting awkwardly on the pitched roof of their little white house. A pink sheet emerged from the top of an attic window below them, floating in the water.

Remy turned the motor on and gunned it and then stopped it abruptly as they drifted closer to the house. Ava used the oar to brace against obstacles—a floating refrigerator, a one-way sign bending into the water—until they were up under the women.

"Take her first!" the younger woman said, anxious, holding the little girl by her armpits, and Ava reached out, while Remy steadied the boat. Ava said soothing words to the girl, who was crying a hoarse cry and looking down at the water. She had braids with little red barrettes at the end, and she was wearing pink pajamas with a picture of a princess wearing a crown and a tutu. Somewhere near them, distraught dogs barked and whined.

"Do y'all have any water for her?" the older woman, whom Ava and Remy assumed was the grandmother, asked as she pointed at her granddaughter. "We ran out almost two days ago," she said.

"Yes, ma'am, we do," Ava said. In the back of her mind she thought about how Mainers rarely say ma'am and sir. It's not a Yankee thing. There was something about it that was so wonderfully civil.

Ava set the little girl down on one of the boat seats.

"My mother-in-law can't swim..." the mother said. She looked defeated but relieved.

"No problem, ma'am," Remy said. Turning to the grandmother, he said, "We'll take your daughter-in-law here first, okay? And then we'll help you."

"Yes, please," the grandmother said.

The girl was still crying as Remy helped her lower her mother from the roof to the boat. The whole time the little girl wailed, and her mother said "I'll be right there, honey" over and over.

"Thank you, thank you," the mother said repeatedly to Remy as she got settled next to the little girl. Her daughter clung to her, pressing her face into her mother's shirt. "Shhh, honey. Shhh. It's okay, baby." The mom introduced herself as Sandra.

"Nice to meet you, Sandra," Remy said. "Wish it were in better circumstances."

Ava handed Sandra a water bottle, and she gave some to her daughter. Meanwhile, Remy helped the grandmother into the boat. She nearly slipped out of his arms; she was unsteady, weak, and on the heavy side. Remy tensed, and Ava moved in to try to help catch the woman, but she recovered herself, and they helped her sit down on the other side of the boat. As Ava picked up the oar to push away from the bigger pieces of floating debris before they started the engine, she saw ruined jasmine flowers floating next to the boat. They released a whiff of sweetness that was soon overpowered by the surrounding stench.

As they headed back to the rescuers' camp, Sandra sat next to her daughter and put her arm around the little girl's shoulder, pulling her close; she kissed the top of her head. The girl's crying subsided, and she drank more water. Ava handed another bottle of water to the grandmother.

"I can't swim too well either," Sandra said to Ava, who sat next to the grandmother on their way back to shore. Sandra was so relieved that she could not stop talking, releasing a flood of emotions from three days of life-or-death stress.

The little girl's eyes stayed focused on her mother, locked on her every movement. Ava scrounged up a couple of protein bars from their limited supply and offered it to the women. Sandra gave it to her daughter first and then to her mother-in-law and took the dregs for herself. As the boat gained speed, a slight breeze blew around them, providing a tiny bit of relief from the heat. All around them the water was shining with slick rainbows of oil and gasoline. It seemed like more than yesterday. Just beneath the surface the big lake fish moved with sureness, exploring their new expanded territory. For the hundredth time, Ava thought there must be gators, and she prayed she wouldn't see one. In this landscape, the gators must be monsters, twelve- or fourteen-footers, and dinosaurs, the stuff of nightmares.

"You from around here?" Sandra asked, raising her voice to be heard above the engine and looking at Ava and then Remy. It sounded like she thought they weren't, and before Ava could answer, Remy nodded and said, "Uptown."

"Your people okay?" Sandra asked, turning to Remy. She had hazel eyes and high, sharp cheekbones.

"Yeah," he said. "Well, I think so. My mom's out of town with relatives. My dad stayed. I need to go check on him."

"You didn't stay with him?"

"No, I live in DC. I got here yesterday. Came down with my friend here," Remy said, gesturing to Ava.

"Oh, y'all from DC too?"

"No, I'm from Maine," Ava said. In that moment, Maine seemed like a place so far away that it was hard to believe it was real. In the midst of all this heat and misery, she imagined what it would be like at home now. Definitely cold enough for a jacket at this time of day.

"Maine! You came here all the way from Maine?" Sandra half laughed. Ava nodded, smiling. It did sound crazy when someone said it out loud.

"There are a lot of people from out of state," Remy said. "A lot of people came down from all over the place."

Sandra nodded. "This one was…this was *the* One."

"Where you going to take us to?" the grandmother asked.

"Everyone's being dropped off at the I-ten," Ava said. "But there are supposed to be…there are buses coming to get people out of the city. To the airport, I think, and then I'm not sure where after that." She had seen one bus arrive last night. It was a genuine clusterfuck as people jockeyed to get on; a handful of law-enforcement people attempted to control the situation, but there were definitely people—elderly, sick—who should have been on that bus before others, but they weren't.

Ava really had no idea when more buses were coming. They had to eventually, right?

"Oh God, when we saw that water coming up at us," Sandra said.

The grandmother shook her head and said, "We were looking out the bedroom window at it all, you know? And the neighbor's house, across the way…the water just kept pushing it, and the roof just popped off! The walls were going in and out. It was as if it was alive, as if it was breathing, you know? The water just came so fast. It was maybe five inches, and then not five minutes later, it was ten feet, and we had gone up to the top floor, and then we had to come up through the window onto the roof; we didn't have time to bring anything…I've never seen anything like it. Never. Hope I never ever see anything like that again."

"I don't know what we're going to do," Sandra said. She looked at her daughter, and Ava could see her catching herself from going into a spiral of fear, from wondering aloud where she would live and how she would take care of her little girl. Instead she brightened and said to her baby, "But we'll figure it out, honey." She squeezed her closer to her.

"We should have left," the mother-in-law said. "We should have caught that ride with Dex and Kelly."

"My brother-in-law offered us a ride," Sandra said, shaking her head. "Biggest mistake I ever made."

"We don't usually evacuate, either," Remy said. "This was the one time my mom did."

As they came up to the drop-off point, they reached the edge of the oil-slicked water. Here it gave up some possessions in its undulations—bits of trash, clothing, dead rats—and deposited them on the shore of this new putrid lake.

Ava hopped out and started helping everyone out of the boat, while Remy held it as steady as he could. One of Irish's new cohorts, a stocky, sunburned fireman named Mike from Eastern Tennessee, came up to greet them. He had more water for the women, and he gave them wipes to clean themselves. "You're in for a long night, but you'll be okay," he said to them. "Official emergency response and management doesn't really have its act together yet, so we're still waiting on buses to get you folks out. There is some water and food here and in the waiting area over by the highway." The state police were trying to keep the highway crowd under control. Bottles of water had been airdropped by the freeway, along with military rations. Ava and Remy had noticed there were more military units making an appearance, but their presence still seemed sporadic and unorganized.

Mike explained that when the buses finally came, people would be deposited at the airport. There was a makeshift hospital set up there—the only place that made sense because it was large and safe from floodwaters and close to transport out of the area. From there, families were to be flown all over the country, sometimes to stay in strange towns where they knew nobody. It was another terribly unorganized step in a pathetically unplanned series of rescue attempts. The truth was, Mike and Irish and the rest of them didn't know much about what happened after they pulled people out from the neighborhoods. They just focused on getting them off those roofs and out of that inky black water.

Remy and Ava pushed the boat back off into the water. As they headed back, Ava watched Sandra walk away, her arm around her baby girl.

After a few hours, they had a sort of drill going; they'd find people via shouts or word-of-mouth from the Cajun Navy or from the people they had already rescued. Sometimes they were directed by the gestures of helicopter pilots, usually Coasties, whom everyone deferred to; all you could see were helmets and gloves, sweeping military gestures, hands signaling as they swooped past. As they motored back to shore, they would offer rudimentary first aid with the little supplies they brought or got from the Cajuns; they cleaned nasty-looking cuts with alcohol wipes, and they offered water to quench thirst.

In the putrid water, Ava and Remy saw floating smiling faces from the forties, men in uniform and women with glamorous Hollywood hair, long-haired hippie girls, and curly-haired boys with horn-rimmed glasses. They saw recent school pictures, blasted from refrigerators by the blunt force of water. A teakettle, a mattress, and a dead cat with a collar, somebody's beloved family pet.

They were several streets into the 8th Ward, heading in the direction of Lakeview, when they heard voices again and saw a man on a roof, who had been waving frantically at a helicopter. The helicopter pilot was flying low, close; he had just tried to pick someone up, but there were electrical wires and trees hanging directly above the home. The basket got stuck on each try. The pilot gestured toward the man. Ava gave him a thumbs-up to show they understood.

The man on the roof was a middle-aged, dark-skinned black man with a receding hairline. He had dark-brown eyes and wore jeans, ripped and dirty, and a green T-shirt. He was thin and haggard, but he smiled with relief as they drove the boat closer to him.

Ava and Remy steadied, lifted, dragged, pulled until the man was in the boat.

"What's your name?" Ava asked as she handed the man a bottle of water.

"Charles," the man replied. The wife and kids, he explained, had evacuated on Sunday, at the last minute. He had a bad feeling that this time the storm wouldn't turn; it was going to be a direct hit, he thought—it was going to be different than all the other times. He stayed behind because he wanted to protect the house; he was afraid of looters and losing everything.

The man's arms looked puffy and swollen. As they headed back down the street, he turned to Ava and said, "Have you seen the gators?"

"No," she said. "But I'm sure they're in there."

"Oh, they're in there. I've been watching them. They took one of my neighbors," he said. He rubbed his eyes with his hands. "Took her right down," he said. "She was already dead, thank God."

"Is there anyone else here who's alive?" Ava asked. "Other neighbors?"

Charles shook his head. He finished the bottle of water and rolled it around in his hands. "I lost everything, man," Charles said. "I stayed so I could look after the place, and I lost everything. When the water was coming, I tried to save some of our photos and my wife's jewelry, but it just came up so fast, I don't know...I don't know what else I could have done."

Ava said, "You saved yourself. That's the most important thing."

As Remy maneuvered the boat back toward the drop-off point, Ava looked around and thought about how this unrecognizable terrain would have to be razed and scraped clean.

Ava remembered her father telling her about the way Mardi Gras ended, especially in the old days. Cops on horses would ride through the streets, spread out from one banquette to another so there was no way to get by them, and would drive the celebrants before them; everyone must go home and go to bed. At midnight on Mardi Gras night, it's over. It's Ash Wednesday, and the streets must be swept clean of sin.

Chapter 23

Thursday Afternoon
Gentilly

I found applesauce for Penny. There was one little disposable container of it, and I can't remember if I saw it earlier, but I remember throwing it in one of the bags and thinking it was something the girls must have left behind after their last visit. Snacks for the grandchildren. Penny is propped up against a box, and she is spooning it out of the container with her finger. She shares it with Baron. My boy doesn't look good, and I'm more worried about him with each passing hour. So is Penny. We're both worried about each other, but it's easier to talk about Baron. We think we have more control, more ability to help him. He is so overheated. This has been the cruelest day. If only it would rain, to provide a respite from the heat. And I laugh to think that right now what I want in all of this—besides rescue—is more water. But, of course, our summer rains don't provide much relief anyway. The air seems even more humid when they pass. We might as well live in the tropics. It's always felt like the edge of the world down here, not quite American, not quite South American, not quite Caribbean. We don't know what it is, but it is home, it is ours, and it's broken and crazy and frustrating but so wonderful.

A few hours ago we heard someone crying out, "Hello?! Hello?" Someone was out in the neighborhood, very near us, looking for survivors! I scrambled to the window and stuck myself out so far that Penny was afraid I would get stuck. And I shouted. I have never shouted so hard in my life. In the heat and the haze, I pictured myself back in basic, shouting my lungs out in time with the other guys, singing raunchy songs while humping it up the hills and through the valleys on our twenty-mile runs.

But nobody could hear me. We never even saw the boat. I tried squeezing myself out through the window to get on the roof but couldn't get a good hold and kept nearly falling into the floodwater. I shouted until I was hoarse. I shouted until Penny was crying, and she shouted too. We each stuck our head out one of the windows and looked in vain for the source of that voice. Such an adrenalin rush of excitement at the prospect of being rescued. I feel a renewed sense of desperation now. How many more boats will come by until it is too late for us?

"Maybe we can fan him some more," Penny says, bringing my mind back to Baron. She is using the cardboard I fanned her with to try to cool Baron down. He lies down, panting. I see the worry in Penny's eyes when she looks at me and she looks at him.

"They gotta come soon, honey," I say. "It's been more than enough time now. The girls must be making calls. They know we're missing."

"We should have been honest with them," Penny says. Her sweet heart and her sweet eyes. She pats Baron lightly on the head. "Rest, little man," she says.

I want to rest too. I lean against the window. I have been feeling dizzy and vaguely nauseous since I spent so much energy trying to alert our would-be rescuers earlier. We still periodically shout, but we have so little strength left. It's the heat, and no meds for three days now. I don't want to strain too much—I can't. Just breathing in this hot attic is a strain. I am starting to think that I'm just going to have to swim for it to save them. I lightly rest a hand on Penny's hand and then reach over to pet Baron's tricolored fur.

As I lean back, my chest is seized with pressure. I try to breathe lightly, shallow, my hand frozen on Baron's back for a moment. But it gets worse, and now my chest is a vise, gripping my lungs, stealing my breath. I cannot breathe in for the stabbing pains. I feel like I am going to black out. Through fog, Penny is saying my name, and I know she is saying it louder and louder, but her voice is receding like an outgoing wave. I lay to the side against the pile of boxes behind me. Slowly, slowly. I try to say something, but my voice won't cooperate; my body is not my own. Penny crawls over to me. Between us, on the blankets I had pulled out for Penny to lay on, there is the container of applesauce and what's left of our clean water. I close my eyes, and Penny crawls over to me. "*I love you*," she says. She is crying.

I am in the backyard. The girls are with me. And the grandkids are here too! And the girls are grown women, but they are also my little girls again. Dad is at the barbeque, and Penny is there, petting Baron...

I love you too.

Chapter 24

Thursday Night
8th Ward

When she finally slept on Wednesday night, Ava had a dream about her father, about the days and weeks and months after he died. The guilt was always there, like another person in her dream, a shadow falling around her everywhere she went. She woke up with the weight of it. He had saved her. What had she done? Logic told her she was just a little girl. But the voice of logic is too soft and still. She could have dived back in and tried to pull him to safety. She didn't. She was too scared to let go. She could have asked him to take her out to ice cream instead of going kayaking. He would have relented. She was daddy's girl.

"I want to go check on Dad tonight," Remy said. "We can't rescue folks at night anyway."

Ava wanted to see the old neighborhood too. Since they had arrived in New Orleans, her father's home had been on her mind; she needed to see it again for him. And though she hadn't said anything to Remy, she was worried about his father. Communications were so difficult here, so it was not surprising that Remy had still not gotten in touch with him. But it still worried her. Remy's dad was in his seventies now.

The sun was sinking. They had almost finished searching their assigned grid. After Sandra and her family, they had rescued four more people: an elderly brother and sister sitting on the top of one house and a young couple sitting on the top of another. They were only two streets apart. As they got down to the levee, they knew there could be no survivors here; everything had been blown away, and splintered wood and ripped asphalt roofing shingles floated around them. Yet Ava wanted to finish their assigned search.

They saw nine more bodies. Bloated, stretched, caught up in chain-link fences or rolling in the wake of the boat, discarded like offal. Always with the dragonflies floating above, outnumbering the mosquitos.

Guilt pushed them forward; they both envisioned, without telling the other of their fear, leaving for the night only to find, just one street over—a street they would have searched if they stayed until dark—someone who didn't make it through the night. Someone who could have been saved.

When they picked survivors off the slumping tops of their devastated houses, sometimes they could tell the survivors had crawled up there through an open window. But other times the only way out had been by ax and ragged, gaping holes desperately hacked through roofs to escape water's greedy mouth.

Sometimes people had written "HELP" on the roofs, either in sheets and pillowcases or by stripping shingles bare, peeled back until their hands were bleeding.

Their next rescue was at a low brick house, where they found four people who had been stranded on their roof. Next door to the brick house, there was a body lying on a second-floor porch. The peaceful and eerie sound of wind chimes carried across the floodwaters.

Above them the National Guard helicopters swung past, heading back to the levees to drop more sandbags. Fingers in the holes of a burst dam.

Ava and Remy motored back to where they had picked the last family up, and they were well past that house, motor cut, floating, calling and listening when they heard something splash in the water. They looked around; nothing but floating debris. Until Ava spotted it: something moving. A little black-and-brown dog.

It was paddling for its life, headed directly for the boat, its eyes fixed on them. Its floppy ears were pinned back in terror. "Remy," Ava said, but Remy had already picked up the oar and started to steer them closer. Ava tried to talk calmly and encouragingly: "C'mere. It's okay, little guy."

Once the dog got close enough, Ava leaned over the edge of the boat, pulling it up, one arm around his back and another under his stomach.

"Careful; he might bite," Remy said, seeing the dog was terrified. But all he did was claw onto Ava's arm for dear life. She pulled him into the boat.

It was a he. Some sort of terrier mix, maybe twenty pounds. "It's okay, buddy," Ava said. "You're safe now." She poured some bottled water into her cupped hand, and the dog lapped it up immediately.

"He doesn't have any tags," she said, inspecting him. "Or a collar, although that could have been lost in all this." He was skinny.

"He's probably a stray," Remy said. "There are a lot of dogs like him down here."

Ava patted the dog's head. "It's going to be okay, buddy." The dog was shaking despite the heat, and his coat was slick with oily water.

"Help! Please!"

Remy and Ava whipped around in the direction of the voice. It was coming from what used to be the end of the street.

"Hang on—we're coming!" Remy yelled, and he gunned the engine, scraping the bottom of the boat on some unseen debris (a stop sign, a tree) until they were practically on top of the house. It was a strange sight; half the building had been washed away, and the other half stood, branches in the roof, siding slouching where the outside wall had been decimated, just a jagged pile of wood and metal surrounded by floodwaters. But then they turned the corner of the house to see a woman crying, hanging onto a gutter that was peeling away from a crumbling section of roof. She was a stout, dark-skinned woman with raven-black hair with gray roots. Behind her was a teenage boy, hanging just as precariously.

"Help my boy," she was crying. "Help my son!"

The boy was a gangly kid of maybe fifteen or sixteen. His legs were shriveled and thin.

"He can't stay up," she said. "He can't keep himself up, and he's too heavy for me!"

They positioned the boat under her son first; Ava was an expert at using the oar now, and though it was only a drop of about five feet, the woman warned that they must catch the boy because he could not stand, and his legs were fragile. Remy reached up and told the boy it was okay to let go, and he awkwardly but firmly grabbed the boy's waist as he dropped, pulling him into the boat and into a sitting position.

The boy's baseball cap was plastered to his sticky forehead. He was wearing a drenched T-shirt advertising a fundraiser at Tipitina's. He wiped his eyes with lean fingers. He arranged his legs closer together as he watched Remy and Ava help his mother into the boat.

The mother was a picture of exhaustion. Every part of her seemed swollen... her puffy face, red eyes, arms covered with bruises and scratch marks, wounds from trying to save her boy and herself from drowning in their house.

"They never came," she said, crying. "They never came. They don't care. They don't care."

"Who never came?" Ava asked, thinking the woman meant family members.

"Social Services! My boy is on Medicaid, and they told us they would send a van for us, because of his equipment and everything. He's in a wheelchair." The boy's face was vacant, exhausted. But when he saw Ava's little dog, he perked up. He reached out his hand for the dog to smell him and started petting him gently.

Ava imagined telling Aunt Rosa about this. She would have been livid. She would tell her all about this, whenever this was over and she could get back in touch. As she handed the woman and her son bottles of water, Ava felt the anger rising within her. The anger she had felt back in Maine, on the road. The anger she did not have the time to feel here, here where she was useful. But now her thoughts strayed cynically; she thought about how somewhere in Baton Rouge right now there was an assistant on her Blackberry or a PR rep protecting one of the many politicians who were failing the people she and Remy and hundreds of others were picking off buildings. This woman's boy could have died, as many did, their battered bodies like driftwood in their living rooms.

The gathering darkness slowed them as they puttered back to the Cajuns' staging area; they had to shine flashlights to make their way around obstacles. Their flashlights caught the glare of eyes, human and animal, dead and alive.

The ever-present and painfully heartbreaking sound of desperate dogs barking followed them all the way back to I-10. Ava held the little dog close.

As they pulled up back at the launch point at St. Claude's, they came alongside a tall, thin, dark-skinned man with long, tied-back dreads. He was with another man, burly with striking green eyes, who was helping two elderly women climb out of their boat. The dreadlocks guy raised a bottle of Red Stripe in salute to Remy and Ava. "How's the fishin'?" he asked, laughing.

Remy and Ava dragged the boat up on the "beach" that used to be a banquette. From there they helped the mother out of the boat, and Remy carried her son up to the evacuation point down the street. Ava took the little dog out and looked for a makeshift leash. Not finding one, she tucked him under her arm. Van, Irish's husband, offered to help Remy carry the boy, but Remy shook his head. He tried to find a good spot for the boy to sit, among the throngs of people waiting for buses. There wasn't any good spot; the entire roadway was a mess of humanity and trash and stink. So they set the boy down on the pavement, and his mother stood guard over him. Remy talked to some of the surrounding crowd, and soon enough a Good Samaritan came up and said she would help them get on the next bus when it came. She said she was a nurse's aide and knew how to help the boy.

There appeared to be more order to the crowds now. There were more cops, mostly state troopers from other states, as well as some ambulance workers from Ohio and northern Louisiana, who were administering basic first aid to people.

The faces of the people on the highway were exhausted, angry, and resigned. There were piles of trash pushed up against the side of the road and busted-opened palettes of water bottles that had been dropped to the crowd from helicopters.

Everything stank, but the whole city stank so bad that Remy and Ava could hardly smell anymore.

When they made their way back to the staging point, they saw Irish and Van leaning against their truck, eating hot dogs they had just cooked on one of the little grills. "Love those crazy bastards," she said, waving at the guy with dreadlocks, who was now talking with a young mother and her little girl down near the floodwaters. "Reginald!" she shouted to him. "Job well done. Again." He turned and waved at her in acknowledgment.

"Who is he?" Remy asked.

"Reg and his crew are from around here—Upper Nine. They are some of the Homeboys I told you guys about." She laughed. "That's the name they gave themselves," she said. "I wouldn't call them that."

Ava set the little dog down and offered him part of a hot dog Irish had given her. She ripped the bun into pieces and split that with him too. He was heartbreakingly hungry, inhaling the food with a sad desperation.

"Is there any rope around here?" Ava asked Van. He looked over to ask what she needed it for and saw the dog.

"Ah! Who do we have here?" He bent down and petted the dog. After some hesitation, the dog wagged his tail. "It's okay, little buddy. Let me see what we can find." He went back to his truck.

Ava and Remy sat down next to some of the Cajuns on a tiny piece of the embankment that wasn't already claimed. As she shifted on the ground, Ava felt the weight of the knife her uncle had given her. Like her cash, it was still taped under her clothes. The duct tape itched like hell after two days, but she was afraid if she adjusted it, it would lose its stickiness. She looked around and wondered who was armed. Some, probably off-duty law enforcement, had guns visible on their hips. But she was sure there were many with concealed weapons, guns or otherwise.

As night fell, they were backlit by the cameras of a nearby news crew. Across the embankment and up on I-10, the lights glared down on the crowds waiting to be evacuated, grouped here and there along St. Claude. A portable radio was playing somewhere, news updates with words so muffled Ava couldn't make them out. For a while people around her seemed too tired to talk. But eventually conversations started. Ava overheard two policemen from another parish talking about more ambulances coming from Texas.

"Every ambulance in New Orleans is underwater."

"Damn poor staging for an evac. Buses are all underwater too."

About five minutes later, some members of the Cajun Navy motored up, sweating, cursing, hauling their boats in, angry about a confrontation with some looters in the Upper 9th.

"We were starting to get worried about you guys," said Van, who had emerged from the truck with a length of rope for Ava to use as a leash. She took it gratefully from his hands and started to tie part of it into a collar. Her scruffy charge was curled up on the ground next to her, watching everyone with wary eyes.

"I saw some of them cruise right on past this old woman. Their boat was full of TVs, jewelry, all this shit. They went right on by that woman," one of the Cajuns said.

"Where is she?"

"Bobby picked her up," the Cajun said. "He came back earlier. She's already up at the I-10."

One of the Cajuns had somehow procured a portable generator and everyone rushed him to see if they could use it to recharge their cell phones.

As Ava and Remy sat with the dog, pouring water out of bottles into their hands for him to drink, Remy said, "We should go soon." Ava nodded. At that moment, Ellis and Erick walked up.

"Hey! We haven't seen you guys since last night," Remy said, his face brightening. "How're you holding up?"

"Ah, fine," they both said, almost in unison. "What about you guys?" Ellis asked.

"We're pretty good," Remy said. "We rescued eight more today."

"Nice," Ellis said and then punched Ava playfully on the shoulder. "Good job, cuz."

"What about you guys?" Ava asked. "What is it like over in Nine?"

Erick shook his head and said nothing. Ellis's bright eyes darkened. "Pretty damn bad over there," he said. He didn't say anything else.

Pretty soon the rescuers were sitting around telling stories—rumors they heard today, more looters they tangled with, and disturbing things they saw.

"I saw the biggest damn gator," Van said.

"Where?" Ava asked, thinking she would avoid that area at all costs.

"Right on up Magnolia," Van said. Only two streets away.

"It was just...swimming around?" Ava asked.

"What else did you expect it to be doing?" Remy laughed.

"I don't know. Eating someone?" Ava said.

"God forbid. Hey, Ellis," Remy said. "Remember when we went down to the camp after graduation?"

"Huh. Yeah. That was a wild weekend." Ellis laughed.

"Remember that big-ass bull gator?"

"Shit, yeah. The one that scared the hell out of me when I was...uh...taking a break?"

"That's why they invented indoor plumbing, man." Remy laughed. "Bet you never did that again."

"You bet right."

"You should be more worried about the rats," Irish said. "They're huge here, man. The big fat ones are the only ones that survived. They probably ate all the others. You shoulda seen the ones I saw down at the wharves. And God, the snakes."

"Snakes eat the rats," Ava pointed out. "So really, the snakes are your allies."

"Ava, you saw that big water moccasin in that last house we went to, right?" Remy asked.

"Which house?"

"The last one, you know, with the lady and her son?"

"Uh, no."

"Oh. Yes, actually I saw a nest of water moccasins. I mean like there was a big knot of them. All tangled up swimming together."

"I'm so glad I missed that," Ava said.

"We need this damn water to go down," Remy said. "Get the fucking snakes and gators and everybody else the hell out of here! They gotta get those pumps working."

Irish sat down next to the dog. Ava noticed the dark circles under her eyes. She must be, what, fifty years old? But she seemed more energetic than anyone else here. The beer had softened her a bit.

"Hell of a week, huh, Irish?" one of the Cajuns asked.

"I still can't believe all this shit. When we heard..." Irish said. "Just nothing, nothing seemed to be happening. Damn government at every level. So we decided to come down here, and we went down I-10, you know, and people knew what we were doing. I mean, there were dozens of boats speeding down the road. People were honking at us, waving, thumbs up and all that." She shook her head. "Didn't think we would have to be the ones doin' this."

Ava looked over at their motley flotilla. The camera lights seemed to underscore their names: *Acadiana, Cajun Love, Gone Fishin'*. All so predictable but somehow touchingly familiar.

Irish leaned back against her husband's knees and accepted a beer from him. Abita, not surprisingly. Ava remembered Remy drinking that in college. Every fall when school started again, he would show up with his car packed to the gills. Hidden underneath his comforter and clothes were always a few cases of Abita.

The volunteers were comparing battle wounds: scratches, mosquito bites, cuts and bruises. The conversation took a turn when people talked about who had accidentally swallowed the water and the effects on their intestinal tracts.

"We were coming in, and, you know, you start to see the damage, way outside the city. What the wind did to the sugarcane, man, it was flattened, the roofs just blown off, water in the road, and a houseboat sitting there, probably more than a mile from the water. What's funny is then we saw Walmart trucks heading toward the city, you know? A few other groups like ours. But mostly Walmart trucks. No FEMA, no army."

Ava had seen the trucks. They were dispensing food, water, diapers, and hand wipes.

"You know they told out-of-state emergency responders to stay out," Erick said.

Everyone turned to look at him.

"It's true. I have a colleague in Arizona; he's a trooper, and they were putting a group together, when they were told by FEMA that they were not allowed to enter the city," he said. "Don't get me wrong; he's here anyway. They came anyway. Because some of the responders here, like Fish and Wildlife, and some of the other troopers, they've looked the other way and let people in, but the word out there is that people should stay home and not come here. And we are talking qualified people, not—" he looked at Ava and Irish. "No offense, but not volunteers. Certified, experienced emergency responders."

"If they were handling it, if we had enough responders, I could understand that," Ellis said. "Like on nine-eleven. There was a saturation point. New York couldn't use the additional help. It was logistically too much. But this is different."

"Well, for starters, the NOPD has been a colossal failure," Remy said. Ellis and Erick said nothing. But then, cops don't badmouth fellow cops. But they didn't contradict him either.

Reg, one of the leaders of the Homeboys who had saluted Ava and Remy with his bottle of Red Stripe, nodded and said, "We went to this apartment building, right near the Desire projects. And there was some de facto guy in charge, some dude who lived there. The survivors, in some of these bigger buildings, have organized themselves, and they have leaders. And the leaders would try to get the Coast Guard to take everyone else or take their families and leave them behind. Well, this NOPD guy lived near there, and he had shown up and tried to get the Coasties or somebody to come take those people down outta that apartment building, and the Coasties gave him shit just because he was NOPD. I felt bad, but there's a reason why they gave him shit, right? So many other police took off or looted and whatever."

"So what happened to the NOPD guy?"

"Well, when the Coasties pointed us in that direction, by the time we got there, he had already sort of triaged everyone, and we all came and went back three, maybe four, times and got everyone out. But he didn't let us take him. He asked us to drop him off near his precinct station. His station, which is totally flooded, and there was nobody there, man. But we left him there. Don't know where he is now."

"Weren't you guys at the elementary school today?" Remy asked. Ava had heard this. A group of locals in the Lower 9 had sought refuge on the roof of a school; it was the tallest building in their neighborhood. A group of Homeboys from Treme and Bywater had gone out to the school and returned triumphant, boats brimming with more than a dozen survivors as well as a number of pets.

Reg nodded. "Yeah. A bunch of neighborhood folks were on the roof up there. Some of the homes around it were all washed away, but the school's pretty solid and high enough. Bad scene up there, though." He shook his head. "Wish we got there sooner." He didn't elaborate, and nobody asked him to.

At that moment, two officers from the Louisiana Department of Wildlife and Fisheries came over. They received a round of applause. Like the Coast Guard, these guys were seen in the trenches rescuing people from the beginning, and they were welcoming to the Good Samaritans who were trying to help.

Some of the Cajuns and Homeboys had pooled their resources together to grill some Andouille sausage and hot-dog buns that were too small. They brought some over to nearby isolated small groups of evacuees, although they were afraid to start some sort of crowd response that they wouldn't be able to control and a demand they couldn't accommodate, so they were somewhat clandestine about it. They saved some for the rescuers, and people started passing around paper plates with bite-sized servings of sausage.

"Don't you give yours to that dog now," Reg said to Ava as he passed the plate along to her. She laughed, but when nobody was paying attention, she split her share with the pup. Ava thought about Tiras and whether the two dogs would get along. But then she stopped herself. Maybe his owner was out here somewhere. Maybe they were in Houston. She asked around, but none of the rescuers had encountered people looking for a dog that matched his description. Unfortunately, many of them had seen many dead dogs and had tried to comfort people who had lost their pets. Some of the rescued had their pets with them on their roofs, and the Cajuns and the Homeboys all let them take their pets. What happened to the pets after that, they could not control. They were not allowed on the buses and were hopefully taken in by the ASPCA and other pet-rescue organizations that had been patrolling the same floodwaters that the Cajun Navy had.

Irish spread out a map on the ground in front of her. "More emergency responders are coming in," she said, "but we need to keep on doing what we are doing and stick to our grids to make sure we didn't miss anyone. So let's plan for tomorrow. Sunrise as usual." Remy looked at the map: his city and all its deeply wounded neighborhoods. Irish had slashed an "X" over areas that were already searched.

In a sad call and response, Irish named sections that had not yet been searched, and volunteers answered to claim each one in turn.

Chapter 25

Late Thursday Night
Vieux Carre, Downtown, and Uptown

Remy and Ava started their walk to Uptown at around 9:00 p.m. When Ellis heard their plan, he elected to join them; he didn't know the state of his parents' house either, and it was about time he went over to check on it. As they left the rescuers' camp and headed down the near-deserted city streets, they looked up to see bright pinpoints of pulsing light defying the ruin below.

"It's like back home," Ava said. "You can see every star." She was carrying the little dog; he seemed so exhausted. She had slung him into her backpack, leaving his head and front paws exposed while zipping it up enough that he wouldn't fall out.

"It's like Port Sulphur," Remy said, envisioning their fishing camp obliterated, part of the Gulf by now. *It always belonged to the Gulf,* he thought. As they walked west, past shotgun houses, creole cottages, stucco apartment buildings, and shuttered stores, everything was dark. The moon and the stars and the occasional lights of cars were the brightest sources of light except for the occasional building that seemed to have some light, thanks to working generators. They were quiet, nervous. Looking out for looters and trouble. Ava thought about how her aunt had tried to make Uncle Keenan and herself feel better by mentioning Ellis and how he was going to protect her. And here he was. It was strange to see him again all these years later. She remembered Ellis and his parents being there when her dad was showing her around his childhood home. Those summers of family trips. Getting Sno balls and eating dinner in the Quarter. Burning asphalt and the cool grass under the oaks in her grandparents' yard. Walking barefoot, she'd have to watch out for fire ants.

Ava still thought of Ellis as the friendly, joking little boy who tried to cheer her up by scaring her with frogs and bugs. Now he was a grown man, tall and authoritative, walking his cop's walk, his shoulders broad, his eyes alert. Ava noticed his hand was hovering near his holster.

"I wonder how long it is going to take to put all this right again," Ava said.

"I don't know if we can," Remy said.

The dog moved in Ava's backpack. She reached around to pat his little head.

"It's okay, buddy," she said.

"That dog needs a name," Ellis said. "And he's probably hot in there. You should let him walk."

"He's exhausted," Ava said. She had tried to get him to walk along with her, but he kept stopping and lying down. Lord knows how many hours he had been wading for his life when she found him.

At that point they passed a plaque in front of a neighborhood store. It had a small bronze likeness of Louis Armstrong, a long-ago patron.

"Louis," Ava said.

"Perfect," Ellis said and laughed. "He's a true son of New Orleans."

Helicopters flashed by, news choppers or rescuers, braving the sniper rumors. By now some real news had trickled back to them. No, a gang of black men had not taken over the Children's Hospital. No, there were not scores of dead people at the Superdome. Two were reportedly murdered or had committed suicide, not nearly as many as everyone thought two days ago.

Moments later, crossing a street under a blinking, ghostly traffic light, they were startled by a shout, a scream, a gunshot. Ellis unholstered his pistol and, in one quick movement, darted forward and looked in every direction. But they saw no one and did not know where that sound was coming from.

Ava pulled her increasingly greasy black hair into a ponytail. The night brought little relief from the heat. She reached down to scratch a welt from one of the many mosquito bites she had. A mosquito got to her overnight; despite the wealth of dragonflies, mosquitoes were everywhere. The undersides of Ava's arms were marked with bites that had turned into welts.

"What was Lower Nine like today?" Remy asked Ellis.

Ellis shook his head. "We helped evacuate this little church, little neighbor-hood congregation. Erick's wife's uncle was the pastor there, before the storm. His daughter was about to have her baby up in Jackson, so he evacuated and went to stay with her. Well, the baby was born on Monday, and by Tuesday night he was back here; you know, he wanted to help the folks in the neighborhood, and now his nephews are dead, and the secretary who had been working for him for twenty-five years is dead. We went around with him to all the houses he hadn't gotten to yet. He had a little pirogue he scrounged up from somewhere, and he was going house to house. We got the Coasties to help out, and they evac'd the ones that they could drop a basket to."

"Those guys are something, huh?" Ava said. She had been watching them drop those baskets around the 8th Ward too and sending guys down to pluck people off roofs. It was no joke piloting a helicopter that close to a roof with all the obstacles—especially dangling power lines—around.

"Yeah. Those guys are killing it. I met one back at the drop-off point. He lost his house too."

At that moment Remy's phone rang. He looked at it, incredulous.

"I have had no reception the whole time I've been here," he says. "But, of course, she can get through." He flipped it open.

"Momma—"

Ava and Ellis heard his mother on the other end, frantic with worry.

"No, no, no, I'm safe. I'm with a bunch of people," Remy said. He started to talk several times but was interrupted by parental concern.

"I'm on my way to Dad's now," he said. "No...no, I think that's a rumor, Momma. Yes, I'm safe. No, that's just what they are saying on TV."

While Remy tried to calm his mother, Ellis turned to Ava.

"Speaking of moms, Ava, I meant to talk to you after your mom died. I know I just sent an e-mail and that was lame. I meant to get back in touch more."

Ava nodded. "I know. Me too. How are your brother and sister?"

Ellis said, "Everyone's doing pretty good, you know, considering all this. Dad is up in Alaska right now, doing some crazy bucket-list trip, and James is with him. I think he's going to hike to see bears or something. Just nuts as usual. And Mom is doing some sort of ladies' trip with her college friends, since she doesn't want to be a part of that insanity. I'm just glad they're not here. I guess I'm the nut now."

Ava laughed. Her uncle Alex was always the family daredevil. His wife, Tess, was the cautious one. Ava's other cousins, Ellis's brother and sister, James and Cecilia, were always up to some shenanigans with their father or their friends. Ellis was definitely the straitlaced boy in the family. Her uncle always had a lot of crazy stories about nearly getting arrested or running into celebrities and embarrassing himself. She remembered her father and grandparents laughing at him, always prodding him to tell another one.

"How is Cecilia?" Ava asked. Cecilia was Ellis's sister. Ava had dim memories of her father talking to her mother about how he worried about how his parents treated Ellis and his siblings, all half Creole. New Orleans had a long, long history of interracial relations that were illegal, yet they were an ever-present product of a cruel and violent system that made black women the targets of white men who had power over them. When she was growing up, she could tell her grandparents did not understand why their son would marry a woman who was not white. They had that in common with her mother's father.

"Ah, she's great. At college, thankfully. I'd worry if she were home right now."

Something about the sadness on Ava's face made Ellis hesitate before talking more about family. It was a sadness she didn't realize was showing.

They both turned at the sound of Remy's rising voice. "I love you, Momma, but I gotta go. I'm fine, okay? I'll let you know when I'm with Dad." He hung up and rolled his eyes.

"She hasn't heard anything from your dad?"

"No. But she heard from one neighbor although they didn't talk long. He said they're worried about looters. He's got the guns out."

Now they were walking through the Quarter. There was so much dry ground here that it seemed almost like a different city.

"So Lower Nine is as bad as they say?" Remy asked Ellis, wanting to see if he missed anything important while he was trying to calm his mother down.

"Yeah. The worst was the nursing home," Ellis said. He and Erick, after helping the preacher all morning, had headed over to St. Anthony's Nursing Home.

"There were a lot of bodies along the way," Ellis said. He could still see them in his mind's eye. They were tangled in debris, trapped in the logjams of splintered houses. He had seen a lot of bodies in his line of work, but this was different. Too many at the same time, caught in the flood without an ark to save them.

"It was next to a church." He didn't describe it to them, but he remembered the brick church, beautiful stained glass broken out in places, the statue of St. Anthony upended, headless. As he and Erick had rounded the corner behind the church, motoring toward the entrance of the nursing home, they could smell it. Death. Then they saw the sign, twisted, floating.

"It was a three-story building; the first two stories were underwater. You know how it is around here. The land rises and falls in spots, and you can have one house that is completely submerged and another down the street that has a dry second floor. But here it was a low patch, because almost two whole stories were swamped. And then on the third story, the windows were all broken open. Some had sheets hanging out." He remembered how the sheets would rise and fall in the wind. The stench.

"Then we heard this moaning," Ellis said. He would never forget the sound of it.

"We tied the boats to a fire-escape railing, and there was just...trash and debris floating around. We went right into the stairwell, and already there were four bodies. And there were snakes and rats. All dead. There wasn't a single staff member there. All those folks were abandoned." He remembered thinking, *These are somebody's parents, somebody's grandparents, lying there exposed to the summer heat.* Open eyes, suffering eyes, creased faces and oxygen tanks, stained and faded hospital gowns. These people didn't drown. At least, the ones on the third floor didn't. They died of heat exhaustion, dehydration, maybe heart attacks or strokes. They survived the flood but not the aftermath.

Ava thought about the stories her father told describing Hurricane Betsy and how it ravaged parts of the city. Some of the same neighborhoods that had been ravaged this week.

Ellis continued, saying, "We're still looking for this moaning, right? Then we head down the hallway and look in every room, and there were just bodies, bodies on beds, in wheelchairs..." He remembered a torn powder-blue cotton robe. He remembered the ruined, plaid-print furniture. Some faces turned toward him, distorted; an elderly black man, an elderly black woman. Hands curled into fists, faces with creased cheeks.

"We kept looking. More dead. These little resident bedrooms, you know, so sad." They were really just hospital rooms with a few personal touches like a photograph of a grandchild or a hand-crocheted blanket over a chair. The heartbreaking vestiges of a life on this earth: seventy-five years. Ninety years. And left like this, discarded, abandoned to the water and the heat. In some rooms there were solitary patient bodies. One old man slouched, as if he had just fallen asleep waiting for his next meal. A silver cross was in his hand.

"So did you find someone?" Ava asked, hoping for a little miracle.

Ellis shook his head. "No," he said. "The moaning was a woman crying. She had come over in a rowboat, looking to rescue her mother."

"I need a fucking drink," Remy said.

"Let's get one," Ellis said. "For the road."

"Just a really quick one," Remy said. "I need to get to Dad's."

"Where on earth are we going to get a drink?" Ava asked, thinking all the bars were closed. But as they walked through the Vieux Carre, she realized a couple of places were open, including Johnny White's. They made a beeline for it. As they headed for the open door, they saw rats scurrying in and out of holes under the building, poking at trash.

As they walked in, Ava and Remy wondered at the supply of ice and beer.

"Connections," said Ellis, "and donations."

The bar was packed. Above the bartender there was a row of twinkling white Christmas lights. It smelled like sweat and stale, spilt beer. Off-duty cops, out-of-town volunteers, and very drunk locals hunched over the bar. The bartender, whose job was currently limited to handing out beers from coolers and acting as de facto bouncer, was a generously tattooed man who looked as though he had experienced some rough living. He wiped his face with a kerchief he had tied around his neck. It was hotter here than outside, with the claustrophobic old wood walls and the body heat; the generator in the corner was saved for the coolers and the meager lighting. The fan hung motionless from the old tin-covered ceiling.

"Only two beers per person," he said. "And the dog doesn't get one."

"Anything harder than this?" Remy asked.

"Nope. Ran out of liquor two days ago."

They accepted the Abitas and clinked bottles. Ava asked if there was any water. The bartender charged her ten dollars for a small bottle of Poland Spring. She raised an eyebrow, but he shrugged. Supply and demand. She asked for a glass, and he said, "Dishwasher ain't running, so we're sticking with the bottles." She explained it was so she could give her dog some water.

"Ah," the bartender said, his demeanor softening. He pulled a glass out from under the bar and handed it to her.

Ava took Louis out of her backpack and set him on the floor. He still had the crude rope leash. She set the glass in front of him. He drank most of it, his tail wagging faintly.

They looked around at some of the specimens around the bar. A little apocalyptic flooding will not stop some people from drinking. And it will certainly drive others to drink more.

Ellis and Remy saw someone they knew and went over to give bear hugs to the guy.

Ava asked the bartender if his house was spared.

"Nope. My place is flooded. I live in Treme," he said. "It's a small apartment building; just a few units. Earlier this week I could come and go, you know, and I was trying to take care of business, my neighbors. There's an old lady who lives next to me, and I had to help her out, you know? I don't know if they got her out because it was too hot in there, man. But when I went back to check on her, they wouldn't let me in. I'm sleeping in the back of the bar. Not that I'm sleeping much. I got a shotgun next to me all night. You know, looters."

Ava remembered the guys she and Remy had seen out in the water.

"I'm sorry to hear about your apartment. Can I ask you something about Treme?" Ava said. The bartender nodded.

"You know that old Opera House? The one Hamilton designed?"

The bartender looked puzzled. "Alexander Hamilton? The president?"

"No...he wasn't...I mean, no, not that Hamilton. Benjamin Hamilton."

The bartender shook his head. "Never heard of him. But do you mean that old Opera House that they're restoring?"

Ava's heart jumped. They're restoring it. Her father would have been thrilled. Even when he was studying it, they were talking about how it needed so much work that it was doubtful it would be saved.

"Oh yeah, that's sitting in about five feet of water," he said. "It's a goner."

Ava nodded and looked away. She bit the inside of her lip and took a deep breath to stop the tears. How disappointed he would be.

Remy and Ellis came back and leaned against the bar next to Ava. They had downed their beers and asked the bartender for their second rounds, which they would take out the door with them. While they were waiting to pay, the three of them struck up a conversation with a pair of firefighters from Arizona. When the firefighters found out Ava was from Maine, they gave her high fives.

"Yes! We're not the only ones who drove thousands of miles to join this shitshow," said one of them, a tall, bald African American with a neatly kept mustache.

"It is indeed a shitshow," said Remy.

"Cholera. Fucking *chol-er-a*," one of the locals, who was eavesdropping and clearly had exceeded the two-drink limit, said to them. "This water," she said, gesturing in the general direction of the floodwaters, "is a public health crisis. We've already got reports of dysentery, fever. There are a billion mosquitoes breeding out there. We need to worry about *cholera* now. God."

"She's a public health nurse," said one of the firefighters. He clinked bottles with her.

"Yeah, fucking cholera, man."

"How very eighteenth century," Remy said.

They used to have sick ships back then. Nothing to do for you except hope you miraculously pull through. But in the meantime, quarantine. Any undesirable island off the coast might be used for smallpox victims or those with malaria, diphtheria, and cholera. The unwanted, the people you were scared of. Left to die on barren islands or on quarantined ships, never allowed into port. Surrounded by water with no way to get to land.

The French explorers who came upon and named New Orleans, who fell sick and died, were felled by disease-bearing mosquitoes, just like the American

Indians, who used to hunt and fish in East Tamarack, were nearly wiped out by smallpox and the other diseases the Europeans brought with them.

The three of them paid the bartender and started to make their way out of the Quarter. As they passed each neighborhood and many of the city's well-known, world-class restaurants, there was a sickening stench of rotting food that punched through the air and assaulted their senses. Debris in the streets, generator lights near Jackson Square, the statue of that famous and infamous president still partially in shadow, his horse rearing near semiorganized piles of tree branches and trash. They passed knots of people gathered in shadows—locals, sane and insane, talking to reporters, rescuers from near and far like themselves.

"Remember that time when you came to visit one summer in high school and we went on that ghost tour?" Ellis asked Ava as they walked.

"I do," she said. "I remember that story about the surgeon who tortured his slaves. So gruesome."

"I remember that too. All these pretty townhouses and mansions and all these sick, twisted stories behind them."

"Well, who knows how many of them are true," Ava said. "Could just be rumor or folklore passed down."

"I don't know," Remy said. "This city has some deeply disturbed folks. That undercurrent of magic and witchcraft and voodoo. There are people here who think they are vampires. Actually think that."

"I used to think that was just an old wives' tale, but it's true," Ellis said. "I have run across some pretty twisted people on the job here. I don't doubt they do things in their basements that will someday make the ghost tour itinerary."

Ava thought about how she had come here with her parents so many times, exploring the kitschy tourist shops that a little girl took very seriously. And people looked mysterious here too. People who sold cloudy vials, small bottles of hot sauce with raunchy labels, and musty voodoo dolls. And folk art: tiny farmers and tiny jazz musicians with blank faces.

At the edges of the CBD, that neighborhood that always conjured up for Ava the chain hotels and convention crowds, the water began to encroach again; there were looters on Canal Street, which was now living up to its name. There were stores with their front windows busted in. Every once in a while they would hear another shout, but the streets were quiet overall. Commercial buildings gave way to more and more homes as they made their way through the edges of the CBD and into the Garden District. As the streets got quieter and quieter, Ellis put his gun back in its holster.

After they had walked for a while, Ellis said, "I'm thinking most of the rumors we have been hearing are complete bullshit." The streets were not filled with rampaging looters robbing the rich folk. No gangs, no mansions going up in flames. The neighborhood was nearly deserted. In the dark, with most of the city without power, the stars shone with a painful and prehistoric brightness. They looked up and were reminded that those ancient lights would burn long after all of what was left had been washed away.

Ava put her hand on her belly, feeling the knife she still had strapped to her. She had loosened the tape enough so that she felt she could pull it out easily; plus it was really itching, so she had to loosen it so it didn't drive her crazy. She would just need to slip her hand up and under her shirt. But now, in this neighborhood, it felt silly and paranoid to have it so handy.

The Garden District had always seemed eerie in a proper, genteel way; while it didn't have the obviously rough history of some other neighborhoods with their red light and pirate pasts, many of its storied families had built their fortunes on human toil. Indeed, it was basically founded by whites who did not want to live side by side with the Creoles and who maintained that boundary long after the South lost the war. This was an undercurrent that hadn't escaped Ellis's Creole mother.

And this was part of the darkness of New Orleans despite its penchant for celebrating life. It was right there under the noses of the tourists at the French Market, where human beings were once sold as chattel and in Congo Square, where slaves had once gathered on Sundays. It was in the tombs of the cholera victims or the long-dead orphans of the Ursuline Convent. But in the Garden District, with its lovely homes and stately trees, its iconic streetcars and well-loved bookstores, its family-friendly Mardi Gras gatherings, there was still more of the Magnolia and Moonlight South—the South that Ava's grandparents had believed in and her father was troubled by, the South that dressed well and called you "ma'am" and "sir" and was ever so hospitable but did not talk about or acknowledge the violence that permeated every particle of red soil and Mississippi mud.

The Garden District was almost completely spared from flooding, but wind damage was everywhere: trees lying on crushed porch roofs or uprooted in grand backyards and shingles blown off and strewn across roofs covered with small branches. They saw plastic bags caught on road signs, pieces of roofing tile in the gutters, and electrical cables coiled like snakes on the street. The houses were mostly dark, but here and there they were lit, and a few of them were guarded by old white men sitting on their porches, guns on their laps. At one grand dame home with an ornate Victorian facade, striking white columns, and wrought-iron fences with points shaped like tulips, there were two black SUVs with black-uniformed men standing around the grounds, well armed.

"Holy shit, those are the Mossad guys," Remy said. "Remember? We saw them when we first got here."

Ava nodded, open-mouthed. "Wow. Yeah, that's them."

"They're not Mossad," Ellis said, laughing. "But you're close. Some of them might be ex-Mossad. A few homeowners around here hired some ex-Israeli military to guard their property."

"Wow. That's…" Remy started to say. He shook his head.

"We could use their expertise elsewhere in this city right now," Ava finished.

"Who even knew that you could hire people like that for something like this?" Remy asked.

"Private contractors, man," Ellis said. "They fight wars now, so why not this."

They made their way into Uptown. These streets were just as abandoned and windblown, but they had an aching familiarity for all three of them. Home.

Suddenly someone was shouting at them. His voice was gravelly, threatening.

"Who the fuck goes there?" The voice was coming from a yellow house with peeling paint. "I have a fucking gun, and I have already used it twice tonight," the man added.

"Mr. Fouche! It's Remy! Remy Devereaux."

"Remy?"

"Yes, sir. I'm here to check on my dad."

"Oh. Well, then go ahead, Remy. Sorry about that, son. He's home."

They walked down the block to a white house with a matching carriage house. They followed along the brick path to the front door, stepping on downed branches as they went. Remy started to reach into his pocket and paused.

"I don't have my fucking keys," Remy said. "I just realized. They're in Maryland."

"It's okay," Ellis said. "He's in there." He nodded toward the parlor window. They could see a faint light moving around. They heard a dog barking.

"Dad!" Remy yelled. "Dad! Are you okay?" He knocked on the door. The three of them stood on the porch waiting for his father to emerge.

Ava looked around. She vaguely remembered this place from the one time during college she had visited her father's family. The last time she had been here until this week. It was strange that Remy had lived so close—just a few streets away—from where her father and Ellis had grown up. What she could see of the house in the darkness looked stately and gorgeous, white with plantation shutters, hand-carved columns on the front porch, the painting of some Acadian ancestor visible from the parlor window.

"Son?" Remy's father opened the door a crack. From where she was standing, Ava could clearly see that he had a long-barrel shotgun cradled in his arm. A brown-and-white springer spaniel pushed his way around Mr. Devereaux and tried to nose the door open.

"Dad! You okay?" Remy asked, bending down to greet the dog, Porter, who went up to Louis to exchange dog greetings.

His father opened the door all the way. Ava hadn't seen him since her college graduation. His wavy hair was completely gray, and he had a bit of a beer gut now. He wore a polo shirt and khaki shorts. He was a head shorter than his son. They hugged briefly, and he ushered them inside.

"What in the goddamn hell are you doing here, son?" Ava realized that Remy's penchant for swearing was a family trait. "You shouldn't be here!"

"I came down to help out. And I wanted to check on you," Remy said. He bent down to pet the dog, whose tail started wagging furiously again.

"Who have we got here? Ellis!" Mr. Devereaux said.

"Hello, sir," Ellis said. Remy's father clapped him on the shoulder. Mr. Devereaux noticed Ava hanging back.

"Young lady!" he said. "You shouldn't be here either," he scolded. Ava could tell he couldn't remember her name.

"You remember Ava," Remy said helpfully, pulling her forward.

His father nodded. "From Bowdoin," he said.

"Yep. She drove down from Maine to help out," Remy said. Ava was touched to see that he was proud of that.

"Well, you shouldn't be here," Remy's father said again with the sternness most fathers would display in such a situation. "It's not safe, especially for women. White women, most of all," he said.

There it was. Ava cringed and couldn't help but look at Ellis's face, but he had a blank expression. He had a lot of practice ignoring this kind of thing since his mother had married into it, and he encountered it often on the job.

"Have you had any intruders?" Ellis asked, still in cop mode.

Mr. Devereaux said, "They're out there! I can hear people skulking around at night. You know it's awful quiet out there. But they probably know that Bobby—" that was Mr. Fouche "—and I are pretty well armed."

"How are you, son?" He turned to Remy.

"I'm okay, Dad. We couldn't get ahold of you. Momma has been pretty panicked."

"Yeah, I'm afraid I can't find my damn cell phone," Mr. Devereaux said. "The landlines ain't working on this street either. So I haven't been able to call your mother. I am sure she's pretty worked up."

"Yeah, after five days of trying to reach you and panicking," Remy said. His father sighed.

"I know. I shoulda come back from the camp sooner. But you know, I'm glad I'm here to look after the house."

"You sure there hasn't been any incidents? We've heard a lot of rumors," Ellis said.

"Well, like I said, I've seen some folks skulking around. They might have caused trouble in other parts of the neighborhood, but I haven't heard anything. And there are a few old-timers like me around, so we've been comparing notes."

"You know, I did hear the hardware store got looted," Mr. Devereaux continued. "You might want to check that out."

Ellis nodded. This was old news. "I think they're on it," he said.

"Well, I would offer y'all something to drink, but…" Mr. Devereaux looked sheepish. "I'm a little low."

"Been hitting the bottle a bit, Daddy?" Remy asked, eyebrow raised.

"It's been a long week, son," his father replied.

Chapter 26

Thursday Night and Friday Morning

Uptown

They ate up some of the canned goods Remy's father had found after rummaging through the pantry. He offered Louis some of Porter's dog food. The two dogs became fast friends, and Louis was soon curled up next to Porter snoring.

Remy handed his father his cell phone so he could try to call Remy's mother. They couldn't get a signal. "She'll call again," Remy said. He and his father laughed.

"Yes, about a million times, I'm sure, if that's what it takes," Mr. Devereaux said.

After a meager snack of crackers, peanut butter, and Slim Jims ("The cupboard's pretty bare," Mr. Devereaux said), they sat around a coffee table with a small array of candles lighting the room. Remy's father talked about how the neighbors were doing and people they knew who had lost their homes. People he hadn't heard from and was worried about. That so-and-so had stayed. That this couple or that couple had left town and evacuated with their kids. How Mr. Aucoin and his son had taken their boat down to the water and were out there somewhere, rescuing people. Finally Ava and Ellis excused themselves; they were bone tired. Remy was, too, but he was so relieved and happy that he stayed up well into the night, talking to his dad. At one point in the wee morning hours, they were able to get through to Remy's mother, who cried with relief at hearing the voices of her husband and son together and safe.

That night they slept in beds, which felt like a luxury now. Louis eventually tired of hanging out with Porter and slept at Ava's feet. Everything was calm and quiet. They were up before first light the next morning, even Remy who had barely slept. All three of them were anxious to get back out there, and Ellis and Ava were itching to check on their family homes. Remy's dad saw them off with what was left of his Slim Jims and some first-aid supplies he kept in the medicine cabinet of one of the downstairs bathrooms. Ava gratefully accepted a Ziploc bag of dog food for Louis to get him through the next couple of days.

"Be careful, son," he said as they were leaving, their backpacks repacked and Louis back on his leash. "Don't push your luck."

First they went to Ellis's parent's house, which was a stone's throw from the Devereaux house. It was in good shape, with only a few downed branches and palm fronds in the yard. His parents had pulled all the shutters closed when they had left for their respective vacations, before anyone knew that the storm was going to revive after Florida and gear up for another assault. Ellis walked through the property, checking behind every door inside, making sure everything was in its place. Ellis pulled some branches off the porch and locked the house back up.

Next they checked on their grandparents' house—the house where they had met all those years ago—as Remy tagged along.

Her father's house. *Daddy, I'm here*, she thought. It was undamaged, save for a few large branches in the yard and a broken storm door on the side of the house. It had been so long since she'd seen it that Ava was surprised at how small it looked. It wasn't small; it was a grand Victorian, like Remy's father's house. But it had seemed so much grander and then so much emptier when she was a child. Whoever lived there now—it was no longer in the family—had let it get a bit careworn, with paint peeling from the trim in some places and a neglected garden taking over the backyard where she had once sat and read her books.

It seemed like nobody was home. Ellis and Ava stood at the edge of the yard, looking down at a couple of large tree branches that lay scattered and splintered as if a small bomb had gone off. There were a few shingles askew, but the ancient oak tree, the tree she remembered sitting under for hours until her cousin got her to go bike on the levees with him, the tree her grandmother said had been there since before the French founded New Orleans, was still standing.

Standing there, Ava imagined her father, allowed by Fate to grow old, coming home to see that the storm—or rather, the Mississippi river levees, the levees that did not fail as the lake and MR-GO levees did—had spared this house. She thought of him in this house as a child and visiting it as the old man he never had the opportunity to be. She thought of him in his Maine house, his pre-Nor'easter preparations and her grandfather Noah mocking him. As a kid she had imagined the former inhabitants of both of her parents' houses, women in empire-waist gowns with bonnets or in hoop skirts or with tall boots and suffragette hats and men with stovepipe hats and striped waistcoats. Northerners and southerners. She tried not to think that her parents had joined that ghostly ledger of former residents.

The morning light was starting to brighten as they walked back out of the neighborhood, back toward the Garden District. As they passed a mansion with lights on the inside and a lawn that had already been cleared, Ava was startled when a man emerged out of the shadows near the gates, close to where they were standing.

"Frisk them," the man said, his voice accented and gravelly. Ava, Remy, and Ellis whipped around to see six more men. Before she could register what was happening, her face was on the pavement, scratched and burning.

"What the fuck?!" Remy was saying.

Ellis said, "I am a cop! I am a cop! Let me show you my badge! Let me show you my badge, man," but they told him to shut up, and he was on the pavement too, and the badge he had pulled from his pocket flew from his hand and into the street as he was grabbed and thrown on the ground.

Remy started to say something but then thought better of it. All three of them were frisked. Ava's backpack was ripped off her shoulders, and Louis's leash was ripped from her hands. He yelped.

"Hey! My dog! Don't hurt my dog!" she said, her voice surging with anger and fear, but Louis had already backed away and ran down the street. Ava lifted her head to shout "Louis! Hey!" although she realized as she shouted that he didn't know his name yet. Or she didn't know his, if he already had one. Shit. How was she ever going to find him? "Louis!" she shouted again, not knowing what else to shout. "It's okay, boy! It's okay." But he knew it wasn't okay, and he disappeared down the street.

Now the man who had forced her to the pavement frisked her, pushing her harder against the pavement. He felt along her sides and back for a pistol. He turned her on her side and patted her stomach but patted where there was no tape, so he did not realize she had a knife. As he pulled her up by her elbows, she prayed her shirt would hang down enough to cover the knife, and it did.

"Hey! Leave her alone!" Ellis said. "She's not armed! She's not armed!" he said. Ava realized she never told him about the knife; it hadn't come up.

Ava realized: these guys thought they were looters. Here they were, three people with backpacks, roaming around the Garden District when the sun was barely up.

"She's unarmed," the man who had frisked her reported to the guy who had stepped out in front of them, who seemed to be his superior.

"I'm a State cop!" Ellis was saying.

"I'm from this neighborhood! We were just visiting my father! He lives in Uptown!" Remy tried to explain.

"Shut up!" said the man in charge. "You don't know how many fucking bullshit stories we have heard from assholes like you." For the first time, Ava got a good look at him. He was dressed all in black: black T-shirt, black military-style pants that billowed around the tops of his black combat boots.

"This dude's armed," said a thick-necked, deep-voiced man with an accent, who was hovering over Ellis. He expertly removed the gun from its holster; clearly he knew enough to disable the holster lock.

"I told you, I'm a cop!" Ellis said. A note of frustration crept into his voice, but at the same time, Ava could tell he was trying to keep his cool. It didn't escape his attention that all the men surrounding them were white.

"Take these two jokers down to the school," the guy in charge said. "The cops there can decide what to do with them." Remy and Ellis were handcuffed, protesting but cautious about protesting too hard with guns in their faces. At the mention of other cops, Ellis was silent. *They'll tell these assholes what a mistake they are making*, Ava thought.

Ava watched as the men left, dragging Remy and Ellis by their hands to a van parked in the driveway. She turned to the guy who seemed to be in charge.

"Who are you? You're not cops! You can't just take people!"

"Listen, lady," the guy in charge said. "Fuck off." And he slammed the door shut on the van and gave it a knock, and the men drove away.

Chapter 27

Friday Morning

St. Liberatus

When it comes to rescues, we are zero for three now. I am sitting in the dark call room, taking a rare five-minute break, slowly sipping a bottle of water I picked up from the roof. The water is warm. I am hot. It is early, and there is just a hint of light outside. At the staff meeting last night, we decided we would start swimming for it today. We'll encourage the able-bodied to go out there and fend for themselves. The doctors and nurses will stay with the patients who can't be moved without a proper evacuation. We haven't shared this news yet, but we will as soon as it's light. There is no sense in waiting another day for a rescue that won't happen.

Marius walks in, flashlight at his side; he has been lifting diabetic patients for their insulin shots.

"We're officially out of antibacterial gel," he says. "Every floor."

Now we have nothing to try to keep our patients clean. They have some baby wipes left in the NICU, but those are for the babies, the most susceptible of all.

"There's another fight," Judah says, coming in to give me updates. "Up in the OR."

"Nerves? Or withdrawal?" I ask.

"Withdrawal, looks like," he says. The addicts are getting more and more desperate and sick. All our remaining meds are under lock and key and watched 24-7 by multiple security guards. Most of Judah's security team has been focused on this problem. We have had a few people who are frustrated that they can't get drugs in a hospital, start fights, threaten staff and their own family members they are here with, and, in a few cases, wander off into the water. It's better if they leave, and it's one of the reasons why we are going to try to encourage the able-bodied to swim for it if they can. We might be endangering some people… hell. Who am I kidding? We're endangering everybody. That water is a disastrous stew of God knows what kind of chemicals, oil, sewage, hazardous trash, snakes, dead animals…dead people. But we won't force anyone to leave, of course, and certainly will tell people who can't swim to stay put. And besides, we must pro-tect the most vulnerable among us. Addicts in withdrawal will do desperate and terrible things, so the more people leave, the fewer potential troublemakers we have left.

"Judah up there?" I ask.

Tennant nods. "But he'll be coming to the meeting in a few minutes."

I think, as I have many times since this ordeal began, that Judah has the toughest job of all in this hospital right now.

At our first check-in meeting of the morning, I look out at the faces of our traumatized staff. I think back to our hurricane party, which seems years ago now. Everyone was happy and only the tiniest bit nervous about what was com-ing. Then the relief we all felt on Monday was shattered hours later. And here we are.

In the early morning hours, we lost two more patients. Both were elderly, and their bodies could not take this heat. Our death toll is now up to seven. Seven patients gone.

At the meeting, Judah announces that three more people decided to swim for home in the early hours. One guy did not get very far, not being a strong swimmer, and flailed his way back toward the building and was subsequently rescued; the other two we hope got to safety, but we have no way of knowing.

We talk about the sorry state of the stairwells (another public-health disaster) and the hallways, the waiting rooms, and the patient rooms. We talk about what to do with the corpses in the chapel.

"This poor old place…" says Susan Robertson, with more emotion than I have ever seen her display in all the years we've worked here together. "It's just tough to see it like this."

It was never a grand old hospital. It is a workhorse for working people. But it used to have dignity and professionalism and a solid presence in this neighborhood. Now it is an unsanitary hellhole.

Before I wrap up the meeting, Arlene announces, with much hesitation and doubt, that her husband, Jerry, who must be the last working NOPD officer in the city based on the rumors we have heard, said we are all going to be evacuated soon. Really, he said. They are coming for you guys tomorrow. He said Tulane had already been evacuated and we were next on the list. When they were evacuating Tulane, he had asked about us specifically and tried, she said, "for the hundredth time" to get military folks over here to pick up our patients. And he talked to a FEMA contact, someone who was "in touch with higher ups" as Arlene put it, and that person said all the hospitals would be empty by Friday afternoon.

"Who's actually coming? FEMA or National Guard?" asks Jain, who had not been able to get back in touch with her mysterious caller yet. Jain never wrote the number down, so we couldn't try the contact on someone else's phone. She kept hoping her earlier assertions about a rescue would be proven true, but that was a lifetime ago now. So much happens in one day here.

"No," Arlene said. "Well, I'm not sure, but I think he said it was FEMA. FEMA's coming."

I'm too cautious to feel relief. We've been burned too many times, and we are working on our own plan anyway.

At the rate we are going, we will run out of food and water tonight.

"Well, that is the best darn news I've heard in days," says Osgood, his ruddy cheeks rounding into a smile. "Finally."

I drum my fingers on the tabletop. "Okay, guys, to be honest, I don't want to waste a lot of time on this. We went through this a few times earlier, and we should be focused on our backup plan. If they show up, fantastic. So let's go to each person, each family member, and see who might be able to make a swim for it. Let's just start getting whomever we can get out of this hospital. At this point, I hate to say it, but if they are ambulatory, they might have a better chance out there at this point. If people want to try to use some of the wood we used on the windows, if they can scrounge that up and it floats, all the better. Housekeeping can help try to jury rig some small rafts together or at least something to hang onto."

I lean back in my chair. "But just remember...I know—believe me—that we all want to get the hell out of here...but remember if FEMA or whoever the hell it is this time *is* coming tomorrow, they can work with us and whatever evac plan we feel comfortable with. We'll still be in charge of these patients. We're still not handing our patients over to untrained nonmedical personnel. Do they even have medical personnel? Anyway, it doesn't matter. *Our* patients, *our* responsibility."

Jain, who has had this conversation with me before, counters, "That's not protocol. I was the chair of Emergency Preparedness last year, and I remember exactly what Waters said when we had the drill—we are to stand down once FEMA arrives." She's challenging me in front of everyone because she's still annoyed about what happened earlier.

I feel my muscles tensing. "Are these physicians that FEMA is sending? And are they experienced with critical-care patients like ours? They don't know these patients. *We* know these patients."

I go on to say, "Since I am the Emergency Incident Commander, I'll be the liaison with the FEMA folks when they get here. But I just wanted everyone to have the appropriate expectations."

"Sorry," Tennant says, entering the room with his hand raised, looking at me.

"What's up?" Against my will, I'm finding myself attached to this hard-working, earnest intern. I feel bad for him, because I'm not sure he'll make it. I sometimes hate him, because he makes me feel old, but I also remember so well what it felt like to be in his position.

"Andy," he says.

"Okay," I say, getting up. "Meeting over," I say to everyone else, stating the obvious.

I quickly follow Tennant down the hall toward the limited bank of windows at the end near Andy's room.

"How are we doing?"

I know the answer. Natalie is bagging him now, and another nurse stands next to her, ready to take over.

Andy's mother looks at me, and I think of our conversation earlier. Andy's breathing is labored. His legs are horribly swollen, his abdomen distended. He is clearly in severe kidney failure, and I have really no therapies to work with. Any hour now, any minute, his dialysis machine will cease to work. If his nephrologist had advice, I haven't heard it, because she hasn't been able to get through. I presume she has been trying to reach us along with hundreds of others.

I excuse myself to confer with Tennant for a moment. Osgood appears behind her.

"We're going to lose him if we don't get him out of here soon," I say. Tennant looks grave and says nothing.

"There is literally nothing else we can do for him. He needs to be on a respirator, and he needs to have fluids drained, and he needs a new damn kidney. Or two."

Osgood looks at me, but I know he won't go there. Not with this patient who is just a kid. I walk down to the nurses' station, where his mother can't hear me, and ask if anyone has a cell phone. I have lost track of mine, so I am begging a phone off somebody every few hours when I take my turn at trying to reach help. Someone is always on a phone or trying to get online on our call-room computer that is slowly losing battery life. Someone hands me a phone. For what seems like the millionth time, I dial 911, the fire department, the state police, NOPD, FEMA, the CEO of our parent company, the mayor's office, and my state senator. I dial the networks: ABC, NBC, CBS. I dial Fox News. I try any media outlet I can think of that has anything approaching a large audience.

All busy signals or silence at the other end of the line. When I call the CEO, I get his voice mail. Earlier in the week we got through to his admin once or twice. She had assured us he was aware of the situation and working with authorities to get us out. The man never got back to us.

I go back into the room. "We're in a tough situation right now," I say. "His kidney failure is definitely worsening, which I'm sure you can see." Andy's mother nods. Her face is stoic, but her eyes are shining with tears.

"We really need to get him out of here to a functioning hospital where he can have a chance," I say.

"Have they forgotten about us?" she says. I shake my head, even though I have been wondering this for the better part of three days.

"No, ma'am, I just think there are a lot of people in the same position we are now," I say.

"Why can't you do anything? Why can't you get him out of here?" She is, understandably, frustrated with me.

"We're trying. We're trying to get evacuated," I say. "We've been trying since this happened."

I need to do something.

I convene another emergency meeting. I get everyone's attention immediately when I stand in front of the room and say, "Fuck FEMA. If they show up, great, but I'm done waiting." Many staff around me nod. It's dangerous sitting here. We had assumed—everything about where we lived and how we lived in the past made it natural to assume—that in this type of situation, emergency responders would help us. Here, where the most vulnerable people were, surely we could count on assistance beyond bottles of water dropped on the roof.

But we were on our own. Even those of us who had been in denial about this since the beginning, or who had been remaining upbeat for the sake of the patients, were starting to think we would never be rescued.

We go over an updated triaged patient list so every senior staff member knows which patients are our top priorities. Then we form teams and pool together any cell phones we have that are working. We designate two staff members to borrow any other working phones that might be among the patient, family, or guest populations. No more trying to call back FEMA or the NOPD or the fire department. From now on, half of us will be calling the news media. The other half will try private transportation companies. We will offer our own money to cover the costs to get our patients the hell out of here.

Every second of our inconsistently working, dying cell phones will be dedicated to reaching the media and the president or CEO of every helicopter company in the South and beyond. Every tiny amount of charging that the few car adapters can do before their batteries completely die is going to be used up now.

After rounds, it is my turn to make calls, so I go up to the roof for a better cell signal and some fresh air. Someone had tracked down the number for

CNN's on-air call-in segments. I had tried it before, and it was always busy. But to my surprise, someone answers this time.

"Jamie Green."

"Uh, hi, is this CNN?"

"Yes, I'm a producer at CNN. Who is calling?"

My heart jumps. "My name is Ray Reid. I'm at St. Lib—St. Liberatus Hospital in New Orleans, and we have people dying, and we need to get evacuated immediately," I say; the words are rushing out too fast.

"Okay, can you just verify again your name and position?"

"I'm Dr. Ray Reid. I'm the head of the Intensive Care Unit at St. Liberatus Hospital in New Orleans," I say. She asks me more about our situation, if any help is coming. I provide a very brief review of the past three days and then explain that my phone will be dead in minutes.

"Okay, Dr. Reid, I'm going to put you on the air with Wolf, okay?"

"Wolf Blitzer?" No, the other guy named Wolf on CNN.

"Yes, Wolf Blizter. Just hang on, okay? Try to remember to speak clearly and enunciate so everyone can hear you, since there's some static on your line."

In this surreal week, I experience the oddness of explaining, with the help of Wolf Blitzer, to millions of Americans that my people need to get evacuated the hell out of here. I am still on the phone with Wolf, when Tennant comes running up the steps and onto the roof.

Wolf is particularly fond of repeating the part about how we were supposedly saved and how the media—including his network, I guess—falsely reported that we had been evacuated. The times we had been told that we were going to be rescued and then nobody came. The time the National Guard came so close, only to turn away from us. You couldn't make this stuff up.

Tennant is waving his arms frantically at me to the point where I tell Wolf to hang on because I think I have a patient emergency. I hit the mute button, and Tennant says, "We've got a transport! We've got a transport!" he says. "They heard you on TV!"

Two hours later, the ambulatory patients are evacuated onto National Guard trucks; they climb, one by one, from the waiting-room windows into the amphibious vehicles.

On the roof, the NICU babies, their mothers, and their dedicated doctors and nurses are in front. Behind us in line are the rest of our nonambulatory patients, including Michaela and her parents. Dr. Osgood and I are carrying Andy; his mother lays her hands on her son as we watch a Blackhawk closing in from the direction of Louis Armstrong Airport.

I hold back tears as the helicopter lands, blowing wind in all of our faces.

Chapter 28

Friday Morning and Saturday Morning
Lower Garden District and Lower 9

Ava made her way back to Remy's father's house and told him what happened. He very kindly asked her if she was okay, and then he was immediately on his phone, mumbling something about calling a district attorney. Ava was afraid, especially for Ellis. She thought of those white cops on that bridge. But he was a cop. And those guys in black weren't. They seemed even more powerful than cops to her.

"Do you want to stay here, honey, until we get Remy and your cousin?" Mr. Devereaux asked.

Ava shook her head. "No, sir, but thank you. I might as well go back to the camp and see if I can help some more."

"Well, be careful, will you?" Mr. Devereaux said. "I don't want to have to make phone calls for you too."

Ava nodded. She gave him her cell-phone number and asked him to let her know as soon as he heard something. She turned to go but then turned back and said, "Those guys scared my dog off. If you see him around, can you try to take him in, and I'll come get him?" Mr. Devereaux nodded.

Ava texted Remy and Ellis. She figured their phones were confiscated, but maybe it would scare off the people who took them if they knew she told Remy's dad, and he is making calls to a lot of people, including the district attorney. She tried to exaggerate without sounding as though she was bluffing. She texted them as though she thought they still had access to their phones. *He is in touch with the NOPD. Making several calls.*

Please be okay, she thought. Vigilantes ruled this city at the moment; she had seen it and heard about it. She prayed these men would not hurt her friend and cousin. Or worse.

She slowly walked out of the neighborhood; she passed her father's house again, even though it was a couple of blocks out of the way. She wanted to be alone there for a moment.

She leaned against the wrought-iron fence. *Daddy,* she thought. *I am here.* A few minutes later, she took one last look and started back down the sidewalk. After she had gone only a few steps, she sensed someone behind her. She turned. There, down the block, was Louis. He was watching her hesitantly. She knelt down and scrounged in her bag for the dog food Remy's father had given her for Louis the night before.

"Here, my boy," she said softly. "It's okay." She held out the treat, thinking he was still traumatized by everything he had seen over the past few days and that he might be too skittish to come near her again. But once she held out the treat and got down to his eye level, he trotted up to her. He had lost his little leash. She picked him up, cradled him, and put him in her backpack.

"Let's get back to work, buddy," she said.

Eight hours later, it was dusk, and Ava was huddled on disintegrating shingles. Louis sat curled up on her lap like a cat. She pushed off bits of crumpled tar with her heels and watched them roll off and drop into the toxic stew below.

Irish did not want a woman (or really anyone) going on a rescue run alone. Not just for safety but also because of the physicality of the job of helping people out of their ruined houses. You had to have two sets of hands. But everyone else was already out, so when Ava belatedly showed up at the drop-off point, Irish reluctantly watched her head out into the 9th Ward with Remy's boat.

Ava had brought two people back. Now, five days in, most of the people out there in the floodwaters who needed rescuing had been rescued. But there were still a few people, mostly elderly or handicapped, like the older couple Ava found, who needed help and who had been passed over in the confusion of various earlier rescue attempts.

On her way back to the intersection where she had rescued the couple, Ava saw another boat come into her field of vision from a perpendicular direction.

When she realized who they were, it was already too late.

"Nice boat," said the taller of the two, who was standing up, sizing her up as if deciding whether or not he wanted to take her as a prize. He held a shotgun. The same one she and Remy had seen the other day. At that point these guys had a boat full of TVs and sneakers.

"Please don't," she said. She looked around, hoping some other rescuer would see what was happening and intervene or scare them off. But they were alone on the street.

They took the boat. She was lucky they didn't do worse. She briefly thought about the knife, but there were two of them, and they were bigger than her. She would not have stood a chance, and she would have made them angry.

At least they let her climb on the nearest roof. They took her bag, but let her keep Louis, thank God. She had her phone in her back pocket and a mini flashlight in her other pocket. They asked if she had a phone, and she lied and said no. Luckily they didn't check her pockets for one.

One of the two men hopped back out of Remy's boat and went into their old boat, and then the two blew out of the neighborhood without so much as a glance in her direction. As they motored away, Ava thought about how Remy's dad had given him that boat. And now neither of them would ever see it again. It would have a new name and possibly a new paint color by the time the next nightfall came.

Ava called Remy's father, but he did not answer. He was probably out trying to find his son. Either that or the communication systems were overloaded again. Ava texted Remy and Ellis. She had to tell them her predicament and pray they were okay and had their phones back. She had nobody else to tell.

As dusk fell and light retreated, every sound was ominous. Every splash, motor, chopper, and siren. Every scream and shout and every piece of debris falling and shifting and every creature swimming and every poor hoarse barking dog (how they had any bark left at this point she did not know) set her heart beating too fast. She could feel Louis's heart beating even faster against hers.

Ava noticed the absence of the birds. No twittering and singing, calling each other home to nest.

She tried to get used to the idea that she might be out here alone for the night.

Alone on the water. Waiting for rescue.

She flipped her phone closed and nearly dropped it but caught it at the last minute, leaning backward toward the large hole in the roof behind her. Louis jumped off her lap, scared, his nails digging into tarpaper. He backed away from the hole. For probably the twentieth time, Ava peered down into the hole and shone her feeble flashlight into the ruined attic beneath. There were boxes floating, a trunk, chunks of wood and unidentifiable bits of broken things. In the far corner of the attic, there was a dresser, and curled up on top of the dresser was a large snake. Ava kept watching that snake, convinced that somehow it was going to slither up to the roof.

She was still thinking about the snake as night drew its curtain down. It had become more quiet as the helicopters started to go back from whence they came. Ava thought she still heard the occasional call for help, but then she would hear nothing, no repetition of them, so she wondered if she was imagining it.

She kept checking her phone and patting Louis, coaxing him back to her. He settled back in her lap, shivering. She wondered what his canine brain was thinking: *This woman gets into a lot of trouble.* She wondered again if he and Tiras would get along. She was getting pretty attached to this little guy but didn't want to steal him from someone who could be looking for him right now.

To distract herself, Ava thought about what she would be doing if she were home on a regular Friday night.

Work late. Alone in the building. Maybe visit her aunt and uncle; on a special occasion she would maybe meet a friend for dinner. But usually she would go home for dinner with Tiras. She would walk him around the neighborhood and then throw a ball for him in the yard. Then she would make dinner. She would check her personal e-mail. She would go to bed reading one of her father's old books. Sometimes he had signed his name in the front cover. He told her when she was a little girl that he did that in the early years of his teaching, because he would always lend books to students, and sometimes they forgot to give them back. If you put your name in them, they're more likely to remember.

One late summer night a couple of years ago, when a Nor'easter hit earlier than usual, Ava was sitting in the flickering light of a strawberry candle at her kitchen table. Leftovers: brown rice, asparagus, one chicken breast, and one glass of red wine. She had a battery-operated radio but no working batteries. She had stared into the flame and listened to the whipping wind as Tiras sat and solemnly watched the chicken, waiting for her to relinquish it. She thought of how ancient the house was, how so many occupants before her had endured such storms, and the house had stood through them all. Still, she wished she had batteries to run the radio and not feel quite so alone.

But just then her uncle had arrived at the door, drenched even in his ancient, dependable L.L.Bean raincoat, flashlight and batteries in hand. He shouldn't have been out, but he was worried about his niece. Alone too much. He teared up when he saw her at the hospital. The wide eyes, the lost little girl, bereft, drenched clothes in a plastic bag with the hospital name on it. Her small hands, whiter than the white hospital gown.

Suddenly Ava's memories were interrupted by a faint sound, as if somebody was stage whispering. A hoarse, tired voice. Her eyes pulled away from the stars visible over the tops of battered palm trees, and she scanned the houses near her. But she could see so little—an outline at best.

She wished for a brighter moon.

"Help! Help!" Ava heard it again—the whispering voice.

"Where are you?" she asked. The strength of her own voice startled her in all this quiet.

"I'm at Ninety-Nine Magnolia! The roof!"

"I don't know where Ninety-Nine is," she said, but she realized it sounded like the other person—a woman's—was to her left. "Can you hang on? I don't have a boat, but when it gets light—"

"I can't swim, and I haven't had water in three days," the hoarse voice trembled. "I'm in the attic," she said. "I'm hurt. I can't move."

Suddenly Ava heard voices, also coming from her left. There was a paddling and splashing sound and then the sound of breaking glass—house after house after house. Things being dragged, opened. Dogs barking, shrieking. Louis growled; Ava ran her hand across his back and felt his hackles. She shushed him, and he immediately stopped as if he understood it was safer not to growl.

The other woman was silent. They were both holding their breath.

Then whoever it was came to the house she was perched on top of. The flashlight swung toward her; she rolled over the apex of the roof and clung onto the other side, pulling Louis by the scruff of his hair. She knew if it was a rescuer, they wouldn't be silent, and they wouldn't be destroying windows unless there was somebody on the other side to get to. She heard them break a window on the opposite side from where she sat, perched on her feet, ready to flee, but to where she did not know.

Then the flashlight swerved again. And there was the scraping of the bottom of a boat over a car roof or an antenna or a light pole or a one-way sign. Low voices, laughing, the smell of lit cigarettes.

Please go away. Please go away.

She peered over the edge of the roof and caught a face just behind a flashlight. Behind him rose another face.

"I see you, lady," the man said. Then his face and the flashlight dipped away, and she heard splashing.

Oh shit, oh shit, oh shit.

A scream came from 99 Magnolia.

An angry voice; shouting. "Shut up, bitch!"

"No! Leave me alone! Help!" Oh shit, oh shit.

Ava whispered to Louis to stay and hoped he knew what that meant. She climbed down the roof until her feet were in water. How would she jump down without them knowing? They'll hear the splash. What was she going to do when she got there? She pulled up her shirt and pulled out her uncle's hunting knife, holding it high and gripping it tightly as she slid into the water.

She swam toward the shouting. Her mind bounced around as she felt the water envelop her.

How is it still so hot when the sun has gone down? Smells like a gas station in a sewage plant. Can't swim in this shit what the hell else is in here. Stop. Dad. Grandpa. There are things alive in there...the knife. Haven't swam anywhere and certainly not this far for twenty years or more. Can't live with the thought of that woman dead. I know what they are doing. Can't imagine explaining to anyone. Nobody will know...Almost there...don't drop the knife...

Splash! Something was near her, and she started swimming faster, so awkward with one arm above her head, ready to strike. Her heart leapt in her throat as she bumped up against something alive.

It's the top of a mailbox. Or a car, a car leaning into the house. She lies to herself. It is alive.

Not a gator. *Oh God*, please don't let it be a gator. *Oh God.*

She thought about her father and how that gator almost pulled him into the death roll, almost dragged him under forever with those jaws. Almost drowned him then. His fate. *They pull you under and drown you so you don't put up a fight for too long and, in the process, snap your arm, snap your leg, you wouldn't even have time to use a gun even if you had one.*

She was almost to the shouting, and then she saw a flashlight waving around. Two men in there. The flashlight swerved behind her, nearly caught her but just missed her as she got up against the house. She felt metal scrape against her, and again something was moving next to her, and she thought about the blood and bacteria and Irish's words, *Don't drink the water; you'll be shitting for days,* and the toxicity and *Can gators smell blood like sharks do?*

As the side of 99 Magnolia loomed up in front of her, she scrambled for a foothold; a ruined porch rail fell away in her arms. She scrambled onto the top of a gutter. The attic was just ahead. Adrenaline had replaced exhaustion, and she pushed herself to outrun whatever she had just felt and then take on whatever she must take on inside: the flashlight dropped to the floor, the woman still screaming, scuffling, and a struggle. Ava clawed and scratched and heaved herself in and threw herself at the man whose figure was visible in the dropped flashlight's static arc of light, all the time her arm extended away from her body, her fingers gripping the handle so tightly it hurt.

"Get the fuck out of here!" she screamed. The man was tearing at the woman's clothes. As he turned to look at her surprised, she lunged and sunk the knife into his stomach.

The man was much bigger than Ava, and he stared at her with a look of anger that turned to surprise when she stabbed him. There was nothing behind those eyes. It was as if he couldn't believe she would interrupt him. The woman on the floor, meanwhile, was pushing to get away from him, but she was obviously hurt; she was dragging one leg along behind her.

"What the—" the man uttered. Ava knew she had sunk the knife deep enough to do some real damage. He started to get up and lunge at her, but the pain was too much.

"Get the fuck away from her!" Ava said, her heart pounding, hard and erratic against her chest.

She was about to stab him again when she fell to the side, staggering, trying to upright herself. Pain beat through her body, stunning her. She looked to where the blow came from, behind her, and just as she was sizing up the silhouette of this other, larger man, he cried out in pain and shock. Louis was sinking his teeth into the man's leg. The man grunted and reached down to hit the dog, and Ava drew back her arm and then sliced it forward, plunging the knife into the man's thigh as hard as she could as Louis darted away from the man's blow. The man screamed out and sank to his knees. A shotgun, which Ava realized is what he hit her with, clattered to the floor. She lunged for it, quicker than him despite the pain in her side from where he hit her. As she grabbed the gun and pointed it, she looked for the other man, expecting he would jump her. He was still holding his stomach and stumbling toward her, positioning himself to grab the gun out of her hands. But she pointed it toward him and backed away, glancing down at the floor to see where she had room to move. She called Louis to her, afraid they would try to grab him and either hurt him or force her to drop the gun to save him.

"Here, boy!" He darted around the men and came up to her side.

"Get the *fuck* out of here!" Ava yelled. She hoped the safety was off. She guessed, with these two, it was. She didn't know how to use a shotgun, but she decided to bluff her way out. Ava felt a rage she didn't know she had surge through her body.

"I'm from rural Maine," she said. "I have been using a gun like this since I was ten years old. Hunting season. Do you want me to show you how I use it?"

"Bitch," one of the men said under his breath.

"What the *fuck* did you say?" She pretended to take aim. "All bets are off in this town, right? You obviously fucking know that. Well, so do I."

"Okay, okay, Jesus. Fuck, let's get out of here. We're leaving, okay?" The man with the knife wound in the thigh was talking now, both to Ava and to the other guy. The two men inched backward, both still grabbing their wounds. Louis growled and stepped forward; the man he bit turned toward him angrily.

"If you touch him, I swear to God I will kill you," Ava said.

The friend said, "All right, all right, we're gone, we're gone," and he pulled at the other guy, and they both dropped back into the water. Ava listened to them splash away.

"Bitch," she heard them say again. She did not move; she stood frozen with the gun pointing in the direction the men had gone. She heard their splashes recede and the sound of a boat's motor starting up and heading off into the distance.

Then silence.

When she was satisfied they were gone, she turned to tend to the woman. The flashlight one of the men had dropped cast part of its light in their direction, so they could see each other somewhat.

"Are you all right? What's your name?" Ava asked.

"Sadie," the woman said.

"Sadie, I'm Ava."

"Thank you, Ava."

Ava nodded.

Louis approached them, whining. "You are such a good boy," Ava said. "You don't even know. I can't believe you swam over here, you crazy dog. I thought you ran away again." She bent down and patted him and hugged his neck.

"Did you break your leg?" Ava asked Sadie.

"No," Sadie said. "But something gouged me pretty bad when I was trying to get out the other day." Ava picked up the flashlight.

"Mind if I take a look?" she said. "I'm not a doctor or anything, but maybe I can help." Sadie nodded, and Ava pointed the flashlight at the wound. Sadie had ripped what looked like an old bedsheet into strips and wrapped it around her leg. It was covered with dried blood. Ava peeled it back gently; Sadie grimaced. It was a pretty deep puncture wound that looked infected.

Ava cursed those looters for taking her bag. She had first-aid supplies in there and could have at least cleaned the wound. She hoped the woman hadn't gotten any water in it, but it seemed likely that was why it was infected.

"I wish I hadn't been robbed earlier; I had alcohol wipes at least. And we can't leave right now, obviously. But we'll see if we can get out come morning," Ava said. In the meantime, they felt like sitting ducks. She turned the flashlight off. They could still make out a dim outline of the room and each other from the light of the moon.

Ava's mind went back to Remy and Ellis's predicament. She checked her phone; no word from either of them or Mr. Devereaux.

What did those men do to them? She remembered the boss of those men had mentioned something about taking Ellis and Remy to some cops at a school. Surely if they were taken to cops, Ellis could sort everything out. He might even know them. But in this city, at this time, who knew what could happen?

Ava was sitting near Sadie. She had laid the shotgun down on the floor very carefully, pointing it away from them. Now she drew it closer just in case. She found a scrap of cloth from the ripped-up sheet and wiped her knife off on it and then sheathed it. Sadie watched her.

"You came prepared," she said. Her voice sounded weaker.

Ava laughed, hoping to make her feel better. "I wasn't prepared for any of this," she said.

Sadie laughed too, though weakly. "Yeah, I guess none of us were." After a few minutes of silence, she said, "I'm sorry. I'm not feeling so hot over here." Seconds later, she threw up. "I think this fucking water is making me sick," she said.

Between the wound and this, Sadie was in trouble. Daylight couldn't come soon enough.

A rat scurried by both of them. Louis made a belated attempt to catch it but, thankfully, failed. He sniffed around and then came and sat between the two women.

Ava gestured to the shotgun and asked, "Do you know how to use this? Because I sure don't."

Sadie laughed again.

"Well, you were convincing. And yes," she said, "I do know how to use it."

"Okay, good," Ava said. "If they come back, you better take it."

Sadie nodded; her smile faded.

"They might come back because we saw them, and they know we're trapped here. They might come back with more men." Sadie nodded. "Yep. We need to get the hell out of here." And Sadie clearly needed medical care.

"You couldn't have come along at a better time," Sadie said. "Are you with the cops or something?"

Ava shook her head. "No," she said. "I'm a volunteer. But I've been going around with a couple of people, including a cop, trying to get people out. I hope my friends will be back in the morning."

"Why did they leave you here?" Ava noticed the sweat pouring down Sadie's face, worse than before. She offered her what was left of her water, but Sadie shook her head, insisting Ava and Louis drink it.

"They got detained. By some private security guys who thought they were looters," Ava said. "Or at least that's what he said." She didn't bother to explain where they were when it happened and how she had come back here; it didn't matter.

Ava tried calling 911 and Remy's father, the only person besides Remy and Ellis she still knew in New Orleans, but she got a busy signal each time. She laughed. Of course. She should know better than to look for help right now.

Thank God she had charged her phone battery again last night at Remy's house. She still had a little bit of battery charge left.

For a couple of hours both women sat in the darkness, talking softly once in a while but mostly listening for trouble. As morning approached, Sadie threw up more and more frequently and talked less and less. All they heard was the occasional splash and passing chopper.

"There used to be crickets," Sadie said at one point when it was dead quiet outside. Ava thought again of summer nights in Maine. The dark water of the Bay. The warm sound of night, owls and crickets and June bugs, in the woods near her house.

Waiting for the light to come. Waiting for those men to come back. They didn't dare close their eyes despite the exhaustion they felt.

Before dawn broke, they were still awake. Sadie asked, "Do you know the heron story?"

Ava thought for a moment and started to say no. Then something clicked. A story her father had told her once, on one of their visits down here.

"I do. You mean about Lake Pontchartrain..."

"Yes, a big ol' Louisiana heron, in this children's story. He sucked all the water out of Lake Pontchartrain with his bill."

Ava nodded. "My dad told me that story once."

"Wouldn't it be nice if he were real? He could clean up this whole city. Fast."

Ava chuckled. "If only fairy tales were true, too."

Sadie said, "You don't sound like you're from around here."

"No. But my father was."

"Where are you from?"

"Maine."

"Maine. I've never been there. I've been to New York."

"New York is nice."

"What's Maine like?"

How could she summarize Maine? It was impossible. She could no more describe the beauty and devastation and *home* that was Maine than she could describe New Orleans.

"It's beautiful," Ava said finally. "And cold. We hit eighty degrees maybe two weeks out of the year. At least in the part of Maine where I'm from. But it's home." She thought of the drive out to her uncle's: the neat colonial houses, their lights in the windows in winter. The rocky shore and those towering pines.

"Eighty degrees would be a blessing compared to these last few days," Sadie said.

"Yeah," Ava agreed. "I've never been so hot in my life."

"Just another summer in New Orleans," Sadie said.

Ava sent another text to Remy and Ellis with an update. She ended it with *Hope you are ok. I'm at 99 Magnolia. Lower 9.*

As the morning light grew stronger, Ava still sat by the window, shotgun and knife at the ready. But the sun rose higher and higher, and still no rescuers came by.

Sadie got so weak that she finally consented to drink the little water that Ava had left. Ava, meanwhile, kept trying to keep Louis from drinking the floodwater. He had lapped some up before she could stop him, but she was praying it wasn't too much and that he would be all right.

It was nearly 6:00 p.m., and Ava had nearly lost her voice from shouting when they finally heard it: a boat engine in the distance that actually turned their way and got louder and louder. At first, Ava's heart started thumping, and she envisioned the looters returning, more armed and intent on making her pay for what she'd done. But then, to her great relief, she heard a familiar voice.

"Over here! Over here!" A motorboat appeared around the corner, one she hadn't seen before. But she recognized the men at the helm. She said to Sadie "I know them!" and turned back around to see Remy easing up on the engine, sending debris in a brown wake behind him. Ellis stood beside him. Remy clambered up to the roof, and even while she was hugging him, Ava started pushing him toward Sadie.

"Sadie here really needs some help," Ava said, and she wiped away tears of relief as she scooped Louis up in her arms.

"I'm so sorry," Remy said after they got Sadie in the boat. "Those fuckers handed us off to these so-called cops, but when they dropped us off, we were in this jail…"

"Not a jail," Ellis said. "Fucking makeshift I-don't-know-what."

"Detention center, then," Remy said. "Ellis didn't know those cops, and they didn't know him—"

"They weren't cops, I'm telling you," Ellis said. "I think they were Blackwater too, like those assholes in the Garden District."

"They had us all day yesterday and most of last night. Mostly ignoring us but then asking us stupid-ass questions about what we stole and where it was. They finally let us go when a couple of my dad's friends showed up. How they knew where to find us, I don't know. But I know you told Dad what happened, so I guess they figured it out."

Powerful friends, Ava thought. Like district attorney and former chief-of-police friends. Friends who knew where to look, because there were probably a few centers like this in the city right now that certain law enforcement and legal entities knew about.

"Questioning you? What for?" But Remy and Ellis both shook their heads as though they didn't want to talk about it yet, and Ava, feeling disgustingly dirty and touching her left side, which was still hurting from the blow with the shot-gun, dropped it for now. She would get the full story later.

"Let's get Sadie here back to the checkpoint," Ava said. Ellis and Remy nodded.

Ellis looked down at her feet, suddenly realizing the dog was there.

"You found Louis!" he said.

"At least something worked out right," said Remy.

"I'm so sorry about the boat," Ava said to Remy.

He shrugged. "You know, I never used the damn thing anyway," he said. That wasn't true, but she appreciated him saying it.

They took Sadie to the drop-off point so she could get medical help, and Ava felt a strange sadness that this woman she had just gone through a life-and-death experience with was now leaving her. But she was also worried about Sadie's condition, between the wound and the dehydration and illness from the water, and she hoped Sadie would be okay.

The three friends talked more about how each of them had spent the night. As for Ellis and Remy, the "goods" they had piled up in their bags (mostly food from Remy's dad's house and first aid for the people they had been rescuing for the past several days) and the fact that they were "roaming" the streets of the Garden District in the wee morning hours (and, of course, the unspoken fact that Ellis was black) convinced the trigger-happy paramilitary that Ellis and Remy were looters.

"It was so strange. So disconnected, you know? This city is imploding all around us, and all they seemed to care about was stolen stuff. I mean, even if we were looters, should that really be their area of focus?" Remy asked.

Once they were free and got their phones back, Ellis and Remy had seen Ava's texts and headed out to help her.

Ava gave an abbreviated version of what she had experienced. She didn't really want to talk about it anymore, although she knew it would be hard to forget what she had done and the threatening look she had seen in the eyes of those men.

The three of them headed down another ruined residential street.

Ellis told Ava stories he had heard from people around the makeshift jail.

There were some looters there, certainly. And a few characters Ellis was quite familiar with. But there were other rescuers too. One guy, who was a teacher from Chalmette, was very practical; he had a kayak tied to his porch railing, just in case, and, of course, he ended up being glad he did. So he started setting out, and he went to his neighbors and rescued their dogs and took dog food from Walgreens, and he took food for himself, two days in, and he thought the dogs must be really hungry, you know. Well, they caught him with his rowboat and the food. There he was in jail, while more dogs died all over New Orleans.

"Just a clusterfuck, all around," said Remy. "Like this whole damn situation."

They went back out that afternoon. They rescued three more people. The city was changed again now; there were dozens of National Guard trucks patrolling the streets. You could see people being taken out of town on buses. The word was they were all going to Dallas and Houston and that places all over the country had offered to take them in.

They went back to Remy's father's house that night and took turns using his shower. Ava stood in there for a long minute, soaking it in before washing her hair and scrubbing every part of her body clean until her skin was red.

Remy and his father canvassed the neighbors for alcohol. Two drinks later, Ava was sleepy and tipsy. She had had so little to eat and drink for the past week that her tolerance had cratered.

She fell into a deep and satisfying sleep, Louis curled up beside her.

Chapter 29

Sunday

All Over New Orleans

Ava woke to Remy tapping on her shoulder. She was curled up sleeping like she used to when she was a little kid.

"Time to get up," Remy was saying. It was barely light outside, but it was already another hot day in New Orleans. Even compared to yesterday, the police, fire, and military presence was again more visible, even in his father's neighborhood.

"I think maybe this will be the last day," Remy said.

Ava said, "The dogs. Can we please help the dogs? The ones who can still be saved." She knew many had been lost this past week.

"I was thinking the same thing," Remy said.

They said a quick good-bye to Remy's dad and headed back to camp. They greeted one of the Homeboys who was standing next to NOPD and National Guard guys at the drop-off point. Irish and her husband had already pushed off on their first mission of the morning. Some Cajuns were packing up to leave.

All day, they went back to the streets where they had heard dogs. Many of their voices were silenced forever now. Ava wished they had saved more earlier. But they did find thirty-six dogs and forty-four cats alive. The pets were taken by the Humane Society, the ASPCA, and several other animal-rescue teams who promised the dogs and cats would either be reunited with their owners or rehomed.

They did not come across any more people who needed rescuing. They saw helicopters dropping water bottles; they passed the empty shelves of mom-and-pop stores. They overheard stories from people waiting for the next bus out of town; one woman told them how the walls of her apartment caved in, how there was only one intact room left, and how she hid in there, in her closet, a mattress over her, her feet in the hall, scared to death; she said she heard screams, human and animal, and she felt something brush past her in the dark.

"I haven't seen Mama or Daddy since Sunday night," one young man in his twenties told them. "They live two streets over from me. I stayed because they were staying, and I thought everything was okay; I had slept at their place, and then it was over, and I came home on Monday, and then...I was taking a nap, and when I woke up, the water was everywhere..." He begged the Homeboys, crying, to cruise by his parents' home. And they did, and they found two bodies.

Sunday night, Remy and Ava met up with Ellis, who had gone back on official duty and had been assigned to another part of the city to help with recovery missions.

"I think we're heading out soon," Remy said. "Now that all the usual suspects have finally got their shit together and are helping out around here." They headed back to the drop-off point to say good-bye to whoever was left. They felt like comrades-in-arms after the past few days.

Irish and her husband, Van, were still there. Irish was on the phone, shaking her head. She said good-bye to the person she was talking to and shoved the phone into her pocket.

"What's the latest?" Remy asked.

"We're being told to get the hell out by tomorrow morning," Irish said.

"How's that for a thank you," Van said. "But we were getting ready to leave anyway. We have to get back to work." They said their good-byes, and before they parted, Remy said, "You know, I heard some jerk on the radio saying that we shouldn't rebuild, that we shouldn't have a city here in the first place."

"Yankees," Irish's husband said and laughed.

Ellis came by that night. He had been making his dutiful daily visit to his assigned barracks. He had been told the same thing: volunteer groups with no formal training were being asked to leave.

He brought beers for them, and they leaned against the truck to say their good-byes.

"It was good to see you despite all this," Ava said.

Ellis nodded. "It was good to see you too. Let's not wait so long to get together again next time, okay?"

He gave her a tight squeeze on the arm and a bear hug when he left. She watched him walk away.

Remy and Ava finished packing up what little they had left into their truck, and Ava secured Louis to the seat belt with a rope. As they worked, they saw trucks, one after the other, loaded down with supplies, moving down the streets around them. When they drove out of the city, they watched the line of vehicles heading in: all army.

Chapter 30

Fall

Maine

They drove north. Behind them they left valleys scraped clean by fire and the lights of the suburbs trailing from the city, sparks from a candle that had blown out. She thought of the cool balsam air, could almost smell it hundreds of miles from home. She thought of the view from her uncle's porch. How even when she could not look at it because of what it had taken from her, she knew it was there, and it was powerful in its beauty. It's September then, and the New Year wasn't far away.

Ava's aunt and uncle were more than a little relieved to have her back in their midst. So was Tiras, who seemed suspicious of Louis at first, but they warmed up to each other. Ava had posted notes on various websites for evacuees, and she contacted the ASPCA in New Orleans and other Louisiana cities. Nobody had seen someone come in asking for a dog like Louis. He seemed almost trained; he was so well behaved. Ava thought that perhaps his owner didn't make it.

Ava, who had not said one word to her boss since the day she called to say she was taking an unscheduled vacation, was happy to hear she still had a job. She was surprised to learn that her boss wanted her to write a "Hurricane Diary" to be published in *Eastland*. Her first cover story would appear in November. She was supposed to put a Maine spin on it but hadn't figured that part out yet.

One night late in September, Ava came in from a run with Tiras and Louis and turned on the radio. As she fed the dogs, she listened to an interview with a woman who lived in California but had flown back to New Orleans to try to find her elderly parents, who had not been heard from since the storm. She had tried for weeks to get permission to fly into New Orleans and finally had flown into Lafayette and rented a car and drove to Gentilly.

Just before she got there, a recovery team had finally found them dead in their attic, twenty-one days after the storm. They were found lying on a blanket together with their little dog. There was a jar of applesauce and a bottle of water beside them. And above them, safe on a box, high above where the floodwaters stopped, were two photos of their daughters.

So little was done.

Chapter 31

Late September 2005
New Orleans

I finally am able to catch a ride back to New Orleans. They're letting residents back in. We don't know if the hospital will ever open again, so I have been working with some of my other colleagues at a sister hospital here in Baton Rouge.

My friend drops me off at the marina. It is closed, and I walk down the little slope past the office, fully expecting that *The Good Life* will be long gone and that I will see nothing but water and ruins.

But there she is, bobbing lightly, waiting for me. I see paint scraped off, I see debris on the deck, I see a broken window.

But she is still there.

Epilogue

Mardi Gras 2006

Ava had been back in Maine physically for nearly five months. But her mind was living in two places now. She had been devouring every bit of news she could get her hands on. From afar she heard stories of continued devastation, the fear of another storm, Rita, which made her nervous for the Cajun Navy, and she wondered how Irish and Van and their colleagues had fared. In her dreams, she saw nothing but water. That part of her life had not changed much.

She decided to go back for Mardi Gras in February. There had been so much controversy in the media about Mardi Gras and whether it was "appropriate" to have it this year. Even some New Orleanians debated it. Weren't there other things to spend their money on? But Ava knew her father's city was the kind of place that would have Mardi Gras, come hell or high water, and both had since come to pass in New Orleans. They were going to be damned if they weren't going to celebrate life.

Flying in, Ava noticed a sea of blue tarps, wrinkled, rough, dotting the roofs of the city, covering whole blocks.

She and Remy were spending the week in the city. Through his family and nonprofit connections, Remy had made plans to work on a couple of houses while they were down there. He helped haul moldy refrigerators out of Lakeview and the Lower 9.

At one point in between parades and house repairs, Ava walked over to the old Opera House that her dad's beloved Benjamin Hamilton had designed. It stood bleach-white, like bones in the sun. Trash was piled on the sidewalks in front of it. There was a black waterline across the front, halfway up the grand front doors. A small crew of locals were sweeping out the main lobby and scraping mold off walls.

"Do you need help?" Ava asked.

"Here's a broom," someone said, and they stuck one in her hand.

At night they stayed at Remy's parents' house. Their Uptown neighborhood was a stark contrast to where Remy and Ava were spending their days; everyone was back, and the homes were in good shape. The wind damage had already been repaired.

Remy and Ava wanted to support the local economy, so they ate out a lot that week, but many restaurants were closed simply because the workers who staffed those restaurants had been flooded out of their homes, or worse. Many had been evacuated to Houston or Nashville or Atlanta and were never coming back, at least not anytime soon.

One night, they met for drinks at Napoleon House. Exhausted from the day, they eavesdropped on the conversations around them.

"He is living with his parents because it is impossible to find an apartment right now."

"I know. If the place ain't damaged, it's the freaking carpetbaggers, builders, dealers, scam artists, reporters…they're all taking up too much space."

It was just past 8:00 p.m., but the clock on the wall said 6:45. The bartender, a lanky white man, saw Ava and Remy looking at it, and said, "Stopped the morning the storm hit."

"I kind of want to take a storm tour," Remy said when the bartender walked away to serve another customer.

"Why would you want to do that?" Ava asked. The idea of those tours disturbed her. Making money off misery. Like wartime profiteers. The type of people who started buying defense-company stocks before the second tower even fell.

"I want to know how they're telling the story to people who don't understand," Remy said.

Ava relented, and they showed up for a tour early the next morning. The tour guide took them to New Orleans East first. He was a tall, lanky Cajun man, with a honeyed accent and two bright-blue eyes peeking out from leathery skin.

The sky was brilliant and bright with sunlight, disturbed only by the passing marks of the beating wings of lost gulls and wandering herons. The wind blew the leaves, revealing their gray underbellies. There was a woman from some far-away state in the van, and she said she felt so sorry for all these poor people, but then she complained to her friend about the quality of her manicure that she got that morning, and she seemed fixated on getting back to Bourbon Street. The tour guide turned to Ava, who was sitting in the front, and made conversation to drown out the other woman's inane comments while they were stopped at a red light.

"Where you from?"

"Maine."

"Oh, a long way away…I've never been to Maine. Cold up there, hmm?"

"Yeah, it gets pretty cold."

"So you here for Mardi Gras?"

"Sort of," Ava says. "I was here a few months ago…after the storm. I wanted to see how the city was doing."

"You were here? Man, I wasn't even here, and I live here! I hightailed it outta here to my cousin's in Jackson. Glad I did, except it took me two months to get home."

After a tour of Da East, with its ruined apartment buildings, waterlogged car dealerships, and destroyed gas stations, they went out to the bayou. Remy mentioned Port Sulphur, where his dad was hanging out in his hurricane hole the weekend of the storm. He wondered what had become of it; his family assumed that, like so much else in St. Bernard Parish, it had been wiped away, but they hadn't attempted to go see it yet. Like the Mississippi Gulf Coast, in St. Bernard Parish there were many haunting places where homes had once stood. Now they were marked only by tangled clumps of clothing, hanging like kite strings from broken trees.

The guide showed them the remnants of shacks on stilts, summer homes for people whose families had been living on this water for more than a century. As they stared at the ruins of fishing camps, the guide told stories of the storm surge that left washing machines and sharks hanging in the trees.

"We was finding dead rats for days, weeks around here. Whole nests of them tried to get to higher ground before the storm, because, you know, animals know. But there isn't a lot of higher ground around here, as you can see. So we was finding them, and lots of dead fish, for weeks. And the smell. Oh, the smell."

"We lost some folks out here who were never found," the guide continued in his honeyed accent. "You know, there's some folks out here, on their own, loners or what have you, and they just were never seen or heard from again."

The woman from California seemed bored. She joked with her friend about a past trip to New Orleans. Remy gave her a chilling stare, but it didn't register.

The woman's friend asked the guide about the cops, about looters.

"I don't know if this got out much, but there was looters all over the place, not just New Orleans," the tour guide said. "That governor of Mississippi wanted everyone to think they was all perfect over there, but they were looting all up and down the Mississippi coast. And even in St. Bernard, and over in Gretna, you know, there was looting. It was the worst in New Orleans because we had the most people, so you do the math and realize that with the most people, you're gonna get the most criminals."

"I'll tell you, though," the tour guide continued, "we can talk about the looters, and there's no doubt they were there, but then we had heroes too. The heroes to us were the Coast Guard and the LDWF—the Louisiana Department of Wildlife and Fisheries. The Coast Guard, I think it's the largest rescue operation they've ever done, and they were there, man. They were there first. They called it Operation Dunkirk…that's how big it was. Massive. And you know a lot of them guys lost their own homes, you know? I mean at first it was all Louisiana guys. Later on they brought in Coasties from Cape Cod, from Oregon, you name it. And you know what? There were volunteers, not just military, who came from all over this country. I've talked to some of these people. I mean, some of them drove for days to get here. California, Texas, New York. I always buy them a beer when I meet one at a bar.

"Then there was the Fish and Wildlife. They usually…well, they're usually counting fish eggs or handing out hunting licenses or what all they do I don't know, but they were all over this Parish, and they were in the city too, and they rescued thousands of people. They have every damn boat you can think of— airboats, canoes, fishing boats, flat bottoms, pirogues, kayaks. They were fishing…fishing for men. They did an unbelievable job. An unbelievable job. There

228

were local citizens who did pretty heroic rescues, too. People from all over New Orleans and Louisiana. I don't think the media covered that."

Remy and Ava both thought about Irish and Van and the other Cajuns. And the Homeboys.

The guide leaned forward in the boat, stretching a bad back. "I had a cop on one of these tours once. I asked him all sorts of questions about the rumors. He was one of the guys who stayed. People forget, some cops stayed, and they lost everything too, you know? Anyway, I asked him, 'Did you see a lot of bodies?' And he said, 'Yeah, there were bodies everywhere, all over the place.' This guy thought there were tons of bodies that never got found. They ended up getting ate up by the gators or the rats. Anyway, I asked him, 'Was you shot at?' And he said, 'Yeah, but there's gunfire every day of the year in New Orleans. That ain't nothin'.' And he said he didn't have his rifle, lost it in the chaos and everything, but he had his pistol, and even after he ran out of ammunition—it wasn't easy to come by more—he kept on going out there, trying to help people. He said his head was nearly taken off by some kid who was guarding his house with his father's .22. Kid probably barely knew how to use it. But he kept going out there, you know? Those are the New Orleanians I think about. Those are the ones who are going to help this city come back."

That night, Ava and Remy met Ellis at the Carousel Bar at Hotel Monteleone. They hugged him in turn, holding on tight, like war vets who understood each time they got together that it was a blessing to be able to do so.

"Erick is working—he's a bigwig sergeant now, but he'll meet up with us later," Ellis said. There were not many people in the hotel. While Ava and Ellis caught up, Remy went up to the concierge who stood near the entrance to the bar, greeting guests in the old hotel's venerable marble lobby. The concierge had powder-white hair and the gnarled hands of someone who had worked his way up. He wore an old-fashioned gray-and-red uniform.

"How is the season looking?" Remy asked.

"Let me put it this way. It's Mardi Gras, and there are still rooms available," he said. "But, hey," the concierge said, laughing, in true New Orleans style, "we're here!"

After a drink, they went for a walk. They left the Quarter and went through the Bywater and Treme, toward the Upper 9th Ward. The landscape was still otherworldly. It felt like a crime scene or a movie set, and seeing it brought them all back to that hot awful first week, the bodies, the crying women, the desperate men, and the howling dogs. Bywater was in the best condition. They had not suffered much flooding, although the wind damage was severe. But as they moved east, they saw more and more evidence of what had been wrought there. There were dead and twisted trees leaning over some of the ruined homes. There were piles of debris in people's yards. There were lopsided stacks of bricks and stop signs pushed sideways; rusted, mud-dried cars; ruined cars slumped on lawns; and dried-up yellow-brown marsh grass on top of roofs and hanging in trees.

On the second night, Ava and Remy had dinner with Ellis and his parents. She had not seen them in more than a decade. Her aunt Tess was still beautiful and looked fifteen years younger than she was; her uncle Alex was still the spitting image of Ava's father. It hurt to look at him. She couldn't help but think of what her father would look like if he were alive now.

"Your dad was always afraid of this," Ellis's father said. "He was so worried all the history here would be lost."

The next day, before the parades, they went to some of the levees: London Avenue and Industrial Canal. Ground zeroes. All that water with all its force pushing all that sand and earth had turned the land around the levee breaks into cracked, caked mud that looked like the floor of Death Valley. A squat brick ranch house that seemed miraculously intact until you came around the corner and found the front tilted in, the bay window at an unnatural angle, and the porch hanging loose above the ground. A barge still left sitting in the middle of a street, months later. A ruined school bus, the bones of thousands of modest homes. In one apartment complex in New Orleans East, trash in the yard piled higher than the trucks out front; black shutters hung askew. On their drive back to the Quarter, they saw FEMA trailers with twinkling white lights strewn over their doors. There were signs in spray paint:

Evacuated to Dallas
Destroy this Memory
RIP James
God is with us—the Ark Bible Church

And the search graffiti that still stained so many doors; red and black and orange quadrants of grief, painted on hulks and wrecks, the shells of homes.

9/10. 2 DEAD. DEAD DOG INSIDE

"They're still finding bodies," Erick said. "Not every day, but every week or so now. They'll still come up on someone. The other day one of my buddies went on a call, and it was a long-lost relative who hadn't heard from his uncle in months and had been trying to track him down but didn't have his last known address. So, you know, welfare-check type of call. Sure enough, they found his address, and they found him. Place wasn't searched properly; he was under some furniture, and they couldn't smell him when the first searchers went through, because the whole damn neighborhood smelled like death everywhere."

"So many damn bodies and funerals," Ellis said. "The priest I know from back home in Uptown? He was telling me how he's been officiating for people he didn't know; there were too many people to bury." Ellis thought of one home he and his partner had searched—how they found an old lady there, dead for weeks, her oxygen tank on its side in another room, furniture rotted and shifted, and walls seemingly held up by mold.

"The rats have made a comeback, I see," Remy said as they headed down St. Charles to watch the Krewe of Morpheus roll. A healthy-sized rat was scurrying along the edge of the sidewalk up against the gutter.

"They're like kings in all this," Ellis said. "You wouldn't believe the ones I have come across on recovery searches. They've gotten fat off this."

Ava shuddered at the thought.

"Them and the snakes," Erick said. "They are taking back whole sections of this town."

Erick was drinking Abita and watching, with the eye of a cop who is never truly off duty, the shenanigans of a few drunks walking down the sidewalk in front of them.

"You know there are a lot that were never found," Ellis said.

"And a lot that were covered up. Those Algiers militia," Remy said. This was little heard in the northern media, but it was well known in the city that some whites in Algiers had declared open season on any black residents they saw.

They armed themselves and didn't focus on rescues or helping the injured. They wanted an excuse to kill black men and teenagers. One of them compared it to hunting pheasants.

"They are written off as drowning deaths. But they were murdered."

Erick nodded, but he didn't want to pursue this line of conversation. There were quite a few investigations into the actions of several different police units.

Remy changed the subject. "Well, a lot of the deaths are environmental, right?" he said. "All the chemicals in that water and all the oil spills that happened around here? If you swallowed a lot of that stuff, man, you're screwed."

As they waited for the next krewe to pass by, Ava thought about the future. She thought about her father and his beloved Opera House, marked by waterlines. Somewhere the palm trees will swing ominously again; the water and the wind will hit Charleston or Cape Fear or New Orleans. Someone will pour over satellite images, stratospheric planes will track the birth of a storm off Africa, and all the warnings will be issued. Still, it will not be enough to save New Orleans when the next one comes.

There were knots of spectators, but most people around them were locals. Many used the same parade ladders their parents had used to hoist them up for a better view in decades past. But there was not the usual overwhelming pressing mass of joyous, inebriated tourists. There were the flambeaux, walking with their weathered faces lit up by flame; the smiling high-school marching bands strutting proudly, upholding tradition; and the venerable jazz bands, so many of whom had lost members to the flood and its aftermath.

Many of the floats were recycled and worn or new and homemade, not the grand structures the celebrants were used to. One of the largest Mardi Gras float warehouses had flooded when the levees broke. The krewes were throwing old trinkets from years past. As night fell, Ava watched the krewes with their expressionless masks, watched people reaching out to catch the prizes: purple, gold, and green, that denoted justice, power, and faith, respectively.

Perhaps it was inevitable, but the krewes decided that Mardi Gras would have a Wizard of Oz theme. Tarps would be the float decoration of the day. There were little dogs and witches everywhere. There was a picture of the

Wicked Witch of the West's stocking-clad legs, under a house, the name of the storm written over her lifeless body. Then there was a large bald man with a sign saying, *We're not in Kansas.* He was wearing a tutu. It was good to know that some of New Orleans's characters had survived. On one float a woman dressed like Dorothy held a sign that said, *Throw ME something...FEMA!* Other parade participants held signs that summed up the past few months:

Proud to swim home.
Rebuild New Orleans.
Thank you, Houston.

"The floats are terrible this year," Remy said, "and amazing."

"They're very...homespun," Ellis said and laughed.

"Yes, and they're very New Orleans," Ava said. As she said it, her eyes fell on the neutral ground on St. Claude. There, behind the parade, were rows of plain wooden crosses, draped with Mardi Gras beads.

www.ingramcontent.com/pod-product-compliance
Lightning Source LLC
Chambersburg PA
CBHW071855220626
47052CB00002B/134